PHILIP JOSE FARMER

Hadon of
ancient Opar

MAGNUM BOOKS
Methuen Paperbacks Ltd

A Magnum Book

HADON OF ANCIENT OPAR

ISBN 0 417 01800 2

First published in Great Britain 1977
by Magnum Books

Copyright © 1974 by Philip José Farmer

Magnum Books are published by
Methuen Paperbacks Ltd
11 New Fetter Lane, London EC4P 4EE

Made and printed in Great Britain
by Richard Clay (The Chaucer Press) Ltd
Bungay, Suffolk

Acknowledgments

I am grateful to Frank Brueckel and John Harwood for writing the article which sparked the inspiration to create Hadon of Opar and the Khokarsan civilization. I thank Hulbert Burroughs for his kindness in permitting me to launch this series of novels. The basic debt, of course, is owed to Edgar Rice Burroughs, without whose tales of Opar and other lost cities this book would n͏ ͏ have been written.

P.J.F.

Maps

Dedicated to HULBERT BURROUGHS in gratitude for his permission to write of Opar, that hidden city of "gold, and silver, ivory, and apes, and peacocks" and of the civilization which founded it.

1

Opar, the city of massive granite and little jewels quivered and blurred. Solid with great stone walls, soaring slender towers, gilt domes, and eight hundred and sixty-seven years of existence, it wavered, bent, and dissolved. And then it was gone as if it had never been.

Hadon swallowed, and he wiped away his tears.

His last vision of glorious Opar had been like a dream dying in a god's mind. He hoped that it was not an evil omen. And he hoped that his fellow contestants were similarly affected. If he was the only one to have wept, he might be mocked.

The longboat had traveled the curve of the river, and the jungle trees had moved between him and his native city. He still saw it in his mind, its towers like hands raised against the sky to keep it from falling. The little figures on the stone wharves—among them his father, mother, sister, and brother —had dwindled in his sight, though not in his mind. It was they who had brought the tears, not the city.

Would he ever see them again?

If he lost, he would not. If he won, years might pass before he took them in his arms. And his beloved Opar might never greet him again.

He had left it twice in his nineteen years. The first time, his parents had been with him. The second time, he had lived with his uncle, but Opar had not been far away. He glanced at the young men standing by him. They were not looking at him, and he was glad, because tears were running down their cheeks, too. Taro, his friend, grinned with embarrassment. Hewako, a dark lump of stone, scowled at him. He was not crying; stone did not cry. He was too strong for tears and

9

wanted everybody to know it. But then, he had nothing or nobody to grieve for, Hadon thought. He felt sorry for him, though he knew the feeling would not last long. Hewako was such a surly, arrogant brute.

Hadon looked about him. The river at this point was about half a mile wide, and brown with the mud it was ferrying from the mountains to the sea. The river was walled with green vegetation except where mud banks shoved out like fingers testing for another advance of the trees. On them lay grinning sacred crocodiles who rose up on short legs as they became aware of the lead boat and slid oilily into the brown water. Parrots and monkeys screamed at the boats from the green. A blue-yellow-and-red kingfisher flashed from a branch, falling like a feathered star. It checked, swooped along the surface, and lifted with a small silvery fish in its talons.

The twelve oarsmen grunted in unison with the chunk of wooden blades in the river and the bronze stroke of the coxswain's gong. Short, squat, thick-necked, bar-browed, first cousins of men, second cousins of the great apes, they pulled and grunted while sweat matted their hairy bodies. Between the oarsmen, on the narrow deck, lay chests of gold ingots and diamonds, boxes of furs, carved figurines of goddesses, gods, monsters, and animals, of herbs from the rain forest, and piles of ivory tusks. Five soldiers in leather armor guarded these with spears.

Ahead of Hadon's boat were six boats carrying oarsmen and soldiers only. Behind his boat came twenty-three more, all heavily loaded with the precious products of Opar. Behind them were six craft forming the rear guard. Hadon watched them for a while and then began pacing back and forth, five steps at a time, along the crowded poop deck. Keeping in shape was vital. His life would depend upon it during the Great Games. Hewako and Taro and the three substitutes soon imitated him. Three in Indian file paced back and forth, and the others did setting-up exercises. Hadon watched with envy the flexing pythonlike muscles of Hewako. He was said to be the strongest man in all Khokarsa, except for Kwasin, of course. But Kwasin was exiled, wandering somewhere in the Western Lands with his huge brass-bound oak club on his shoulders. Had he been a contestant, it was

10

doubtful that anybody else would have entered.

Hadon wondered if he would have dared. Perhaps; perhaps not. But though he did not have the body of a gorilla, he did have long legs and speed and endurance and a swordsmanship that even his father applauded. And it was the final contest, that with the sword, which decided.

Still, his father had warned him.

"You're very good with the *tenu*, my son," he had said. "But you're not a professional, not yet, and a man with experience could chop you to pieces despite your long arms and your youth. Fortunately, you'll be up against green youths like yourself. It is ironic that there are many men who could easily best you with the sword, but they are too old to win at the other games. Still, if some old man of twenty-eight should decide to try for the prize, he just might squeak through, and then Kho help you!"

His father had felt the stump of his left arm, looked grim, and then had said, "You have never killed a man, Hadon, and so your true temperament is unknown. Sometimes, a lesser swordsman can defeat a better because he has the heart of a true killer. What will happen if you and Taro are finalists? Taro is your best friend. Can you kill him?"

"I don't know," Hadon had said.

"Then you shouldn't be in the Games," his father had said. "And there's Hewako. Beware of him. He knows you are better with the *tenu* than he. He'll try to break your back before the final test."

"But the wrestling matches are not to the death," Hadon had said.

"Accidents happen," his father had said. "Hewako would have cracked your neck during the eliminations if the judge had not been watching. I warned her, and though I am a lowly sweeper of the temple floors, I was once a *numatenu*, and she listened to me."

Hadon had winced. It hurt him to hear his father speak of the old days, of when he had two arms that could wield a broadsword more expertly than anyone else in Opar. An outlaw sword, swung from behind, had severed his father's arm above the elbow during that struggle in the dark tunnels below Opar. The king had been killed in that murky fight, and a new king had ascended the throne. And the new king had

11

hated Kumin, and instead of retiring him honorably on a pension, had discharged him. Many a *numatenu* would have committed suicide then. But Kumin had decided that he owed more to his family than to the somewhat nebulous code of the *numatenu*. He would not abandon them to poverty and the dubious charity of his wife's relatives. So he had become a floorsweeper, and this, though a lowly position, put him under the special protection of Kho Herself. The new king, Gamori, would have liked to expel Kumin and his family into the jungle, but his wife, the chief priestess, forbade that.

Kumin had sent Hadon to live with his brother, Phimeth, for several years. This was to give Hadon a chance to learn swordsmanship under the tutelage of the greatest wielder of the *tenu* in Opar, his uncle. It was in the dark caves where his uncle lived in exile that Hadon had met his cousin, Kwasin, son of Phimeth's and Kumin's sister, Wimake. Wimake had died from a snakebite some years before, and so Hadon had lived for years without a mother or an aunt or any woman whatsoever. It had been a lonely time in many ways, though delightful in others. Except for Kwasin, who often had made Hadon miserable.

Just before the Flaming God, Resu, disappeared behind the trees, the longboats tied up at the docks which had been built some hundred years before for the overnight stop. Half of the soldiers took their stations behind the stone walls enclosing all but the riverside of the docks. The other soldiers built cooking fires for themselves, the officers, and the contestants. The oarsmen made their fires in some corners of the walls. A fine boar and a great drake were sacrificed, and the best portions were tossed into a fire as offerings to Kho, to Resu, and to Tesemines, goddess of the night. The legs of the pig and the remnants of the duck were cast into the waters to placate the godling of the river.

The swift current carried the legs and the body away in the dusk. They traveled to the bend, where the shadows fell from the branches of the trees. Suddenly the waters moved, and the legs and the fowl went under the surface.

One of the oarsmen murmured, "Kasukwa has taken them!"

Hadon's skin prickled coldly, though he felt that crocodiles, not the godling, had seized the sacrifice. He, with most of the others, quickly touched his forehead with the ends of his three longest fingers and then described with them a circle which swept out and over his loins and ended on his forehead. A few of the grayhairs among the officers and the oarsmen made the old sign of Kho, touching their forehead first with the tips of the three fingers, then the right breast, the genitals, the left breast, the forehead again, and ending up on the navel.

Soon the air was thick with smoke and the odor of cooking pig and duck. Most of the party belonged to the Ant Totem, but a few were members of the Pig Totem and hence forbidden to eat pork except on one day a year. They supped on duck, boiled eggs, and pieces of dried beef. Hadon ate sparingly of the pork, millet bread, goat cheese, the sweet and delicious *mowometh* red-berries, and raisins. He refused the sorghum beer, not because he did not like it but because it would put fat on him and reduce his wind.

Though the smoke fell over them in the still air, made them cough, and reddened their eyes, they did not complain. The smoke would help keep off the mosquitoes, the evil little children of Tesemines, now swarming from the forest. Hadon rubbed a stinking oil over his body and hoped that this and the smoke would enable him to get a good night's rest. When dawn came he would oil himself with another repellent for the flies that attacked as soon as the sun had warmed the air.

Hadon had just finished eating when Taro pulled at his arm and pointed downriver. The moon had not yet come up, but he could see a great dark body on the bank across the river. Undoubtedly, it was a leopard come to drink before hunting.

"Perhaps we should also have sacrificed to Khukhaqo," Taro said.

Hadon grinned and said, "If we sacrificed to every deity and spirit who might possibly harm us, we would not have room enough in the boats for all the animals we would need."

Then, seeing by the firelight Taro's offended expression, he smiled and slapped Taro's shoulder. "There is good sense in what you say. But I wouldn't dare suggest to the priestess that we offer to the leopard goddess. She wouldn't take it kindly if we stuck our noses into her business."

Taro was right. Late at night, Hadon was jerked from a troubled sleep by a scream. He leaped up and grabbed his broadsword and stared bewilderedly around. He saw a black-and-yellow body leaping over the wall, a screaming oarsman between its jaws. And then both were gone. It was useless and dangerous to pursue the leopard. The captain of the guards raised hell with the sentinels, but it was merely to relieve his own fear and anger.

Somehow, the leopard goddess had been offended, and so they made haste to placate her. Klyhy, the priestess, now sacrificed a pig to Khukhaqo. It would not bring the poor oarsman back, but it might prevent another leopard from attacking. And the blood of the pig poured into a bronze bowl surely would please the ghost of the oarsman and keep him from prowling the camp that night. Hadon hoped so, but he did not go back to sleep. Neither did the others, except for the oarsmen. The labors of the day ensured that almost nothing would keep them awake long.

At dawn the priestess of Kho and the priest of Resu stripped and took their ritual bath in the river. The soldiers looked out for crocodiles while the rest of the party bathed in order of seniority. They ate a breakfast of okra soup, dried beef, hard-boiled duck eggs, and the unleavened millet bread. Then they pushed out into the river again. Four days later, in mid-morning, they heard the rumble of the cataract. A mile above it, they docked their boats, unloaded the cargo, and began traveling slowly along the road. This was paved with huge granite blocks. The vegetation along it was cut back at regular intervals by jungle rangers. It curved away from the falls and then terminated at the edge of the cliffs. Here the party followed a narrow, steep, and winding road cut into the face of the mountain. Soldiers preceded and trailed the caravan. The oarsmen huffed and puffed, carrying the boxes, chests, and tusks. The herdsmen moved behind them, calling out or prodding their squealing charges with pointed sticks. The ducks in the cages on the oarsmen's backs quacked. The sacred parrot on the priestess's shoulder screamed and chattered, and the sacred monkey on the priest's shoulder hurled shrill insults at invisible enemies in the jungle.

What with all the noise, Hadon thought, they could be heard miles away. If any Kawuru pirates were waiting in the dense forest below, they would have plenty of warning. Not that there was much likelihood of an ambush. An escort of soldiers from the seaside fort would be at the foot of the mountains. But the Kawuru had been known to slip past these.

14

Presently, the priest's swearing was added to the racket. The monkey had relieved himself on the man's shoulder. Nobody except the priestess dared laugh, though they couldn't help grinning. When the priest saw them grinning, he swore at them. A soldier brought a jug of water, and he cleaned off the mess with a linen cloth. After a while the priest was laughing too, but the monkey rode the rest of the way on an oarsman's shoulder.

At dusk they came into a cleared area near the bottom of the falls. Here fifty soldiers waited for them. The party bathed in the thunder and the coolness of the waters, sacrificed, and ate. At dawn they were up, and two hours later were loading the cargo into longboats. They had a three-day journey ahead of them. This would have been tense enough. But a fool of an oarsman increased their nervousness. He declared on the last trip he had glimpsed the river godling.

"It was Kasukwa himself! I saw him just as Resu went to bed. He rose from the waters, a monstrous being four times as big as the biggest bull hippopotamus you ever saw. His skin was as thick and brown as a hippopotamus', though it was warty. The warts were black and as large as my head, and each of them had three eyes and a tiny mouth filled with teeth as sharp as a crocodile's. He had long arms like a man's, but where hands should be were the heads of river pigs, with red eyes that flamed. He stared at me for a moment, and my bowels still turn to okra soup when I think of his face. It was a hippopotamus' except that it was hairy, and he had only one great scummy-green eye in the center of his forehead. And his teeth were many, and like spearheads. And then, while I prayed to Kho and also to G'xsghaba'ghdi, the goddess of our forefathers, and thought I would faint, he sank slowly back into the river."

The other oarsmen grunted in affirmation, though they had not seen Kasukwa.

"We will sacrifice an especially fine boar to him tonight," Klyhy said. 'Even if, as I think likely, your vision was inspired by beer."

"May Kho strike me dead, here and now, if I am lying!" the oarman cried.

Those near him jumped back, some looking upward and others downward, since Kho can strike from the earth or the

15

sky. Nothing happened, and everybody breathed relief. Hadon suggested to the captain that he should tell the oarsman to shut his mouth before the entire party was in a panic. The captain said that he resented youngsters giving him advice, even if they were to be heroes. Nevertheless, he spoke sharply to the oarsman.

Grim and horrible Kasukwa was not seen during the journey to the sea, though he disturbed the sleep of many, and the oarsmen turned pale every time a hippopotamus surfaced near their boats. Late in the evening of the third day, they rounded a bend. There, beyond the wide mouth of the river, was the sea, the Kemuwopar.

On the northern bank were docks and the great galleys and warehouses, totem halls, houses, and the stone fort. The coxswains stepped up the beat of the bronze gongs. The oarsmen, though weary, grinned, showing their thick blocklike teeth, and summoned strength in their massive and hairy arms for the final lap. For a while they would be safe from the Kawuru, the leopard goddess, and the river godling. And tonight there would be a feast in their totem hall, followed by a beer-sodden sleep.

But not for Hadon. Stuffing the belly with food and beer was not for a youth who must keep himself light and swift for the Great Games. However, Klyhy had promised to receive him tonight in the little temple of Kho by the fort. She was ten years older than he, and a beautiful woman, if you could overlook the beginnings of a beer paunch and the sagging of the large breasts, and Hadon could. Besides, it was a great honor to be accepted by a priestess. And if her sister priestesses stationed here liked his companions, they would not sleep much tonight either.

Hewako was not pleased by this. He had hoped Klyhy would take him in her dark bronze arms and that those big gray eyes would be on fire with love of him. When he had heard Klyhy say yes to Hadon, he had scowled and flexed his massive biceps. He did not dare anything while Klyhy was in hearing. Hadon had grinned at him, but the thought of the long sea trip ahead was not pleasant. Though he had an easy nature, Hewako's jibes were rubbing it away.

16

2

Whether Hadon won or lost the Games, he would be a hero. If he lost, however, he would be a dead hero, buried in a mound of earth under a tall pointed marble monolith. Passersby would pray to him and pour mead or wine on the earth. Much good that would do him. And when he considered that he would be pitted against the strongest and the swiftest youths of the empire, he felt his confidence bending and shaking as a reed in the wind. He had a strong ego, otherwise he would not have become a contestant. But only an egomaniac would take it for granted that he could go through the other contestants as the farmer went through the millet with his scythe.

Nevertheless, the ceiling-high bronze mirror this morning showed him a man who looked like a hero. Even if he said so himself. At six feet two inches, he was the tallest man in Opar. This was due to his Klemsaasa ancestors and, no doubt, to the gods who had been his forefathers—although, now that he thought of it, there were few men of the upper classes in Opar, or in the empire itself, who could not claim from one to a score of gods as ancestors. All his foremothers had, as was their holy duty, resided in a house of god for a month as a temple prostitute. Though theoretically they must accept any male worshiper, in practice they had ensured that only a king, a hero, a great merchant or soldier, or a *numatenu* was admitted to their cubicle. The children of these unions, if any, were supposedly fathered by the particular god of the temple. Hadon could recite the names of twelve gods, not to mention two score of godlings, who had been many times his ancestors. Theoretically, that is. Few educated people believed that conception was due to the intervention of divine Kho Herself. It was admitted by all but the most die-hard conservatives that the human male himself was responsible for pregnancy. But this made, in theory, no difference. The male's body was taken

17

over by the god of the temple during the holy coupling, and the child was the god's, not that of the man. The man was a mere vessel.

Hadon was not a temple child. His oldest brother, his mother's first child, had been fathered by the great Resu himself. But Resu had not favored him. He had died at three of a fever, the first of seven brothers and sisters to go as children to the arms of Sisisken, grim ruler of the shadow world.

Hadon's curly red-bronze hair indicated that the Flaming God was his grandfather. His large hazel eyes showed that he was of Klemsaasa stock. At least, they were supposed to do so, though he had observed that many of the old Khoklem stock had hazel or even blue and gray eyes. His features, which he immodestly admitted were exceptionally handsome, were those of the people who had come down from the Saasares mountains eight hundred and sixty-four years ago and seized the city of Khokarsa. His forehead was high and narrow, though swelling at the corners. His ears were small and close to his head and slightly pointed at the tips. A prominent supraorbital ridge was mounted by thick eyebrows which almost joined. His nose, though straight, was not as long as most of those supposed to be descended from the Klemsaasa. Just as well, since many also had beaked noses. And his nostrils were more flaring than the Klemsaasa's. No doubt this was due to his Khoklem ancestry. But then, no one was pure-blooded, however much the Klemsaasa denied being mixed with the shorter, darker, heavier-bodied, snub-nosed, straight-haired aborigines.

To complete the roster of pleasing features, he had a short upper lip, full but not thick lips, and a chin strong and deeply clefted.

His body was, he told himself in his more critical moments, too lean. Still, his shoulders were very broad and heavy. His was the physique of the long-distance runner, though he had never been beaten in the dashes. His legs were extraordinarily long, and so were his arms. The former gave him his speed, and the latter were a great advantage in swordsmanship. Indeed, they were so long that he had often been accused of having a great-ape grandfather.

Hadon thought of the many fights he had had as a child because of this insult and the many more because his play-

18

mates had jeered at his father's missing arm and lowly status. But most of the jeerers admired and envied him now. Only Hewako among them had succeeded in becoming a contestant from Opar. Hewako still made remarks about long-armed men with monkey ancestors and about floors that needed sweeping. But he always looked away from Hadon when he said this, and he never mentioned names. So Hadon had determined to ignore him until they got to the Games. Then he would get his revenge. Of course, realistically, Hewako might be the one to get revenge. But Hadon preferred not to think about that possibility.

He combed and brushed his shoulder-length hair and shaved with one of the recently introduced iron razors. An hour later, wearing only a loincloth and a rosary of electrum beads, he was jogging along the dirt road that paralleled the shoreline for many miles. Behind him ran Taro and the three substitutes. They passed many farms where millet and sorghum were grown and many pigs and goats were raised. The farmers and their wives, clad only in conical straw hats and animal-skin loincloths, straightened from their labors to stare at them. Seeing the red-eyed hawk feather tied to the hair above the right ear of each, the mark of a Great Gamester, the farmers bowed.

Hadon felt good again. His legs were getting the stretching they needed, and his wind was not as weak as he had thought it would be after the long journey. He wasn't as strong as he would have liked to be, but Klyhy had not let him sleep until an hour before dawn. Not that he minded.

When the four, sweating and blowing, returned to the docks, they saw Hewako working out with weights. He scowled at them, and he did not offer to join them in throwing javelins or slinging stones. Instead, he ran off to do his roadwork alone. Hadon shouted after him, "The farmers' daughters had better look out!" but Hewako ignored him. Hadon was referring to Hewako's rejection by a priestess. When he had bruised her with a too passionate hand, she had kicked him out—literally. Perhaps he had then gone to the totem hall of the oarsmen, the Gokako. They practiced group marriage and were free with their wives, who were not above taking money for the use of their bodies. But it would have been socially demeaning for Hewako to join them. And if

19

some drunken Gokako happened to be in a bad mood, it could be dangerous. Once Hewako entered the hall, he would leave behind him any protection of the law. Should a Gokako stick a knife in him, that was the end of the matter. Besides which, a man would have to be hard up to bed one of those short, squat, and ugly women.

The others laughed at Hadon's remark and resumed their exercises. They ended with a wooden-sword fight while wearing helmets, cuirasses, gloves, and armguards of leather. Hadon beat them all, though he did get a nasty whack across his forearm from Taro. Taro was almost as tall as Hadon, and more muscular. And he was, Hadon reflected, a splendid acrobat and a great javelineer, one who consistently beat him when throwing at a target. He could still be in the Games while Hadon was lying on a granite slab.

The thought that they might have to try to kill each other saddened him. They were lifelong friends, but they would soon be trying to shed each other's blood. All for the glory of being the husband of the queen of Khokarsa.

Three more days passed. The cargoes were loaded on the morning of the second day, but the captain of the merchant vessel wished to wait until the next day. And that day had dawned, a lucky day, the first sea day of the month of Piqabes, goddess of the sea, in the Year of the Green Parrot. There was no more propitious day for starting a sea voyage unless it was in the Year of the Fish Eagle. But that would not occur for seven more years.

The day was bright and cloudless. The wind was blowing from the southwest, and the waves were not high. The sacrifices had been made, a heron flew across the ships from the right (a very good omen), and everybody filed aboard in a good mood. A drunken sailor fell off a gangplank and had to be fished out, but the fleet's priestess, Simari, said that that wasn't a bad omen.

The army band on the shore played a song in honor of Piqabes; their drums, flutes, harps, xylophones, marimbas, and gongs boomed, shrilled, twanged, tinkled, rattled, and clanged in a similitude of rhythm and melody. Simari, the last aboard, danced around and around, whirling a booming bullroarer at the end of a cord. A tall fat woman, she wore a fish-head mask and, over her pubes, the stuffed tail of a fish. On one large breast was painted a giant sea turtle and on the other a sea otter; a crocodile and a hippo were painted above and below her navel, which was circled with blue. Hadon and Taro waved at Klyhy and Taro's lover, the beautiful Rigo. The gangplanks were swung off, and the oarsmen dipped their blades in the shallow water and pulled. Simari, panting behind her mask, went to the prow of the ship, just above the huge bronze ram, and chanted while she poured out a libation of the best Saasares wine into the sea. The captain, Bhaseko, invited the priestess, the first mate, and the future heroes to the poop deck for a cup of wine. Hadon could not refuse this, but he drank no more than one cup. His fellows did not feel so restrained.

Hadon felt hot in his bronze helmet and cuirass, but presently the wind became stronger and cooled him. The captain began bellowing orders. The great sail of the only mast, placed near the bow, was hoisted. Simari went into her cabin, set forward of the captain's on the poop deck, to change and to wash off the paint. The others went down to the main deck and walked to the foredeck, where their quarters were in a cabin. Its roof was only two feet above the deck; they had to go down into a small room with bunks. The portholes were open except in time of storm or cold, and then they were closed with heavy wooden shutters.

Hadon stored his armor and his *numatenu* sword and a small chest of belongings under his bunk. Below him rose the grunting and squealing of pigs and the bleating of goats. The odor that rose from the pens was something that would have to be endured for a long time.

He went back out on deck with Taro, whose wine-flushed face was almost as red as his hair. By now the fleet was in formation, the merchant ships, the bireme, and two uniremes forming a V in the center. Ahead were two uniremes, on each side was a bireme, and behind were two uniremes. The fish-eagle-head standard of the Khokarsan navy fluttered from the mast tops of each of their escort. The gong of the coxswain clanged, the oars chunked into the sea and pulled out dripping, the oarsmen grunted and sweated and stank of sweat and millet beer, the officers shouted orders, the animals squealed and bleated, the pet fish-eagle of the priestess

21

screamed down from the mainmast, the green waters rolled into the muddy beaches a mile off, and they were well on their way.

Their ship, the *Semsin,* was a long, narrow vessel with two tiers of oarsmen. The main deck ran from the poop deck to the foredeck, both of which were six feet above the main deck. Along both sides of the main deck were open portions. The heads of the oarsmen were just level with the main deck. Each tier had twelve oars on a side, two men at an oar. The lower tier was so close to the upper that the top oarsmen could touch the heads of the lower with their feet if they wished to. Below the lower tier was the deck where the cargo, the supplies, and the animals were kept. Also on this deck was the sick bay and a room where the wounded were treated during a battle.

The galley carried two great catapults, one on each of the two highest decks.

The *Semsin* was steered by a rudder, which had recently been invented; two sturdy sailors manned the rudder handle.

The sailors, oarsmen, and marines slept on the deck or in the hold.

The quarters for the ship's officer were forward of the cabin that the contestants shared. The galley was forward of the priestess's cabin on the poop deck. Though it had a breezeway, smoke from the stone fireplace often filled the priestess's and captain's cabins unless the wind happened to be favorable.

Hadon had made one trip before, when his parents had gone to Khokarsa to live for two years, and he wasn't looking forward to this trip.

Five days later, they passed rugged and sheer cliffs. Halfway up one was a huge and dark hole, the entrance to the caves in which Hadon and his cousin Kwasin had lived with their uncle, Phimeth. Hadon purchased and sacrificed a small boar and prayed that the ghost of his uncle would find the blood pleasing.

The days and nights passed as best they could under the conditions. Bored and wishing to get more exercise, Hadon asked the captain if he could help row. The captain replied that this would be socially degrading. Hadon said that his companions would share the oar with him. He wouldn't be working alongside a common fellow. Besides, this was for exercise, not pay, which took it out of the category of manual labor.

The others were not eager for the task, but Hadon explained that if they did not row, they might be in a weakened condition when they arrived at their destination. After the first half-hour at the oar, Hadon wished that he had never thought of the idea. His palms were rubbed raw and bloody, and he was sure that his back was going to snap. On the other hand, he now knew that he was not in such excellent condition as he had thought. He gritted his teeth and rowed, staring at the broad, hairy, sweating back and bull neck of Hewako, working at the oar ahead of him. Hewako was the most powerful man Hadon had ever seen, but evidently he was hurting. Hewako swore for fifteen minutes, then quit to preserve his lungs. Hadon grinned through his pain and weariness and vowed that he would not give up before Hewako. He did, but only because his nerveless hands could no longer grasp the oars. Hewako fell over about three minutes later.

The oarsmen, all rude and impolite fellows, laughed at them. They asked if they were the type of heroes being sent to the Games nowadays. Now, in the old times ... Too exhausted even to feel shame, Hadon staggered off to his bunk. For the first time, the uproar of the beasts below did not keep him awake.

He was back at the oar next day, though he had never hated to do anything so much. By the time they sighted the red city of Sakawuru on top of the black cliffs, he was able to row two hours at a stretch, three times a day. His hands were building up a heavy callus, and his chest and arms seemed to have added an inch. He worried that this type of labor might interfere with his swordsmanship, but he had to have the exercise. Besides, if he quit, he would be mocked by the rowers.

At the red-granite city of Sakawuru, the ships resupplied, and the crew was given four days' liberty. Hadon spent his time either touring or running along the dirt roads outside the city. He felt tempted to drink the cool beer available in the hall of the Ant Totem, but he decided not to. Hewako apparently fell prey to his great thirst. Hadon saw him once staggering out of the hall of the Leopard Totem.

The fleet set out again. The lookouts in the crow's nests were still alert for pirates, though the chances for encountering them were less than in the waters just crossed. They stopped at the city of Wentisuh for one day to disembark two sick sailors and hire replacements. Hadon had never been in Wentisuh, so he and Taro wandered its narrow, crooked streets, listening to the exotic tongue of the farmers in the markets and the common citizen. Hadon was a superb linguist, and in Opar he had taken the trouble to gain some fluency in Siwudawa from the family of a Wentisuh merchant. These people were a strange one, noisy and volatile among themselves, grim and silent when strangers were among them. Their skin was a brownish-yellow. Their hair was coarse and straight and black. Their noses were long, thin, and beaked, and many had a slight fold of skin in the inner corners of their eyes. Though they worshiped Kho and Resu, they had many aboriginal deities, the most prominent being Siwudawa, a parrot-headed androgyne.

The fleet left Wentisuh and traveled in a straight line for the city of Kethna. The wind changed direction then, and the sails were hauled down. Clouds, the first of the rainy season, covered the face of Resu; the seas became choppy; the rowers had to work twice as hard to maintain the same speed; the shifts were changed to an hour apiece. Then the rains struck. Simari sacrificed another pig to Piqabes. The storm, lasting for one day and night, was hell for Hadon. He got seasick and spent most of his time on the railing giving to the sea the pork that he had eaten that morning. Hewako whooped with laughter at the sight, but in half an hour he was hanging on the railing by Hadon's side.

Hadon had recovered by the time Kethna appeared, but he swore that he would never again consider the navy as a career. Kethna was a city of high white-stoned walls and black towers and domes, perched on a cliff five hundred feet above its port. Kethna was fifty miles from the Strait of Keth, where it kept a large fleet. Its rulers paid tribute to Khokarsa, but it ran local maritime affairs with a high hand. Every merchant ship that passed through the strait had to pay a heavy tax for the privilege. Nor did Kethna officials bother to hide their arrogance. They treated the Khokarsan fleet as if it came from a conquered province.

"If our king would quit occupying himself with the building of that great tower," the captain said, "and pay more

24

attention to business, he'd teach the Kethnans a bloody lesson. They need taking down in the worst way. It doesn't make much sense for Kethna to send tribute to Minruth with one hand and take away from him with the other. Why should we pay a tax to these hyenas?"

Why indeed? Hadon thought. But he had more important matters to consider. Hewako's veiled taunts and his sneaky tricks were about to set Hadon afire. He had even thought about complaining to the priestess so she would impose a ban of silence between him and Hewako. He felt, however, that this would be unmanly, even if it was the rational way out. He couldn't challenge Hewako to a duel, because fighting between contestants for the Great Games was forbidden. This was a wise rule, since so many contestants in the old days had picked fights in order to eliminate competitors before the Games started. Even if this rule had not existed, the challenged had the right to pick the weapons, and Hewako was not fool enough to choose swords. He would want a bare-handed battle, and Hadon knew that he would lose that. Of course, he might be wrestling with Hewako at the Games, but that event was for points only.

Then, the night before they were due to arrive at the strait, Hadon awoke to find himself smeared with pig dung. He sat quietly in his fury, thought, and then went outside to dip a bucket into the sea and wash himself off. On returning, he looked at Hewako. The hippopotamuslike fellow seemed to be sleeping. He certainly was snoring, but Hadon believed that he was just pretending, that he was laughing inside himself. He forced himself to lie down, and after a while he fell asleep.

He was, however, up and about before any of his bunk-mates. He went into the galley, found that the cooks were down in the hold, and ate a quick breakfast of bread, hard-boiled duck eggs, and cold okra soup. Then, taking a bucket, he disappeared into the hold. He emerged while the drums for awakening the morning shift were beating. He took all of his cabinmates aside except Hewako and spoke quietly but fiercely to them. They sniggered and promised silence and coopera-tion. Two of them agreed to delay Hewako a minute or so by "accidentally" spilling hot soup on him. None of them liked the surly, arrogant man. Besides, they thought it only fair

25

that Hadon pay Hewako back in kind.

Hewako arrived late at the oars, cursing, his legs red with a slight burn, and swearing vengeance on the soup-spillers when they got to the Games. He found his bunkmates at their positions and the man he was to relieve angry because of the delay. He grabbed the oar handle, then swore and sputtered, but the gong of the coxswain sounded the first stroke, and he could do nothing but stay at his post.

Taro was Hewako's oarmate, and Taro had complained that though the joke would be on Hewako, they would all suffer.

"The air for a mile around is going to be bad for everybody. Hewako won't be the only one gagging."

"Yes, but only Hewako will have his hands in it," Hadon had said.

Hewako kept his indignation and fury down to a mild roar, but after two minutes he decided that he had had enough. He bellowed out for a replacement. The gong master yelled back at him to keep quiet, that he had had his chance at sick call. Hewako shouted back an insult. The gong master screamed that if there was another word from him, he'd have him up before the captain for a lashing.

Since the youths had been told that they would have to accept oarsmen's discipline when on duty, Hewako became silent. At least, he said nothing to the gong master, but he threatened Hadon under his breath. Then he pleaded with Taro to trade places. Taro said he'd sooner drown. After a while Hewako had no breath for anything but his labor.

All might have gone as planned if the first mate had not walked by Hewako. He stopped, wrinkled his nose, and said, "Whew! What's that?"

Nobody answered. He sniffed around until he located the source of offense. He stood for a moment, leaning over and looking down at Hewako, before he roared for the gong master. The master turned over his gong to his subordinate and hurried down the deck. When he ascertained what the trouble was, he requested that the captain be summoned. The captain passed from irritation because his breakfast was interrupted to anger when he saw—and smelled—the cause of commotion. By then Hadon had quit grinning. He hadn't thought that anybody but he and Hewako would be involved, except for the breathers in the immediate area, of course.

The captain sputtered and then shouted, "You future heroes can horse around among yourselves all you want to, as long as it doesn't interfere with the operation of my ship! But this does it! A rower can't be efficient if he has to handle a slippery oar, nor can those around him be efficient if they are sickened! You all report to me at the end of the shift! Gong master, douse this man with water until the dung's all gone! And you, Hewako, make sure all traces are gone before you report!"

The result was that Hadon had to confess. The captain had promised to have every one of the youths lashed if the culprit had not declared himself. Hadon, at high noon, had his hands tied above him to the mast. A burly oarsman struck Hadon's back five times with a hippopotamus-hide whip. Hadon had thought that the humiliation would be worse than the pain. But it wasn't. The whip cut to the muscle, and blood ran down between his legs. He clamped his teeth, refusing to cry out, and he slept on his face for many nights thereafter.

It was some, though not much, consolation when Hewako got three lashes. The captain did not ask Hadon why he had played the trick, since Hadon would have had to refuse to answer and he would have received more lashes. He investigated and found a watchman who had seen Hewako in the pig sty and had also seen Hadon washing himself off, Hewako confessed and shortly afterward had a bloody back. Later, in the privacy of the cabin, Hewako said that he was going to get the captain someday. Hadon replied that he didn't exactly love the captain, but he did respect him. If he had failed to do his duty because the culprit might someday be in a position to execute him, he had no business being the captain.

"I'll get you during the Games," Hewako said.

"You'll only be trying to do what everyone else will," Hadon said. "But, in the meantime, why don't we lay off each other? If we keep this up, we'll wear each other ragged. And a ragged man has no chance in the Games."

Hewako did not reply. However, thereafter he spoke to Hadon only in the line of duty. Though their backs were on fire, they returned the next day to the oars. The priestess rubbed a soothing ointment on the wounds, though it was not soothing enough. She advised them to wash their backs every

27

two hours with water and soap and watch carefully for infection. Fortunately, there weren't any flies at sea, but the cockroaches would nibble at the wounds at night unless they also smeared on a repellent.

"And stay out of the pig sty," she said, and slapped them playfully on the back. Caught by surprise, they screamed, and the priestess laughed uproariously.

"Boys will be boys," she said, "but you're men now. By Kho, if I weren't married to the captain, I'd see just how manly you two are!"

Hadon was glad of that. He didn't care for the fifty-year-old fat woman, and he would not have dared refuse her invitation.

3

The high rugged cliffs continued to rise from the sea. The galleys kept away from them by two miles, since there were reefs close to them. Many a ship had been driven against them by storms and all hands perished without a trace. Then the strait itself appeared, a narrow break in the cliffs, and the fleet put into a port that had been built at great expense of money and life. Two stone breakwaters curved out from cliffs, against which a floating great raft was moored, and on this raft were the headquarters of the Kethnan strait fleet. The Khokarsan fleet was obliged to put in here and to submit to another search. The captains of the merchant and naval vessels fumed, but they could do nothing.

"Fifteen years ago, Piqabes destroyed this place with a great storm," the captain said. "Would that she'd do it again! Though not while we're here!"

At dawn the next day the fleet put out, its path curving

outward so that it could enter the strait head-on. The strait was a gloomy chasm created by some enormous riving of the mountains in the distance past, perhaps at the creation of the world by Kho. It was the only water connection between the two seas, the northern Kemu and the southern Kemuwopar. It was unknown to the civilized world until the hero Keth led two galleys through its awesome darkness, and they burst out into a great bright sea. That was one thousand and ninety-nine years ago. A few other explorers had followed, but there was no active colonization until two hundred and thirteen years later, when Kethna founded the city named after him. Fourteen years later, the priestess-heroine Lupoeth discovered diamond-bearing clay and gold at the site of Opar, and the southern sea became worthwhile considering by the rulers of Khokarsa.

So narrow was the strait that at a distance of a mile its entrance looked merely like a darker vein of stone in a dark cliff. Then, as the first of the naval vessels, a bireme, plunged into it, it seemed to gape like the foaming mouth of a stone monster. Hadon's vessel was the third to enter. One moment they were tossing on the choppy waters in the bright sun, and the next they had been swallowed up. The waters rushed through, carrying them between sheer walls so high that the sky was only a thin ribbon. The dusk rapidly settled about them, so thick as to seem palpable. There was no turning back now, because there just was no room to maneuver. They must either go ahead or go down under the waters; there was no choice. A signalman stood on the prow, above the bronze ram, and called back to the first mate, who relayed instructions to the gong master. Torches guttered on the prow and along the side of the vessel; the oars lifted and dipped, their blades only a few feet from the black hard walls. The chunk of oars, the dripping of water as they lifted, the voice of the signalman and the mate, and the clang of the gong were the only sounds. The orders were for everybody else to be silent, but that was not necessary. Nobody felt like talking, and even those who had made the passage many times felt what Keth and his men must have felt the first time they dared it. Truly, is seemed to be a gateway to a world of the dead, of the queendom where dread Sisisken ruled over her phantoms, pale citizens of the greatest empire of all. No wonder that Keth had had to put down a mutiny before he could lead his men through this twilit passage.

The strait did not go as a measuring stick, but curved back and forth. Several times the walls moved in closer, and it was necessary to ship the oars while one side of the vessel touched stone. Though the contact was not hard, it would have crushed the fragile hull if bumpers of mahogany had not been put up before the vessel entered the strait.

Hadon and his companions stood before the fore deck-house and watched. They had been relieved of their duties during the traverse, since the captain wanted only professionals at the oars. Hadon and Hewako were happy about this, because their lash wounds were far from healed. But their happiness was tempered with apprehension. They kept looking upward and muttering prayers. There were said to be ogres who lived in caves along the cliffs, and if they heard a ship coming, they would stretch down their long arms and snatch up a mariner and eat him. And sometimes the wild Klemqaba would hurl large rocks at the vessels.

Presently clouds shut off the blue line far above, and they seemed to be crawling through the night. The captain ordered more torches lit, but these were soon sputtering in a heavy rain. The wind, which had been only a soft fingertip on their necks, suddenly became a heavy cold hand. The contestants went into the deckhouse and put on caps and ponchos of animal skin and then came back out on the deck. They did not want to be trapped in the house if the vessel should be pushed hard against a cliff. Not that much could be done if the ship did sink. They would be crushed between hull and cliff if the following vessel tried to pull them out of the water. Still, it was better to die in the open.

The strait twisted for fifty miles, and it took two days and nights to get through. The rain stopped, the clouds moved off, in the middle of the noon of the second day the walls suddenly fell away, and they moved onto a broad sea in golden light. Simari sacrificed the finest of the boars and poured the best of wine into the blue waters, and the rowers chanted a thanksgiving song. Everybody smiled, and those not working capered. Hadon felt so good that he drank two cups of wine. The steward, a dour little man, noted the cups down in his records. The city of Opar was paying for the expenses of

Hadon's trip, since he was too poor to bear the cost himself.

The captain consulted the lodestone compass card to check that the lead naval vessel was on the proper bearing, and the bireme turned north by north-northwest toward the island of Khokarsa. The last lap, the longest, lay ahead of them.

Days and nights passed. The broad blue-green Kemu was the only thing they saw except for birds and an occasional ship.

Several days out of Khokarsa, they sighted fishing fleets. These consisted of small ten-man sailing ships and a mother ship which prepared the fish and salted them. Clouds of birds, fish-eagles, sea vultures, and white birds with hooked beaks, the *dakoekem*, swirled around the boats.

And then came the day when a long dark line lifted on the horizon. Sea-girt, cliff-girt Khokarsa was rising to meet them.

The fleet rowed into the broad bay of Asema, passed its red-and-black walls and white towers and domes on their port, and by nightfall were in the long arm of the sea, the Gulf of Lupoeth, that cuts the island almost in half. The traffic became thick with naval vessels putting out for years-long patrols; merchant vessels, some of them gigantic triremes; fishing-boats; and the trade boats carrying cargo between the cities of Khokarsa or river boats ferrying the products of the inland plain cities to the coastal cities, where they would be transferred to the seagoing merchant vessels.

It took three days until the sea arm began to narrow, but before that they saw the peak of the great volcano, Khowot, the Voice of Kho, which lies just east of the capital city. Then they saw the top of the Great Tower of Kho and Resu, two-thirds completed, centuries in the building, its construction often abandoned during times of tribulation.

The captain had by then run up the great linen flag bearing the red ant, the sign that this ship carried contestants from the treasure city of Opar. The flag ship of the fleet saluted the merchant ships, and the naval vessels veered toward the port on the naval-base island of Poehy. The merchants continued, bearing east of Poehy and proceeding slowly through the thick traffic. Presently they were docked, while an army band played, and the contestants filed off the gangplank to be greeted by the officials who would take charge of them.

Hadon was very excited, though he hoped that it was not

noticeable. He was dressed in his finest hippo-hide sandals, a kilt of leopard skin, a bronze cuirass bearing a relief of the great red ant, his bronze helmet with its plume of hawk feathers, and a broad leather belt supporting a bronze scabbard in which was the long, square-ended, slightly curving broadsword, the *tenu*. There seemed to be thousands waiting along the docks, and in the narrow streets beyond, more thousands hoping to catch a glimpse of the Great Gamesters. They waved and shouted and cheered, except for some rowdy drunks who booed. Doubtless, these were partisans of contestants from other cities.

Things went swiftly after that. The officials took over the youths from the priestess Simari, and then, the clangorous band leading, they were marched through the city. Hadon had hoped that they would be presented to the king and his daughter. No such thing. They passed near the high black granite walls of the Inner City, but after a while it was evident that they were to go straight to their quarters near the coliseum of the Great Games. Their progress was slow because of the crowds, which threw petals on them and tried to touch them. Their route led through the commercial and residential area of the east, lined by two to four-story-high buildings of adobe brick with a thick covering of white plaster. Many were tenement buildings. Though the city of Khokarsa was the richest in the world, it also held the most poor people. Evidently many of them neglected their daily ritual bath, because the stench from them in the hot narrow streets was strong. Added to that was the odor of rotting garbage on the pavements and barrels of excrement waiting to be shipped out to the rural areas for fertilizer.

After a mile, the street began climbing, and suddenly they were going by the residences of the well-to-do and the wealthy.

These were large two-story buildings set behind high walls and guarded even in daytime by men with spears and swords. Here the crowd thinned out, consisting mostly of wives of the wealthy and their sons and daughters and the servants and slaves. Hadon saw one beautiful girl who made his pulse beat faster. She wore only a kilt, but it was of the finest linen, embroidered with red and blue flower patterns, and a necklace of diamonds fell between her breasts. A large scarlet flower adorned her long blond hair. If there were more girls

32

like her, he thought, he might enjoy his free time. If he had any. He had no idea what restrictions he faced during the training period.

The street kept winding up and up, and soon they were so high that he could look down on the Inner City. He could see the moated and walled citadel in the northeast corner, the rocky hill on top of which were the palaces, the temples, and the main government buildings. Beyond was the great tower, a ziggurat now five hundred feet tall, its base covering half a mile. Dust hung around it, dust stirred up by thousands of men and oxen laboring there.

The street began to descend again, and they were crossing the Road of Kho, the wide stone-block-paved highway that meandered from the wall of the Inner City up the steep side of the volcano. Above them, glittering white, was the tomb of the hero Gahete, the first man to land on this island, almost eighteen hundred years ago. Up beyond it was the plateau on which was the great temple of Kho and the sacred oak grove. But he could not see them.

They passed through another wealthy residential area, crossed a bridge over a canal, and then, coming onto a broad field, saw the coliseum. Hadon's heart beat even faster than when he had seen the beautiful blond girl. Inside the high circular granite walls his fate waited for him. But he would not see its inside today. He was marched into the barracks reserved for the youths and assigned a bed and a closet. He was glad to remove the hot bronze armor and to take a shower.

4

A month passed before the contestants were received by the king and his daughter, the high priestess. In the meantime, the youths spent the daylight hours training and the evenings talking or shooting dice. Everyone trained by himself; there were no practice matches among them; but they carefully watched each other, making evaluations. Hadon had been mildly shocked to discover that there were three youths taller than he, two of whom were much more thickly muscled. The third, Wiqa of Qaarquth, was the man who might beat him in the 440-yard dash and the two-mile run. He wouldn't know until the day the races came, of course. But Wiqa was fast, very fast. He also seemed to be a swift swimmer, though Taro thought that he could beat him. Hadon didn't believe this, but he did not say so. Taro, who had always been so jolly in Opar and on the voyage, had become glum. It was evident that he regretted now having entered, and it was too late to back out. There was no law forbidding him, but he would be thought a coward if he did, and he could never return to the city of Opar.

Hadon had his own moments of doubt and gloom. It was one thing to be the tallest and the swiftest in Opar, but here he was, a rube actually, up against the pick of the mighty empire. He could not quit, though he could manage to disqualify himself during the field and track events. If a man did not pick up enough points from these, before the dangerous events, he would be eliminated. And doubtless others before him, losing heart, had done just that. He hoped that Taro would do this. He could not. When he was in a contest, he had to do everything he could to win. He wouldn't be able to live with himself if he deliberately lost. And suicide, unless committed under honorable circumstances, assured one of the most miserable of existences in the empire of dread Sisisken. Whereas if he died fighting bravely during the Games, he would be buried as a hero, and his pylon would rise along the Road of Kho.

He kept his doubts to himself. When he wrote long letters to his family in Opar, he tried to convey the idea that he was sure of becoming the victor. By the time the mail had been delivered—if it were, since the ship bearing it might be intercepted by pirates or sunk in a storm—he would long since have been buried or become the husband of Awineth and the new king of kings of Khokarsa. That is, he would be if Awineth accepted him, because she had the right to reject anyone who did not please her. And it was possible that Awineth might marry her father. Rumor had it that Minruth had wooed her but that she had said no. Minruth would not wish to give up the throne, and he had precedent for his suit. Three kings of Khokarsa had married their sisters or daughters to retain the crown.

Meanwhile, whatever happened elsewhere, Hadon had to consider the immediate goal. Wiqa was a threat in the races. Gobhu, a mulatto of a family that had been free for a hundred years, was a threat in the broad and high jumps, and he seemed to be very fast in the hundred-yard dash. There were at least three men who seemed destined to win in the wrestling. Hewako, he thought, would finally prevail, though a bull of a man from Dythbeth, Woheken, was immensely strong and very quick. Hadon watched the youths wrestling with professionals. They all seemed to be very impressed by Hewako and Woheken.

Hadon wondered what the *numatenu* with whom he worked out, using wooden swords, thought of him.

They always beat him, though never by more than four points, and he thought that they respected him. The only contestants who seemed to be as skillful as he were Taro and Wiqa. The sword fight was the most important, because it was to the death. But, as his father had said, the man with the most killer's drive would probably be the winner. And all the youths were untested; none had ever killed a man in a sword fight.

Hadon made his evaluations of his competitors and was not overly worried for a while. Then, one day, it struck him that some might be deliberately holding back so they could

35

surprise their opponents. And he had trouble getting to sleep because of worrying about it.

The day came when they were to be presented at court. They rose at dawn, bathed, sacrificed, and ate. Clad in full armor, they marched behind a band to the Road of Kho and over its ancient marble blocks to the city. Again they passed through cheering crowds. They halted before the fifty-foot-wide moat and the hundred-foot-high walls that ringed the base of the acropolis of the Inner City. They marched across the oaken drawbridge, the massive bronze gates at the other end opening as they did so.

Beyond was the steep granite hill of the citadel, a truncated cone two hundred feet high and over a half-mile in diameter. Around its perimeter was a wall of massive granite blocks fifty feet high. The heroes walked up the steep marble staircase lined with diorite and basalt statues of the *r"ok'og'a** and waited at its top for their elders to catch their breath. Then they passed through a twenty-foot-broad and forty-foot-high gateway. Above this were two carved fish-eagles in profile, a massive diamond set in the eye socket of each. They walked down the wide straight Boulevard of Khukly, the heron goddess, past crowds of government officials and workers. They halted once more, this time before the thousand-year-old palace of the rulers of the empire of Khokarsa. This was, next to the Tower of Kho and Resu, the largest building in the world. It was nine-sided, built of red-veined white marble, and capped by a dome plated with gold, the base of which was inset with patterns of diamonds, emeralds, and rubies. They walked up the nine wide steps, each dedicated to a primary aspect of Kho, and came to a portico. Each of its colonnades was carved in the stiff style of the ancients; each was a representation of a beast, plant, or hero of the nine-year Great Cycle: a fish-eagle, a hippopotamus, a green parrot, the hero Gahete, a sea-otter, a horned fish, a honeybee, a millet plant, and the hero Wenqath.

Hadon was awed by all this. By the time he had marched into the central room, where royalty sat and the great men and women stood he felt very small and humble.

* Probably a now extinct giant reptile, the dragonlike *sirrush* depicted on the Ishtar Gate of ancient Babylonia. In Hadon's time they could be found in the jungles along the southern sea.

The bronze trumpets blared, bullroarers throomed, and their escort grounded the butts of their spears with a crash.

The herald cried out, "Behold, priestess of Kho and of her daughter, the moon, the heroes of the Great Games! Behold, king of kings of the empire Khokarsa and of the two great seas, the heroes of the Great Games!" And he finished by three times reciting the passage that must end all official greetings in this palace. "And remember that death comes to all!"

Awineth sat on an oaken throne on whose high back was perched a chained fish-eagle. The throne was unadorned, though the woman it held was adornment enough. Her hair was long and jet black, her features were striking and bold, her eyes were large and dark gray, her skin was white as milk, her breasts were full and shapely, and the legs were slim and rounded. Certainly she left nothing to be desired physically, though her hips might have been a little broader. It was said, however, that she had a hellish temper.

Her throne was a half-step higher than the king's, a superiority which Minruth was supposed to resent very much. His throne was, in contrast with hers, a splendor of gold and diamonds and emeralds, its back topped by a diorite carving of Resu, the Flaming God, as a crowned eagle of the mountains. Minruth was a man of medium height, but he had broad shoulders and a big paunch. His features were much like his daughter's, except that his nose was larger and slightly curved. Fat now hid the muscles that had enabled him to win the Great Games thirty-eight years before. Still, he did not look as old as most men of fifty-six. He did, however, look unhappy. His thick dark eyebrows, so much like his daughter's, were bent in a scowl.

Near him, a huge black lion, chained, lay on the marble dais and blinked sleepy green eyes.

Awineth spoke in a strong but pleasant voice. "Greetings, heroes! I have watched you unseen and have listened to your trainers. You are all men of pleasing physique, though I'm not too sure about the quickness of wits or of speech of some of you. I would not want to bear children to a man of dull mentality, so let us hope that none among you who fit that description becomes the victor. I would not marry such a man! However, it is seldom that a slow-wit wins, so I am not troubled much by thoughts of having to reject the victor."

She made a sign, and the herald thumped the butt of his staff and cried, "Does the king of kings, the father of the high priestess, wish to speak?"

Minruth spoke in a harsh, rumbling voice. "Yes. I have seldom seen such a sorry bunch of heroes. Now, when I fought in the Great Games, I was pitted against men! I am sorry that my daughter must have such a bad lot to choose from. If, that is, she does so choose."

Hadon's face burned with shame.

Awineth laughed and said, "It is always thus—the good old days, the good old days, when giants walked among us. Well, there is one among you who specially pleases me, and I have prayed to Kho that She give him the victory."

"Is it I?" Hadon thought, and his heart leaped.

Awineth arose and said, "Dismiss them."

Hadon was startled. He had thought that there would be more to it than this, a banquet perhaps, during which he might get to talk to Awineth. But no. They were to be herded out after their long walk, marched back hot and thirsty to the barracks.

Hewako, behind Hadon, muttered, "If I ever get my hands on that beautiful bitch, she'll not be so arrogant."

Taro, beside Hewako, said, "She'd probably rather marry a gorilla. Didn't you hear what she said about the lame-brains among us?"

"And you, Taro, I'll break your back," Hewako said.

"Silence, there!" the herald said in a low voice. Hewako shut up, the band began playing again, and they started the march back. As they emerged from the palace, they saw that the wind had shifted, and clouds of dust from the works around the great tower were powdering everything. Hadon thought that it must take an army just to keep the palace clean. Also, the odor from the thousands of workers and beasts, and the clamor, must be disturbing to the palace occupants when the wind blew their way. But they would not be the only ones unhappy about the Great Tower. The expense of building it was a heavy burden to the taxpayer, and diseases often broke out among the workers. Minruth would do better to stop its construction and to spend money on destroying the pirate city of Mikawuru and humbling the arrogant Kethnans. But it was said that he was mad and that he was intent on finishing the tower in his lifetime. Now, if he, Hadon, became king of kings, he would slow down the work on it, enough to relieve the tax burden but not enough to anger Kho and Resu. Then he would devote money and energy to proper matters.

That was the last the youths saw of Awineth and Minruth until the first day of the games. But they heard rumors of events in the Inner City. The most exciting was that a man, the sole survivor of an expedition across the savannas and mountains to the far north, had returned. And had brought word that he had seen, actually seen, Sahhindar, the Gray-Eyed God!

This was electrifying news. Sahhindar, god of plants, of bronze, and of time, had long been exiled by his mother, Kho. The priestess said that he had incurred Her wrath when he taught the first men to domesticate plants and animals and to make bronze. She had planned to do that Herself when the proper time came, but the Gray-Eyed God had disobeyed Her and showed men too soon how they might become better than the beasts. And so She had thrust him from the land, and She had taken away his ability to travel through time, to go back and forth between past, present, and future. Sahhindar, thereafter, was doomed to keep pace with time as all but Kho Herself must. And he was doomed to wander the jungle and the savannas outside the borders of Khokarsa, on the edge of the world itself.

Yet here was a man, Hinokly, who claimed that he had met the god, had talked to him, and had been told that someday he might come back to Khokarsa. Could it be true? Or was it some wild tale?

"I know the deities walk among us," Taro said to Hadon. "But do you know anyone besides the oracular priestesses who have ever seen a god or goddess? Have *you* ever seen one?"

"Only in my dreams," Hadon said.

"If this is true," Taro said, "it might mean that Kho has forgiven Sahhindar. Or it might mean that he is coming back despite her ban. In which case, Khokarsa will suffer from the wrath of Kho. It is always the mortals who get hurt most when the deities quarrel among themselves."

"Perhaps Hinokly is a liar?" Hadon said.

39

"No sane man would dare to make such a lie. Kho would strike him down."

"Then he may be insane. It is said that he suffered terribly in the Wild Lands."

Wiqa said, "I will deny it if you quote me. But I've heard that the priests of Resu would welcome the return of Sahhindar. They say that he would ally himself with his great brother, Resu, and chain up Kho until She acknowledged that they were master. And I've heard it said that Minruth would be pleased if Sahhindar returned. He would then remain king, force his daughter to marry him, and he would raise the status of men."

Hadon and Taro turned pale. Hadon said, in a low voice while he glanced around, "Don't repeat such things, Wiqa! Do you want to be castrated and then thrown to the pigs?"

He stared suspiciously at Wiqa. "Or are you one of those who think Resu should be paramount?"

"Not I!" Wiqa said. "But it's no secret that Minruth believes that Resu should be chief and master. And it has been said that he has been heard to say, while talking with the priests of Resu, that he who controls the army and navy is the true master of Khokarsa. Spears are to be feared as much as, if not more than, the wrath of Kho, according to him."

"It is said that Minruth drinks much and talks boldly when in his cups," Hadon said.

"Minruth is a descendant of the Klemsaasa, who seized the throne and did away with the custom of sacrificing the king after he had ruled nine years," Wiqa said. "If one custom can be changed, so can another."

"I'm a descendant of the Klemsaasa, as you are," Hadon said. "But I abhor the idea of blaspheming against Kho. If She becomes offended, then we may have another Great Plague. Or She may speak with fire and lava and earthquakes and destroy this ungrateful land. It is said that Wimimwi, Minruth's wife, prophesied just such a thing if the priests of Resu did not abandon their efforts to make Resu chief of creation."

"Here comes Hewako!" Taro said. "For the sake of Kho, let's drop this kind of talk. If he should report us, he would be rid of three of his chief competitors."

"I've said nothing to be ashamed of," Hadon said.

"Yes, but by the time the priestesses determined that, the Games would be over."

It was Wiqa's turn to become pale. It had suddenly occurred to him that Hadon and Taro could eliminate him if they reported his words.

"Don't worry," Hadon said. "Getting you into trouble would not be honorable. Besides, you only passed on rumors and hearsay. But Hewako would report you."

And then the first moon day of the month of Adeneth, goddess of sexual passion, in the Year of Gahete the Hero arrived. On this day the crowds streamed out to the coliseum, which could hold 150,000. At the ninth hour of the day, the high priestess and the king arrived and took their seats under the canopy. The gates were closed, the trumpets flourished, the drums beat, the bullroarers throomed, and the heroes marched out to hail Minruth and Awineth and to pour out liberations to Resu and Kho. The herald announced the first event, and the Games had begun.

There were three champions from each of the thirty queendoms of the empires. The first event was the hundred-yard dash. Deciding the winner from ninety contestants was a lengthy procedure. There was room abreast for nine men on the quarter-mile track that circled inside the coliseum. The contestants from three cities, Opar, Khokarsa, and Wethna, ran the first race. Hadon, atremble to go, crouched, clad in only a doeskin loincloth, waiting for the yellow linen cloth to strike the ground. The crowd fell hushed as the trumpets blared, the starter gave the directions, the cloth fell, and all nine hurled themselves down the track. However, a clang of gongs summoned them back before they had gone a few paces. A man from Wethna had made a false start.

On the second fall of the cloth, they started true. Hadon was happy at the end, because he had passed the finishing post first. Taro was second, a man from Khokarsa third, and Hewako, surprisingly, the fourth. Though squat and massive, he could pump his short legs like a hippopotamus', which can run swiftly indeed for short distances.

The winners of the first four races were then matched. Up until the last moment, Hadon thought that he was going to win that. He was a slow starter, behind the other three for about fifty yards, but then his long legs gobbled up the earth,

41

and he passed Taro, then Moqowi of the city of Mukha. He drew even with Gohu of Dythbeth and was exultant for several seconds as he thought he was going to pass him. But Gobhu put on a burst of speed—evidently he had been saving some strength—and he beat Hadon by a foot.

Hadon wasn't depressed. He had done better than he thought he would. The hundred-yard dash was not his forte.

He looked up at the box in which Awineth sat. Was it his imagination, or did she look disappointed? Probably it was the former.

The second-place winners of the first races were then matched; after them, the third-place winners. Gobhu was given a gold crown to wear in life and in death.

The second event was the quarter-mile dash. Hadon felt more confident now, but even so he was beaten by about six inches by long-legged Wiqa. This did not depress him, even though this was the first time that he had ever lost this event. Considering the competition, he had not done badly. And he did win first place in the race for the second-place winners.

Hewako, he was pleased to see, won nothing. But then, the fellow would pick up many points in the wrestling, boxing, and javelin-throwing.

Late that afternoon, the two-mile race was run. This was to be done in four heats at first, twenty-two men in each race. Two had been eliminated on points in the previous races, reducing the number of contestants to eighty-eight. The two disqualified walked off with hanging heads, but Hadon thought that one of them looked relieved. He wasn't going to be king, but then he wasn't going to die either.

Twenty-two men made a very crowded track. Moreover, for the first quarter-mile, pushing and tripping was allowed. Hadon took the outside curve at first. Though this would require him to cover more distance, it kept him free of the shovers and the trippers. He trailed along behind Wiqa and Taro and a tall fellow from Qethruth, and then slowly increased his speed the second mile. At the third quarter of the last mile, he crept up behind the three still in the lead, and in the fourth quarter he drew up even with Wiqa but was still on the outside. Then, in the last half of the last quarter, he burst into a pace that brought him four paces ahead of Wiqa.

He could have gone faster, but he wanted to save his strength. And he was glad that he had eliminated Wiqa, his chief competitor, in the first heat.

An hour later, his wind was recovered, but he was not as strong as he had been in the first two-miler. Still, he sped along the outside. This time, however, the others, knowing that he had won the first race, tried to gang up on him. Someone shoved him hard from behind, and he fell on his face, skinning it and his knees. Angry, he jumped up, overtook the last man by the end of the first mile, and then stepped up his speed. He went agonizingly slowly, but he did not want to burn himself out. In the final quarter-mile, he drew on strength which he had not known existed in him. The golden crown glittered visibly at the end of the track, and he won it by ten paces.

Was it his imagination that Awineth was smiling because she was pleased that he had won, or did she always smile at the winner?

Hadon slept heavily that night while torches flared along the walls of the great hall and guards prowled softly among them. In the past, contestants had sometimes done things to their fellow competitors—poisoned them, released venomous snakes on their beds, or poured itching powder on the bedclothes so the contestant would lose vital sleep. The guards were here to ensure that nothing like that happened. And outside, more guards watched, because relatives and friends of the Gamesters had been known to attempt similar deeds. The guards themselves were watched by others, because guards had also been bribed.

Thus Hadon slept deeply, knowing that nobody—such as Hewako, for instance—was going to try to cripple or kill him.

The next day was a day of rest, during which he worked out very lightly. The day after, the Games were resumed with the broad and high jumps. In these, the contestants knew fairly well beforehand what the results would be. They had watched each other during the workouts. But the information had been kept from the crowds, or at least it was supposed to be kept. Actually, the big gamblers had been spying and had bribed the officials for advance information, and they were now making bets with the suckers. The big money was on

Gobhu in the broad jump, with, significantly, none on Hadon or Kwobis as second-place winners. These two had jumped equal distances so many times during practice that the professional gamblers did not care to chance their money on the second place winners.

In the high jump, those in the know were backing Hadon of Opar, with Wiqa of Qaarquth in second place.

However, man proposes and Kho disposes.

The wind was tricky that day, with intervals of calm and sudden gusts. Each contestant was given only one broad jump, and so was at the mercy of chance. It was Gobhu's bad luck that the wind was against him but with Hadon and Kwobis. He came in third, with Kwobis first and Hadon an inch behind him.

In the high jump, each man could stay in as long as he did not knock the bar off. The bar was set at five feet ten inches, however, and the contest quickly became one among Hadon, Wiqa, Taro, and an exceptionally long-legged man from Qethruth, Kwona. At six feet four inches, Hadon was the only one to clear the bar. His feat was remarkable, considering that the jumpers were barefoot. The record was six feet five, and the betting became furious in the stands while the bar was set at that height. Hadon waited for the wind to die down and then made the greatest effort in his life. He lightly touched the bar as he rolled over, but it remained on its pegs. Amid cheering from the winners of bets and groaning from the losers, he made ready for an attempt to beat the record. The wind suddenly blew again, but this time it was behind him. He ran at the bar, gauging his steps so he could leap ahead of the usual mark; otherwise the wind might carry him too swiftly and against the bar. He knew as he left the ground that he was going to make it—Kho was with him—and though he again touched the bar, and it seemed that it would quiver off, it did not fall. And so he got a double golden crown that afternoon, one tier for being the winner, one tier for breaking the record.

The following day was one of rest for the youths. The next day they marched out behind a band to the lake, while good-looking girls strewed their path with petals. They found the stands packed with people, most of whom had made heavy bets, whether they could afford it or not. The first event was

44

one of endurance, a swim across and back the quarter-mile-broad lake. All eighty-eight Gamesters lined up, and when the starter's trumpet blared, they dived into the water. Hadon trailed along behind half of the swimmers. He knew his own pace, and he did not want to burn himself out. At the other end he had passed many and had only about ten ahead of him. After touching the baton of a referee on the dock, he turned and began to increase speed. Halfway back, he was a little behind Taro, a youth from Dythbeth, Wiqa, Gobhu, and Khukly. The latter was from the pile city of Rebha and had spent more time in the water than anybody else. He had heavy shoulders and exceptionally large hands and feet and was the one Hadon had worried most about. Now Khukly, deciding to turn on the power, drew even with the others and then passed them. Hadon felt as if his lungs were burning, and his arms and legs were becoming as stiff as driftwood. This was the time when the spirit had to be strong enough to overcome the body's pain, and he urged himself on, though it would have been so pleasant to quit. He passed all but Khukly and drew even with him and lashed himself on, on, on. The crowd's roar mingled with the roar of his blood in his head. And, suddenly, it was over and he was panting like a cornered boar and so weak that he almost accepted an offer to pull him out. Pride prevented him, and he hauled himself up onto the dock and sat down until he could recover his wind. Well, he had almost made it. If the distance had been about twenty yards more, he could have passed Khukly. His endurance was greater. But the lake was not longer, and so he had been beat out by half an arm's length.

Two hours later, the first of the youths climbed up a seventy-foot ladder to a narrow platform hanging over the middle of the lake. He wore a bonnet of fish-eagle's feathers and his face was painted to resemble a fish-eagle's. Around his ankles were fish-eagle feathers. He poised on top of the platform while the crowd fell silent. When the trumpet blared, he soared outward. The crowd roared as he cut the water cleanly, though the bonnet and the ankle feathers were torn off.

The high dive was a feature of the Games founded on an ancient Fish-Eagle Totem ceremony, when the courage of youths during rites of passage was tested. The betting was the heaviest so far, though it was not on the winner, since there was no gold crown for this. The money was down on whether the diver would survive without injury, and since no practice dives had been made, no one knew what the ability of the individual divers was.

The third youth hit the water with his body turned and leaning outward. The crack of flesh against the surface was heard by everybody, and the youth did not come up at once. A boat put out from an anchored raft nearby, and divers went down after him. They pulled up a corpse.

As the sixth youth fell, he was struck by the wind, still tricky, and he hit the water sideways. He wasn't killed, but broken ribs and injured muscles had eliminated him.

When Hadon's turn came, he waited for a few seconds after the trumpet call. Many in the crowd booed him because they thought he had lost his nerve. But he was waiting for the wind to pass, and when it did, he jumped. He was just in time to avoid the second trumpet call, which, if sounded, would have disqualified him for the rest of the Games. And he would have been open to accusations of cowardice.

He entered the water cleanly, but nevertheless came up slightly stunned. Years of practice had paid off.

At the end of the contest, the crowd went away pleased, except for the lovers, relatives, and friends of the dead and the injured, of course. Five were among the latter and four among the former.

The next day, the dead were buried in their earth tombs, and pointed marble monoliths were erected over the mounds. The contestants strewed white petals over the tombs, and the priestesses sacrificed bulls so the ghosts could drink blood and go happy to the garden that Kho reserved for heroes.

The next three days were devoted to boxing. The youths' fists were fitted with thin gloves that had a heavy layer of resin-impregnated cloth over the knuckles. In the preliminaries, they were matched according to height, so Hadon found himself facing Wiqa. Hadon had great confidence in his pugilistic ability, though he dreaded the wrestling, which would come after the boxing. Wiqa, he quickly found, was also confident, and with good reason. Hadon caught a right to the jaw and went down. He waited until the referee had counted to eleven and then rose. Less cocky, he boxed more cautiously. Presently, after an exchange of hard blows, he shot his long left arm up through Wiqa's guard. Wiqa tried bravely to get up but just could not make it.

The odds went up on Hadon when the crowd saw his whip-lash left.

Hadon fought twice more that day and won, but that night he nursed a black right eye, sore ribs, and a sore jaw.

The next afternoon, his first opponent was Hoseko, a short, powerful man from Bawaku. Hoseko was outreached by Hadon, but his thick body and heavy-boned head absorbed punishment as a bull elephant absorbed darts. Hadon ripped his face with a series of slashing blows, but Hoseko, blinking through the blood, kept on boring in. And, suddenly, a sledgehammer left caught Hadon on the jaw, and his legs crumpled as if they were made of papyrus. He got to his hands and knees after hearing the referee, unaccountably far away, count to seven. By eleven, he was on his feet again.

Hoseko advanced slowly, chin down, shoulders hunched, his left fist out, his right eye blinded with blood. Hadon, his legs still crumply but slowly regaining their power, circled Hoseko. Hoseko kept turning and advancing. The crowd booed Hadon, and the referee cracked his whip against the ground. Fight! Or feel the whip against your back the next time!

Hadon continued circling, jabbing at Hoseko but not connecting. Out of the corner of his eye he saw the referee lift the whip handle again. The hippopotamus hide traveled back, back, over the referee and behind him, the arm jerked forward, the tip sped toward Hadon; timing himself exactly right, he ducked. The tip whistled above him, going inward past him, and it cracked against Hoseko's face. Hoseko cried out with pain and surprise; the referee shouted with surprise; the crowd roared protest. But Hadon had taken advantage of Hoseko's confusion and the dropping of his guard. Hadon's left came from far out and ended against Hoseko's sturdy chin.

Hoseko's eyes crossed; he staggered backward, his hands falling down to his sides; Hadon buried his left in Hoseko's solar plexus; Hoseko fell down doubled up onto the ground and was there long after the count of twelve.

There was a delay. The referee summoned the two judges,

and they talked for a few minutes, gesticulating and looking frequently at Hadon. The crowd, becoming restless, booed the three men. Hadon, panting and sweating, stood unmoving. He knew that the three were discussing the admissibility of his trick. Was it valid for a boxer deliberately to cause the referee to use his whip, dodge it, and cause it to strike his opponent?

The referee and the judges were in a difficult situation. This had never happened before. If they ruled that Hadon's trick was admissible, then they could expect other contestants to try it. Not that it would be easy to pull it off again. Every referee would be on his guard from now on. If anybody was foolish enough to try it again, he'd get his back laid open to the shoulderbones.

Possibly it was this that decided the judges. The referee, scowling, lifted Hadon's right arm. The crowd cheered and then laughed as rubbery-legged Hoseko was carried off between two officials.

Hadon's second fight late that afternoon ended when Hadon sank a whiplash left to his opponent's solar plexus. He had taken so much punishment, however, that he walked off in a daze. Taro grabbed him, sat him down, washed and bandaged his facial cuts, and dabbed cold water on his face.

Hadon opened his eyes and became aware that an old man, one of the trainers, was standing by him.

"Why are you staring at me?" Hadon said.

"You got a lot to learn yet," the old man said. "But I haven't seen a left like that since the great Sekoko. He was before your time, kid, but you must have heard of him. He was boxing champion of the empire for fifteen years. He was tall and slim like you, and he had long arms like you and a left that murdered them. I'll tell you what, kid. If you get eliminated on points, don't feel bad. I can make you a champ in a few years. You'll be rich and famous."

"No, thanks," Hadon said.

The old man looked disappointed. "Why not?"

"I've seen too many punch-drunk boxers. Besides, I intend to be king."

"Well, if you don't make it, and you're still alive and healthy, see me. My name's Wakewa."

On the third day, Taro was carried off senseless in his

48

second match. But he had enough points to stay in the Games. Hewako had knocked out his opponent's front teeth and smashed his nose in two minutes, and now he rested. As Hadon walked by him toward the circle, Hewako called out, "I hope you win this one, floorsweeper's son! Then I'll have the pleasure of mangling that pretty face before I break your jaw and eliminate you from the Games and send you in disgrace back to Opar!"

"The jackal yaps; the lion kills," Hadon said coolly. But he felt that there was an excellent chance that Hewako might be able to make good his boasts. It was plain that he expected Hadon to be better than he in the final contest, the sword fight. Hadon had better qualifications—height, arm length, and most important, many more hours of practice with the *tenu*. Hewako had also worked out from childhood with the wooden sword; there wasn't a healthy child in the empire, male or female, who didn't. But Hewako had known that his talents were in boxing and wrestling, and so he had devoted more hours to them than to the *tenu*. He wasn't a professional boxer by any means, but he was closer to being one than Hadon.

It was obvious that he hoped to so cripple Hadon that he would not be able to continue competing. Whether or not he did cripple or perhaps even kill him, he had to win the match the following day. Either Hadon or Kagaga would win today's match, but whoever won, Hewako had to win tomorrow. He did not have enough points to stay in unless he did so. But if he won the boxing and then went on to win the wrestling, he would have enough points to stay right in to the finish. Provided, that is, he wasn't crippled or killed before then.

Hewako was hoping that Hadon would win today so he, Hewako, could eliminate him the hard way tomorrow. Hadon could afford to lose today, since he had accumulated so many points. And this was why the man who hated him so much was rooting for him.

Kagaga meant Raven, and Kagaga certainly looked like one. He was a tall, dark, stoop-shouldered, long-nosed youth from some small town above the Klemqaba coasts. He had a croaking voice and a pessimistic temperament. But he was a very good boxer. And he charged Hadon as if he meant to batter him to a pulp within a few minutes. Hadon retreated,

49

but he danced in now and then and flicked at Kagaga's face or hammered his arms enough to keep the referee from using his whip on him. Kagaga called to him to stand still and fight like a hero, not a wild dog. Hadon merely grinned and back-pedaled or sometimes suddenly advanced to jab Kagaga lightly on the face before retreating again. The crowd booed, and Hewako bellowed accusations of cowardice. Hadon paid attention only to the referee and to Kagaga. He kept dancing in and out, using his longer reach to thump Kagaga, not too hard, on his forehead or nose. And, suddenly, Kaga's right eyebrow was cut and blood was streaming down into his eye.

"Now, I suppose, you're going to run around him while he bleeds to death," the referee said. "Get in there and fight, or I'll flay you."

Hadon had hoped to drag the fight out until both he and Kagaga were too tired to lift their arms. Then Kagaga would win on points because of his aggressiveness, or Hadon would lose because of his lack of aggressiveness. Neither would be badly hurt, and Hadon could rest tomorrow while Hewako wore himself out on Kagaga. But this was not to be. Hewako might get his chance to cripple him tomorrow after all.

Reluctantly, Hadon attacked. There was a fierce exchange of body blows, thudding of fists, gruntings, and then one of Kagaga's fists slipped through, rocked Hadon's head back, and Hadon fell to his knees. He tried to get back up—no one was going to say that he had deliberately taken a dive—but he could not make it. He heard the referee count to twelve, and a few seconds later he rose shakily to his feet. Kagaga was looking dazed at his sudden good luck, and Hewako's face was as red as a baboon's bottom.

A minute later, Hadon, walking unaided to the showers, grinned at Hewako. Hewako's face became as red as if the baboon had been sitting on a rock.

The single event the next day was the match for the boxer's golden crown. Kagaga adopted his opponent's tactics of the day before, since he knew he could not last long in a toe-to-toe slugging fest. Unlike Hadon, he failed to gauge the limits to the referees patience. The whip caught him by surprise across the back; he jumped forward into Hewako's fist; he fell senseless with half his front teeth knocked out.

After the ceremony, Hewako approached Hadon and said,

"Day after tomorrow the wrestling starts. I didn't get a chance at you in the boxing, but you're not going to get away from me in the wrestling. And when I get my hands on you, I'm going to break your back."

"If you do, the referee will knock you silly with his club, and you might be eliminated," Hadon said. "Of course, I don't blame you for your eagerness to get rid of me now. You know that if we ever face each other with swords, you're a dead man. Though I may just chop off your nose to teach you a lesson."

Hewako spat at Hadon, though he was careful not to hit him, and he strutted away wearing his gold crown.

"Why does that man hate you so?" Taro said.

"I don't know," Hadon said. "I never did anything to offend him, not in the beginning, anyway. It's just one of those things, where you dislike a person for reasons you don't know."

Hewako never got his hands on Hadon. Hadon was eliminated after two victories by a bull buffalo of a youth from Mineqo. Hewako looked disappointed; Hadon merely grinned at him knowing that that would infuriate him. And Hewako almost lost the golden crown. During his last contest, he grabbed his opponent's fingers and tried to twist them back. This was illegal, and so the referee slammed his billy against the back of Hewako's head. He lost his senses long enough for his opponent to pin him, and Hewako came close to losing the third fall. Hadon, standing on the side, grinned again at Hewako when he winced as the gold crown was placed on his head.

He sobered up when he thought about the next seven events. Except for the last, no golden crown would be awarded. A man either survived or he didn't. From now on, there would be no referees to ensure that the rules were abided by.

And there was Taro. What if the final contestants were Taro and he? One would have to kill the other, and he certainly did not intend to be the corpse. The thought of slaying Taro depressed him. As he had done several times, he wondered why he had ever entered.

The answer was obvious. He wanted to be the greatest man in the kingdom. And Taro had also volunteered, knowing that he might have to face Hadon with a sword.

Two days later the crowd was again assembled in the stadium around the lake. The centers of interest were, first, the huge and hungry sea crocodiles that slid through the waters. The second was two ropes stretched across a part of the lake between two sturdy poles. One was farther out than the other and at a lower level than the first. One end of a third rope was tied to the middle point of the nearest rope running over the lake, and the other end was held by an official standing on a tower high above the edge of the lake.

The band blared; the crowd roared; vendors passed among the crowd selling fruits, cakes, and beer. Then there was a flourish of trumpets, and the crowd fell silent. Hadon, as the one with most points, had the honor of being the first contestant. He climbed up the high ladder to the platform, where he was handed the end of a rope. This was attached at the other end of the rope which ran at right angles across this corner of the lake. Beyond that rope was the lower parallel rope. And below were the crocodiles, the great gray armor-plated, many-teethed saurians.

Hadon looked at the canopied box in which Awineth and Minruth sat. They were far away, tiny, so he could not see her expression. Was it fear and hope for him? Or, like that which must be on Minruth's face and on most of the crowd's, did it show a desire that Hadon would fail and that he and the crocodiles would provide a brief but entertaining spectacle?

He hated the crowd at that moment. Crowds were people who had lost their individuality, who had become no more than vultures. Less, in fact, since vultures acted by the nature given to them by Kho, and by so doing were performing a useful deed. Yet, if he were in the mob, would he be any different from the others?

The starter's trumpet screamed. The crowd's roar subsided. He bent his knees, grasped the rope with both hands, and waited. The trumpet screamed again, as it had so many times in the past two thousand years, because this, like the high dive, was an ancient Fish-Eagle Totem custom.

He pushed out, clinging to the rope. The water swooped toward him; he drew up his legs, though the crocodiles could not reach him, and he curved up and out. Then he reached the end of the arc and fell back. He jerked his body on the return and swung back out again. Twice he increased the height of the swing. The third time, as he arrived just before the top of the arc, he prayed briefly and let loose. He soared out towards the rope before him, fell, and his hands closed on the outermost rope. And he was dangling while the crocodiles bellowed below and whitened the water with their furious lunges and thrashings of tails. He was too far away to be reached, of course, but his ordeal was not yet over. He had to go hand-over-hand along the rope until he got to the platform at the end. Then—he hated to think of it—he must take a balancing pole and walk the rope back to its other end.

He had no difficulty getting to the platform, though his palms were sweaty. An official handed him the pole after he had recovered his breath, and the trumpet screamed the third time. He stepped onto the rope, which was not as taut as he would have liked, and walked slowly, his bare feet lifting and gripping slowly. Below, the crocodiles thundered.

Hadon had practiced tightrope walking since he was two. But the crocodiles made a dangerous trick even more dangerous. If he lost his balance and had to grab the rope, he would not be eliminated. But he would have to go back to the platform and start all over again.

The rope swayed, and he strove to balance his weight so that the rope would not go into an increasing oscillation. The cheers of the crowd and some boos from ill-wishers reached him faintly, but the bellowing of the hungry beasts below was loud. He would not look down at them. He must concentrate on getting across.

When he reached the other platform, he almost collapsed. Suddenly, he was shaking and weak. But he had done it and would not have to do it again.

He climbed down and took his place among the contestants, who were sitting on the benches near the edge of the lake. Beyond them was the bronze-wire fence put up to keep the crocodiles from coming ashore.

"How was it?" Taro said.

"Not bad," Hadon said, hating himself for his bravado. It would never do for a hero to confess that his guts had turned into a beast trying to claw its way out through his belly.

The third man lost his balance, grabbed the rope, and hand-over-handed back to the platform. The second try, he fell with a scream, and the water roiled around his body. Hadon felt sick for him but glad for himself.

Hewako had to make two attempts, but he got across. His skin was gray beneath the bronze as he climbed down.

The man who followed him missed the rope when he let loose of the swinging rope, and he fell to his death.

By the time the last of the contestants had reached the ground, the sun was quartering the west, and ten were food in the bellies of the crocodiles.

The funerals the next day were curious in that they lacked the presence of the deceased. Stone statues representing the dead, all with the same stylized faces, were lowered into the graves, and earth was mounded over them and the monoliths set above them. Hadon watched the weeping relatives and wondered if his parents, too, would have occasion to grieve for him.

The next day the youths competed in the javelin-throwing. Each had a small round shield for defense but could not step outside a small circular fence. Each contestant was given three javelins to throw and had to endure three cast at him by another contestant from a distance of a hundred feet.

Twelve were wounded seriously enough to be eliminated; two were buried the next day; one man disgraced himself by jumping out of the ring. He hanged himself that night, and so saved himself from a coward's grave.

The games of the next three days were tests of the youths' skill with the sling. On the first day, Hadon was among the initial group of contestants to enter the field. There were ten of them, and each wore only a loincloth and a leather belt. The belt supported a dagger in a sheath and a leather pouch. The pouch held three biconical molded lead missiles. In the hand of each youth was a sling made of soft dwarf antelope leather. The youths marched to the center of the field and halted when a trumpet blew. The crowd fell silent. Another trumpet blast. A huge door in the wall which they faced swung open. Presently, thirty male gorillas, blinking in the sunlight, growling, nasty-eyed, emerged.

The crowd began yelling and cheering. The ten youths arranged themselves in a line facing the gorillas. Hadon was at its extreme left. The trumpet blew for the third time. Each youth tied one end of the sling's strap to one of the four fingers of his throwing hand. The other end, knotted, was then placed between the thumb and forefinger of that hand. With his other hand, the youth removed a lead projectile weighing three and one-half ounces from the pouch. He placed it in the pad which formed the pocket at the end of the two straps.

The gorillas, meanwhile, nervously ran back and forth on all fours or stood up and slapped their chests with their open palms. Though fearsome-looking beasts, they were naturally timid. However, for the last thirty days trainers had been trying to condition them to attack human beings. The trainers had pelted them with stones and poked them with sharp sticks until they had driven them into a fury. Eventually, the gorillas had gotten accustomed to taking out their frustrations on dummies in clothes stinking of humankind. For the last twelve days they had been tearing these apart, apparently with vast satisfaction. And so it was hoped that the gorillas would attack the contestants now. Especially since their trainers, safe on top of the wall, were throwing stones and pointed sticks at them. The giant anthropoids, however, for the moment seemed only bewildered and frightened.

The trumpet blew again. Hadon, with the others, held the ends of the sling above his head with one hand and the missile in its pocket in the other. Then he released the pocket end and began whirling the sling counterclockwise parallel to his body. Around and around, four times, the sling whirled, deriving most of its speed from wrist movement. At the part of the circle closest to the ground, he released the free end of the sling. The lead projectile, traveling more than sixty miles per hour, hurled in a parabola toward its target three hundred feet away. This was a huge reddish gorilla with a broken right canine and scarred face.

The thud of missiles sinking deep into flesh or smashing against the stone wall could be heard over the entire stadium. Six of the giant apes fell backward under the impact, and none of them moved after that. The crowd roared as the youths placed their second missiles in the slings. By then ten of the apes were advancing toward the youths, roaring, slapping their chests, picking up blades of grass and blowing them, or making short bluffing charges. The second fusillade knocked down seven of them, but two got to their feet, and roaring their hurt and rage, bounded toward the youths.

Before they could reach their objective, they fell dead with several missiles in them.

Hadon was not among those who released his last bicone. He wanted to save it for an emergency. He did not think that this would be long in coming. Thirteen of the anthropoids had been killed or rendered *hors de combat*. This left seventeen with only eight projectiles still unslung. And even if all eight hit their targets, there would still be nine gorillas left. And, facing them, ten humans with only six-inch knives.

More gorillas, driven by another hail of stones from the trainers, advanced toward the youths. One suddenly broke into a charge that did not end after a few yards. Hadon called out, "Save your missiles! Taro, you alone use your sling!"

Taro's projectile disappeared within the wide-open mouth of the ape, which fell dead. Hadon then called out the names of those who had missiles left, one by one, and they released them. Eight more gorillas died or were so badly wounded that they could not get up. But nine of the beasts remained, and these were brave with hysteria.

Four died under the knives, though not before they had killed three youths and badly maimed three more. If they had attacked together, instead of singly, they could have wiped out the humans. But they did not think like men, and so they died as beasts.

Hadon, Taro, and the two other youths still on their feet proceeded to dig out missiles from the carcasses with their knives. Hadon had just removed one bicone when he heard, "Watch out!" He looked up to see another hairy, long-canined monster rushing at him and his companions scattering. Hadon dropped the lead missile, transferred his bloody knife to his left hand, removed from his belt the clean knife he'd taken from a dead man, placed its blade in his palm, and cast it. The gorilla quit roaring, began screaming, somersaulted, and slid to a stop on its back just before Hadon. The hilt of the knife stuck out from its huge paunch.

After that, the four youths used the retrieved missiles to slay the four remaining gorillas. Then, saluting the king and queen, they walked out. Attendants poured in to drag away the dead, carry out the wounded humans, and set up the field for the next ten youths and thirty gorillas.

The next day the funerals for those who'd died were held, and the day after that the youths faced hyenas. There were four starved hyenas to each slinger, and each slinger had four missiles and an ax. The hyenas were more dangerous than the gorillas. They were carnivores, used to hunting in packs, and had been fed human flesh for two weeks before being starved. Their jaws could crush a man's leg or arm as if they were made of linen, and they had an awe-inspiring tenacity. Of the ten youths in Hadon's group, five were killed or bitten so badly that they were eliminated from the Games.

The following day, more funerals were conducted. The next day, the contestants faced leopards. These were man-eaters who'd been trapped in the jungle hinterlands of Wentisuh. They had been starved for three days, and goat blood had been smeared on the contestants to arouse beasts that did not need arousing. Three of the big cats were released at a time against two slingers, each of whom had two missiles and a sword. Hadon was paired with Gobhu, who was an even better slinger than his tall companion. Hadon's first throw broke the hind leg of a big male, and this caused the other two, a male and a female, to charge Gobhu. The mulatto knocked the eye out of the female and sent her rolling over and over. But the male knocked Gobhu down and tore his throat before Hadon's missile broke some of its ribs. Hadon cut off its head with his sword, dispatched the stunned female in the same manner, and finally cornered the male with the broken hind leg. Though crippled badly, it charged, and Hadon half-severed its neck while it was in the air.

That night, he and Taro sat at a table talking in a barracks which had grown larger and emptier with death.

"I overheard a judge saying that he understood that Minruth was considering making the Games a yearly event," Hadon said.

"How could he do that?" Taro said. "How often does a chief priestess lack a husband?"

"Oh, it wouldn't have anything to do with that. He would hold the Games just for the amusement of the people, not to mention his own. The winners would get large sums of money. And glory."

57

Taro made a disgusted sound. There was silence for a while, and then Hadon said, "What I don't understand is how Minruth thinks he can institute such games. He won't be king after these are over."

"Maybe he thinks none of us will survive," Taro said.

"That wouldn't do any good. New Games would have to be held."

There was another silence, broken when Hadon said, "Once the kings ruled only nine years and then were sacrificed. But the first of the Klemsaasa to rule—his name was Minruth, too —abolished that custom. Do you suppose that Minruth intends to refuse to give up the throne?"

Taro was startled. "How could he do that? Kho Herself would destroy him! Nor would the people put up with it!"

"Kho didn't destroy the first Minruth," Hadon said. "And the people who rose against him were destroyed. Minruth controls the army and the navy, and while a part of the services would revolt, the other might not. Minruth favors Resu, and he has taken care to make sure that the officers and the soldiers who favor Resu are in key positions. I'm only nineteen years old, but I know that."

"But, if he did that, what about the winner of the Games? He would have gone through all this for nothing!"

"Less than nothing, if such a thing can be," Hadon said. "He would be slain by Minruth. You can be sure of that."

"Oh, that's all nonsense," Taro said. "He wouldn't dare!"

"Perhaps not. But why should that judge have heard that rumor? Who else but Minruth would originate it? He would put it out as a feeler, so he can judge the reaction of the people. One thing is sure, Minruth is exceedingly ambitious, not likely to surrender easily. He's old, fifty-six, and you'd think he'd want to do the decent thing. Retire full of honors, enjoy a leisurely life, and cherish his grandchildren. But no, he acts as if he will live forever, as if he's a randy young bull."

"You have to be wrong," Taro said.

"I hope so," Hadon replied.

5

The next-to-last game lasted two days. On the first day, fifteen contestants chosen by lot took their turn facing a bull buffalo the tips of whose horns had been fitted with sharp bronze spikes. The contestant was given a three-foot-long wand on the end of which was wet ocher paint. He went into the center of the arena and waited until the bull was released. From then on, his aim was to mark the exact center of the bull's forehead with ocher. And he must do it when the bull was facing him.

Once this was done to the satisfaction of the three judges, who sat in a box a safe distance from the bull, the contestant was free to go. All he had to do was to run to a low wall and dive over it before the bull got to him.

"Speed and agility," Hadon said to Taro. "That is what this takes. Plus courage. Hewako has the courage, I'll give the surly pig that. But he is heavy and slow. Faster than he looks, but still slow."

But Hewako did succeed, though not before being gashed lightly along one arm. And in the short dash to the wall, he seemed almost a blur, he ran so fast.

Taro laughed and said, "If that bull had been behind him during the races, he would have won all of them."

Taro was the last of the fifteen that day. Before going through the gate, he turned to Hadon and put his hand on his shoulder. He looked very pale.

"I had a dream last night," he said. "I was drinking blood from a bowl that you had filled."

Hadon felt a shock going through him. "All dreams are sent by the deities," he said. "But a dream does not always mean what it seems to say."

"Perhaps not," Taro said. "In any event, we two would have faced each other with the swords. One of us would have been pouring out blood for the other's ghost. Why did we not shake dice in Opar to see who went to the Games? One of us would have lost a chance to be the king, but he would never have been forced to take his dear friend's blood. We have loved each other too much even to think of that. Yet greed made us ignore that, greed and ambition. Why did we do that, Hadon? Why didn't we leave it to the throw of the dice? Whoever won could then have brought his friend to the palace to share in his good fortune."

Hadon choked up but managed after a struggle to speak.

"Kho must have blinded us. No doubt, for Her own good purposes."

The trumpet blared, and Taro said, "Why blame the gods and goddesses? Think often of me, Hadon, and do not forget to sacrifice now and then to me."

"You may have misinterpreted the dream!" Hadon cried desperately, but the gates had swung shut. Taro walked out into the center of the field stiffly, and when the bull, black, snorting fury, ran out from his gate, Taro did not move. The bull pawed the earth and then raced around for a minute. At last, downwind from Taro, it hastened bellowing toward him and then charged. Taro extended the stick toward him and marked the forehead, but he was slow, oh, so slow, far slower than the swift Taro had ever moved when danger threatened.

Afterward, Hadon wondered if it had not been the dream itself that had made Taro so sluggish. Had dread Sisisken sent him that vision because she had marked him for death, knowing that the dream itself would ensure his end? And why had Sisisken wanted him? Why had she allowed him to survive the Games thus far and no farther?

Was it because her sister, Kho, wished to spare Hadon the agony of killing him?

He did not know, but he wept that night in the barracks. Yet, when he fell asleep, he felt a tiny spark of gladness falling through the dark grief. However much he sorrowed for Taro, he would not be responsible for killing his best friend. Kho had spared him that.

The next day Hadon performed a deed which brought the crowd, gasping and cheering, to its feet. As the bull charged, he ran toward it. Just before the lowered horns were to meet him, he gave a great leap up and forward, brought his feet up, stroked the black hairy forehead lightly with the end of the stick, and landed on the beast's back. His inertia, plus the bull's rolled him forward, and he fell sprawling on the sand. But he was up, though slightly stunned, and running. Behind him he heard the bellowing and then the thundering of hooves. He dived over the wall, which shook as the bull rammed into it.

He rose and looked at the judges' box. They were standing up, both hands raised, the fingers outspread. He had marked the beast perfectly.

The cheering continued for a long time, and after a while Hadon understood what the crowd wanted. They were demanding of the queen that she dedicate this event to him, so that in future Games it should be called Hadon's Day.

Hadon felt a glow of exultation, tempered with sadness that Taro was not here to see him. Perhaps his ghost was, and Hadon would see to it that a bull was sacrificed to Taro tonight—though it would cut deeply into his personal money—and that Taro would be told about this while he drank the substance-giving blood.

And so, a day later, the final event began. There were only twenty of the original ninety left. The buffaloes had taken a toll exceeding that of the gorillas, hyenas, and leopards combined. At the ninth hour, the trumpets sounded, and the twenty, clad only in scarlet loincloths and carrying the broad and long *tenu* in one hand, marched out. They stopped before the box of Awineth and Minruth and saluted. Awineth rose and tossed out across the heads of the mob below a thin golden crown. It sailed out into the arena, rolled, and stopped by the edge of the track. Hadon noted that the impact had twisted the soft gold. But the victor could easily bend it back when he placed it on his own head.

Awineth looked beautiful. She wore a long scarlet skirt, a necklace of red emeralds, and a scarlet flower in her black hair. And was her smile for him? Or was it for one of the others, say, the tall and handsome Wiqa?

If it were the latter, she was doomed to sorrow, because Hadon severed his right arm after ten minutes of furious fighting. Wiqa was very good, and if he had not lost some blood two days before when a horn sliced along his thigh, he might have been faster. But he was carried off, gray, dying, blood spouting from the stump.

Hadon stared after him and felt no exultation. He had killed his first man, a good man whom he had liked. That

Wiqa had been trying to kill him made no difference in his feelings.

The contests were run off one at a time. At the end of the day, the twenty were down to eight. Of the losers, eight were slain and four had been so seriously injured that they could no longer hold the hilt of the sword with both hands.

The next day was occupied with funerals, and a day of rest followed for the survivors. Hadon exercised lightly and reflected on the weaknesses and strengths he had observed among the others. Hewako and Damoken, a tall lithe youth from Minanlu, were the two greatest dangers. Both of these had made just enough points in the various contests to remain in the Games. But they were superb swordsmen, and that was what counted now. Nor were any of the others to be taken carelessly.

When the second day of sword fighting came, Hadon was matched, by lot, with Damoken. The battle was a long one, with both feeling the strength drain out of their arms and legs as they danced, parried, and sliced. At last a swift stroke of Hadon's, though partially blocked, cut off Damoken's ear and gashed his shoulder. Damoken stumbled backward, the sword dropping out of his hands. Hadon stepped forward and put his foot on the blade, and the referees hastened to take Damoken from the field.

"Do not weep," Hadon said. "It is better to be earless than to creep around palely and hope for blood to drink. I wish you a long happy life."

Damoken, holding a hand to his bloody head, replied, "When you become king, Hadon, remember me and make a place in your service for one who, under different circumstances, might have been your king."

Hadon bowed and picked up the sword and handed it to a referee.

The next contestants took their places, and Hadon went to the sidelines. He watched carefully as the others fought, noting especially Hewako's style.

When the sun was more than three-quarters across the sky, Hadon of Opar and Khosin of Towina fought, both for the second time that day. Five minutes after starting, Hadon, though bleeding from a gash on his left arm, was standing and Khosin lay dead.

Hewako of Opar and Hadar of Qethruth engaged in the final battle of the day. At the end of two minutes, Hewako gave his opponent's blade such a stroke that it fell from his nerveless hands. Hadar dived for it, and the edge of Hewako's sword severed his neck.

In the tumult cascading from the crowd, Hadon and Hewako were silent. They looked speculatively at each other. The day after tomorrow, one of them would surely be dead, and the other might be king of kings of Khokarsa. Which would it be for Hewako and Hadon? The arms of dread Sisisken or of warm and glorious Awineth?

6

For the final bout, a platform had been built close to the wall near which the queen and her father sat. It was fifteen feet high, only five feet below the top of the wall enclosing the field, five feet below and ten feet away from the royal box. Its surface was a square of closely joined mahogany planks, thirty by thirty feet. A circle with a diameter of twenty-four feet had been painted in white on it. Bisecting the circle was a white line. The area outside the circle was for the referee. His only duties were to start the contest and, thereafter, to lop off the head of either contestant if he stepped outside the circle during the fighting. He was also there to ensure that only the victor left the circle alive.

As the Flaming God reached his zenith, twelve trumpets blared. Awineth and Minruth sat down in their box on comfortable cushions and under a shady canopy. The trumpets blew again, and the crowd sat down on hard stone and in hot sunshine. At the third blast, Hewako and Hadon appeared from gates at opposite ends of the fields. They were naked, and each carried his sword upright before him. Behind each was a naked priestess who slowly banged a large drum while the youth proceeded to the platform. They met at the bottom of the broad mahogany steps that led up to the platform, bowed to the referee, bowed to each other, and then followed the referee up the steps. The priestesses stayed below, slowly beating the drums.

Within the circle, the two youths faced their rulers, Hewako on the left of the bisecting line, Hadon on the right. The trumpets blew again, the priestesses' drums stopped rolling, the two raised their blades above their heads with one hand and shouted, "Let Kho decide!"

"And Resu!" Minruth bellowed.

Those around the king gasped; Awineth jerked upright from her reclining position and said something to Minruth. He laughed and waved at the referee to continue.

The referee had been startled by Minruth's irregular interjection, but he recovered quickly. He stood just outside the circle at the end of the bisecting line, raised his sword high, and shouted, "Take the line!"

The two turned to face each other across the line.

"Cross ends!"

The two swords rose until they were at a forty-five-degree angle to their holders, and their square tips touched. Hadon stood straight, his green eyes staring into Hewako's brown eyes. His left hand held the end of the foot-long hilt in a pivot grip, his right hand was placed around the hilt just behind the circular guard.

The iron hilt was covered slightly with python hide. The carbonized-iron blade was five feet two inches long, two-edged, slightly curving on the lower edge, and square-ended. It was called Karken, or Tree of Death, and it had been made at great expense by the legendary smith, Dytabes of Miklemres, for Hadon's father. With it Kumin had slain fifty-seven warriors, of whom ten were *numatenu*, seven warrior-women of the Mikawuru, forty Klemqaba, and a lion.

"That one-legged worker of magic told me that he dreamed of Karken the night before he completed work on it, before he cooled its hot blade with snake's blood," Kumin had told his son. "Dytabes said that he saw a vision in which the holder of Karken was seated on a throne of ivory. And by him was the most beautiful woman Dytabes had ever seen, truly a goddess. And around him was a multitude praising him as the greatest swordsman of the world and as the savior of his people.

"But Dytabes could not see clearly the face of the man who held Karken. Evidently it was not I. I hope that it was you. In any event, take this sword, Hadon, and do nothing to disgrace it. As for that dream, do not think too much about it. Smiths are notorious drunks. Dytabes, though the greatest of smiths, was also the deepest of drinkers."

Hadon thought of his father's words, and then he heard the referee shout, "Begin and end!"

Iron clanged. Hewako had stepped over the line, right foot forward first, and had swung the blade toward Hadon's left shoulder. Hadon had also stepped forward, though only a half-step, and had parried successfully.

"Watch the eyes," his father had said many times. "They often tell what is coming next. The footwork is second in importance, but unless you know what the man is going to do, or what he thinks he means to do, footwork means nothing. Courage and strength are important also, but the sight and the footwork come first."

And Kumin also said, over and over, "Immediately after the defense, the counteroffense."

He had also said, "Do the unexpected, though not just for the sake of novelty. The unexpected must have a point, a goal in mind which the conventional, the expected, cannot reach."

Hewako reached back and raised his sword above his head. He had to retreat when doing this, because Hadon, swift as he was, would have swung his blade sideways and cut deeply into his ribs. But by stepping back, Hewako prevented Hadon from doing this. Then Hewako planned to rush forward and bring his sword down straight ahead of him toward the crown of Hadon's head. Hadon would have to parry to keep his skull from being split. He dared not cut at Hewako then, even though Hewako was wide open. If he did wound Hewako, he would still take the full blow on his head. And he would be dead.

Or so Hewako thought. But as Hewako retreated, Hadon stepped forward. Instead of bringing his sword in in a cutting

65

motion, he thrust. And Hewako, who could have parried a cut, was caught wide open.

The thrust was not fatal, nor even badly wounding. The blunt end of Karken, though delivered with strength, could do no more than break the skin. But it drove into Hewako's throat at the base, just above the breastbone. Hewako's mouth opened wider; his eyes bulged; a hoarse pained sound came from the injured throat. And he failed in his surprise and agony to bring the blade down.

Hadon had moved back immediately after the thrust in case Hewako did complete the downward cut. Now Hewako, bleeding from the break just above the breastbone, his face red with anger, charged, bringing the edge down furiously.

Hadon moved one step forward and brought his blade up so that Hewako's struck it glancingly and went off to one side. And at the clang Hadon suddenly *knew* that Hewako was doomed to die. Something had leaped down the sword and had run up his arm and into his breast. Something told him that he could not lose this fight, that Hewako had only a few minutes of life left.

Nor was he the only one to know. Hewako had turned pale, and the sweat that polished his skin, the sweat which had looked so hot before, now looked cold. In fact, goose pimples had appeared all over Hewako's body. And the eyes had become shadowed.

Nevertheless, he fought bravely, and none among the crowd would have known what had passed between him and Hadon. They would have noted only that Hadon took the offensive, that he parried every stroke of Hewako's, that he thrice went in through Hewako's guard and inflicted deep gashes, one on the right ribs, one on the left ribs, and one on Hewako's right shoulder.

Suddenly Hewako stepped back three steps, raised the sword high above him, and shouting, ran at Hadon. Hadon stepped forward, brought up his blade, and caught Hewako's mighty swing against it, sent it off to one side, and once again thrust into the base of Hewako's throat. The squat bull-like man staggered back, his sword dropping from his grasp, and his hands caught at his throat. Hadon slid one foot forward and then placed it on Hewako's sword. The crowd roared, though there were many boos and catcalls among the

66

cheering. Evidently many felt that there was something some-how unsporting about Hadon's use of the thrust. It was so seldom seen. The professionals looked with approval at Hadon, however, and they spoke quietly of his unorthodox technique. None of them admitted that they would have been caught off-guard by it, but it had been appropriately used in this contest. After all, Hewako was an amateur.

He would also soon be a dead amateur. He stood close to the edge of the circle, breathing heavily, sweating so that water pooled by his feet, one hand pressed on the bleeding wound at the base of his throat, his eyes sick.

Finally he said hoarsely, "So you have won, Hadon?"

"Yes," Hadon said. "And now I must kill you, as the rules decree. Do I have your forgiveness, Hewako?"

Hewako said faintly, "I see you, Hadon."

Hadon said, "What? *See* me?"

"Yes," Hewako said. "I see you and your future. Sisisken has opened my eyes, Hadon. I see you in a time far from now, though not so far that you will be an old man. For you will live past your youth, Hadon, but you will never be an old man. And your life will be troubled. And there will be many times when you will envy me, Hadon. And I see ... I see ..."

Hadon felt chilled, as if the ghost of Hewako had left his body and had passed by him. Yet Hewako still remained alive, though the crowd yelled at Hadon to strike, and the referee was gesturing at him to get it over with.

"What do you see?" Hadon said.

"Only shadows," Hewako said. "Shadows that you will see soon enough. But listen, Hadon. I see that you will never be the king of kings. Though you are victor today, you will never sit upon the throne of the ruler of Khokarsa. And I see you in a far-off land, Hadon, and a woman with yellow hair and the strangest violet eyes, and—"

"Strike, Hadon!" the referee yelled. "The king and queen are impatient; they have twice signaled that you should strike!"

"Do you forgive me, Hewako?" Hadon said.

"Never," Hewako said. "My blood be upon your head, Hadon. My ghost bring you bad luck and a grisly end, Hadon."

Hadon was horrified, and the referee cried out, "Those are not the words of a warrior, of a hero!"

Hewako smiled faintly and said, "What do I care?"

Hadon stepped forward and swung Karken sidewise, and Hewako's head fell off and rolled across the floor and almost went over the edge but was snatched by the hair at the last moment by the referee. His body toppled forward, the blood jetting from the neck and bathing Hadon from head to foot. Hadon closed his eyes and endured it, and when he opened his eyes, he thought he saw a flash of something small and dark leap from the corpse and drop over the edge of the platform. But it was surely a trick of his imagination. At least, he hoped it was.

And then the priestesses came up onto the platform with buckets of water to cleanse the platform and him and to utter the cleansing words.

7

The next day the final funeral ceremonies were held. Though Hadon did not like to sacrifice to Hewako, he had to. It was expected of him, but even more important, if he neglected to spill bull's blood for Hewako to drink, he would be haunted forever by his ghost, and ill luck and an early death would be his fate. Hadon's own money was too little for him to buy the fine bull needed, but as the king-soon-to-be, he had no trouble getting credit.

In fact, there were many who were eager to give him the money, though it was evident that they expected favors after he had ascended the throne. He was besieged by people who wanted favors, who were crying out for a justice that he was in no position to give, or who just simply wanted to touch him because of the good luck it would give or because the touch might heal their diseases. He retreated to the barracks, though he could not get away from the clamor.

Officials came who were to prepare him for the days ahead. They told him how he must march to the palace tomorrow, what dress he must wear, and what traditional words he must say and what gestures he must make.

Mokomgu, the chamberlain of the queen, also told him what restraints would be placed on him for some years to come.

"If you will forgive me for saying so," Mokomgu said, "you are a youth of nineteen, and you have no experience in governing anything, let alone the mighty empire of Khokarsa. Fortunately, your wife has been trained in the duties of governing since she was five, and she of course has control of everything in government but military, naval, and engineering matters. But what do you know about the ins and outs, the complexities of the army, the navy, and the building of roads and forts and government buildings and temples to Resu?"

Hadon had to confess that he knew nothing of these matters.

"It will take you at least ten years to grasp all that is needed to regulate matters efficiently, and then there is, of course, politics. There are many power groups within the court, and you must understand what these want and why they want them, and you must make decisions, simple decisions based on complex reasons, all for the greatest good of the empire."

Hadon, numb with the responsibility and the awareness of his ignorance, merely nodded.

"Minruth can advise you, but he is under no obligation to do so," Mokomgu said. "However, he is not a man to endure idleness, and he no doubt will wish to give you the benefit of his wisdom and experience. You, on the other hand, do not have to accept his advice."

Mokomgu paused, smiled, and said, "You have an advantage at the start. You can read and write as well as any clerk, which is a blessing. We have had kings who were illiterate when they came to the throne, and they died only half-lettered. But we have investigated you, and we find that you, though poor and without funds to hire a teacher, taught yourself the syllabary and arithmetic. That is the mark of ambition and intelligence. Awineth was pleased when she heard that, and so were we. There were some who were not so pleased, since they would like to be at the elbow of a king who cannot read reports but must depend on those who can."

"Hewako could not read well," Hadon said. "What if he had won?"

"Awineth does not have to accept the winner," Mokomgu said. "That she did not announce your rejection after the final event means that she finds you pleasing. She likes you and thinks you are very handsome and have the makings of a great warrior, not to mention those of a husband."

"What does she mean by that?" Hadon said.

"Our intelligence service has questioned every woman known to have bedded you," Mokomgu said. "They all report that you are exceptionally virile. That is not necessary, of course, since the queen may take lovers if she wishes. But she admires you, and she is also pleased that you are good-natured."

Meaning weak-natured, Hadon thought. Awineth was used to having her way; his brief meeting with her had shown him that.

"And what else did your spies find out?" Hadon said. He was beginning to feel quite warm—hot, in fact.

"That you are a good conversationalist, drink quite moderately, are adaptable, a hard worker, responsible, though still given to youthful pranks at times, able to take punishment if it's deserved, in short, though only nineteen you have the makings of a fine man. And of a fine king. You are a great athlete, of course, but things are no longer as they were in the old days. Muscles and a strong wind are the least of qualifications for the throne.

"Awineth is also pleased that you are a devout worshiper of Kho, unlike, I might add, her own father. Though, of course, she was dubious at first about your relationship to Kwasin. But she was assured that you could not help it that you are first cousin to that ravisher of priestesses and murderer of temple guards. Besides, we ascertained that you did not like Kwasin. As who does?"

70

"Is there anything you don't know about me?" Hadon said.

"Very little," Mokomgu said.

Don't look so smug, Hadon thought. What I was does not assure what I shall be.

The next day, after a service in the great sacred oak grove high on Khowot's slope, Hadon was given a ritual bath by priestesses. He was anointed with sweet-smelling balsam oil and dressed in a bonnet of fish-eagle feathers, a kilt of fish-eagle feathers, and sandals of hide from a sacred hippopotamus. Since he was a member of the Ant People Totem, a stylized ant head was painted in red on his chest. He was then marched behind a silent band of musicians to an empty grave along the Road of Kho. Here he was shown his golden crown, placed at the bottom of the grave. He had to jump into the grave, pick it up, and climb out. During this, a priestess chanted, "Remember, though you are king, that all, kings and slaves, must come to this!"

Then, with the crown in one hand, he walked behind the band, which played loud martial music, while behind him came priests and priestesses, a guard of spear-carrying soldiers, the queen's chamberlain and his staff, and a crowd of the curious.

They marched along the road, the sides of which were massed with cheering and petal-throwing spectators. Hadon felt his numbness thawing out in the heat of exultation. At the great gates of the wall of the Inner City, he knocked with his crown, crying out to open in the name of the winner of the Games. The gates swung open, and he walked through and soon was ascending the broad and steep marble steps to the citadel. At its top he repeated the knocking and the demand to be let in, and the citadel gates swung open.

And presently he was in the enormous high-dome-ceilinged throne room and crying out the set words that Minruth should descend from the throne and allow him to sit upon it beside the high priestess and the queen of the two seas. However, Minruth was not expected to actually give up the throne then. His role was to acknowledge Hadon's right to the throne. Until the marriage ceremony took place three days from then, Hadon would not officially be the king.

Minruth, grinning as if he were delighted, answered, and

71

it was then that Hadon realized that affairs were not proceeding automatically. He should have been warned by Awineth's look of fury and the set and pale faces of the courtiers.

"Gladly, O Hadon, would I step down from a place which imposes wearisome burdens and the glory of which is more lead than gold. And my daughter desires a young and handsome man, a vigorous youth, to rule with her and to pleasure her, as she has so often told me."

Here he looked venomously at Awineth, who glared at him.

"But what I, the king, wish, and what great Resu and Kho wish are often not the same. And we mortals must bow to the words of the deities.

"Now, as you no doubt have heard, Hadon, a man has recently come to us from the Wild Lands beyond the Sassares mountains. He is Hinokly, sole survivor of an expedition I sent some years ago to explore the shores of the great sea beyond the Wild Lands on the edge of the world. While you were displaying your heroic prowess in the Games, he came to us, to my daughter and me. And he told us of a harrowing journey, of men dead from disease, from lions and the great nose-horned beast, the *bok'ul''ikadeth*, from the great gray-tusked *qampo*, from drowning, and most of all from the arrows of the wild tribes. From arrows which our enemies may use but which Kho has forbidden us to use, much to the disadvantage of her people."

"Beware, Father" Awineth said. "You tread on dangerous ground!"

"I only tell the truth," Minruth said. "Be that as it may, the expedition did reach the mighy sea that rings the world in the north."

He paused and said loudly, "And on its shores they encountered the great god Sahhindar himself!"

Hadon felt awe invade his fury. Sahhindar, the Gray-Eyed God, the Archer God. Sahhindar, god of plants, of bronze, of time itself. Sahhindar, exiled god, disgraced son of Kho. And men had seen him!

"They not only saw him, they *talked* to him! They fell to their knees and worshiped him, but he bade them rise and be at ease. And he brought out of the trees nearby three people, mortals, who had been hidden there. One was a tall woman, beautiful beyond dreams, golden-haired and with eyes like a goddess, violet-colored eyes. At first our men thought that she must be Lahla herself, goddess of the moon, because Lahla is golden-haired and violet-eyed, if we can believe the priestesses. Is that not true, Hinokly, did she not look like Lahla?"

He spoke to a short thin man of about thirty-five who stood on the edge of the crowd.

"May I be struck down by Kho Herself if I am lying!" Hinokly said in a reedy voice.

The courtiers around him stepped back, but Hinokly stood calm.

"And did she not have a name which sounds much like Lahla?" Minruth said.

"She spoke a strange language, O King of Kings," Hinokly said. "The sounds of her tongue are weird. But to my ears her name was Lalila."

"Lalila," Minruth said. "*Moon of change* in our tongue, though she told them that in hers it meant something else. And she claimed that she was no goddess. But gods and goddesses have been known to lie when they come down among mortals. In any event, goddess or woman, she acknowledged Sahhindar to be her master. Is that not true, Hinokly?"

"That is true, O King of Kings."

"Then she is no goddess, Father," Awineth said. "No goddess would bow her head to a mere god."

Minruth, face contorted, said, "Things change! And I find it significant that this woman of divine beauty is the moon of change. Perhaps her name is an omen. In any event, this woman was accompanied by two others—her child, a daughter with the same golden hair and violet eyes as her mother, and a manling named Paga."

"Pardon, lord, it is Pag," Hinokly said.

"That's what I said, Paga," Minruth said.

Hinokly shrugged, and Hadon, fluent in several languages, understood. The Khokarsan language had no syllable ending in -g, and so the ordinary Khokarsan would pronounce the name according to the rules of his native tongue. There was no syllable such as *pa* either, open syllables beginning with *p* being confined to *pe, pi, poe*. But such a syllable was easy for a Khokarsan to pronounce.

"This Paga is a dwarf with one eye, the other having been

knocked out with a rock thrown by some bitch-tempered woman," Minruth said, glancing at his daughter to catch her reaction. Awineth merely frowned.

"He carries with him a huge ax made of some iron that is far tougher than any we have. Paga says that it is iron from a falling star, and he fashioned it into an ax for a hero named Wi. This Wi is dead now, but he was the father of the child, whose name sounds like Abeth. And before he died he gave the ax to Paga and told him to keep it until he met a man who was great enough to receive it as a gift. But the ax is—"

"Get to the meat of the matter, Father," Awineth said harshly.

"We must not displease the high priestess of Kho," Minruth said, rolling his eyes. "Very well. Sahhindar himself ordered my men to take Lalila, the child Abeth, and Paga to this city. He ordered them, under pain of terrible punishment, to take good care of them and to see that they were received as honored guests. He could not come with them because he had business elsewhere, though he did not say what that business was. But he promised to come here someday to make sure that Lalila and the others were honored. When, he did not say. But what the gods promise, they perform."

"And what," Awineth said loudly, "about the ban of Kho! Would Sahhindar dare return to the land from which his great mother drove him?"

"Sahhindar said that he was not aware of such a ban," Minruth said, obviously pleased. "So perhaps the priestesses have not told us the truth."

Awineth said, "Beware, Father!"

Minruth said, "Or, more likely, they misunderstood the oracles. Or perhaps Kho, being a female, changed her mind. She has relented and would see her son walk again among the people to whom he gave such great gifts in the days of our ancient foremothers.

"But on the way back, evil befell the party. They were shot at by savages with arrows, the arrows which Kho has forbidden us, her chosen people, to use. Our men took to dugouts they found, but the savages killed many from the banks and then pursued them in boats. The boat with Lalila, the baby, and the manling overturned, and the last that the men in the other boat saw of them they were struggling in the water. And of the men who escaped, only Hinokly survived to bring us the news. Is that not true, Hinokly?"

"The Wild Lands are terrible, O King," Hinokly said.

"It is too bad that you must journey through them again," Minruth said. "But consider yourself fortunate. You should have been flayed alive for deserting the people whose safety was charged to you by Sahhindar. I am a merciful king, however, and after consultation with my daughter it was decided that you should guide the rescue expedition, since you alone know where Lalila is. Or was."

"I thank the king and the queen for their mercy," Hinokly said, though he did not look grateful.

Hadon's awe was being replaced by a mounting anger. He did not know exactly what the king had in mind, but he thought he could guess it in general. And he could not understand why Awineth seemed to be going along with her father.

"What does all this mean?" he cried. "Why has the ancient ceremony been interrupted for this tale, however wonderful it is?"

Minruth roared, "Until you sit on this throne, you will speak only when requested to do so!"

Awineth said, "In short, it means that our marriage must be delayed until after you bring back this woman and the ax from the Wild Lands. It is not my doing or my wish, Hadon. I would have you on this throne and in my bed as soon as possible. But even the high priestess must obey the voice of Kho."

Minruth smiled and said, "Yes, even the high priestess! An ancient custom may be disregarded when Kho says so!"

"If I may speak?" Hadon said, looking at Awineth.

"You may."

"Am I right in guessing that I have been chosen to lead this expedition?"

"You have quick wits, Hadon. You are right."

"And I am not to be your husband until I have returned with this woman, the ax, and I suppose, the child and the manling, since Sahhindar has ordered that they also be brought safely to Khokarsa?"

"That, to my sorrow, is true."

"But why have I been chosen? Surely you would not ...?"

"Not I! It was my father who suggested that this be

75

done, and I said no! But then he said that this was no mere matter of mortals, that the deities were involved. And so we journeyed up Khowot's slope to the Temple of Kho and there we spoke to the oracular priestess. 'What should we do?' we asked. 'What does Kho Herself wish in this business, if, indeed, She wishes anything?'

"And so we went into the cave where the priestess keeps her vigil, where the dangerous breath of the fires underground issues. And the priestess sat on her three-cornered stool and breathed the fumes, while my father and I, our faces covered with cloaks, sat in a corner on the cold hard stone. And presently the oracle spoke in a strange voice, and a light seemed to fill the cave. My father and I put our hands over our eyes, since whoever sees Kho in Her glory is blinded, and we listened trembling to Her voice. And She said that the greatest hero of the land must go out immediately to find the witch from the sea and the witch's daughter and the little one-eyed man and the ax. And the hero must not tarry to take his ease with any woman, nor marry nor transact any business. And the voice said that the woman and the ax might bring ill or good or both to the land, but she and the ax must be looked for.

"She said nothing about your returning, only that the hero must go at once on his quest. Nor did She say anything about Sahhindar."

Hadon was silent with awe for a moment, and then he spoke.

"And when was this, O Queen?"

"Last night, Hadon. While you slept with the golden crown of the victor in your bed, and no doubt dreamed of me, my father and I hurried up the slope of forbidding Khowot."

"But why am I the greatest hero of the land?" he said.

"That hardly needs answering," Minruth growled.

"But you, O King, are the victor of the previous Games, and you sit upon the throne, and you led your soldiers in the taking of the rebellious city of Sakawuru, and you defeated the Klemqaba so severely that they are now giving tribute—at least on the coast—and you it was who slew the ravaging black leopard of Siwudawa with your bare hands. Surely you are the hero of whom the oracle spoke."

Minruth stared, and then he burst into laughter.

"Surely you are cunning, Hadon, and you will someday make a great king. If you pass through the Wild Lands without harm and fulfill Sahhindar's request, that is. No, Hadon, I am getting old, and my deeds were done a long time ago. And new bright deeds are what figure greatly in the minds of the people and the deities, not old stale deeds. You will find that out someday, Hadon. Perhaps. But do not try to talk your way out of this, as the fable says that the fox did out of the trap.

"The news about this is being printed now to be shipped out to every city of the empire. And the people of Khokarsa are being informed of this by the criers at this very moment."

"Then when do I leave?" Hadon said.

Awineth, tears running down her cheeks, arose. "This very moment, Hadon."

She came down the steps and held out her hand to him. "Kiss it, Hadon, and remember that you will have all of me when you return. I will grieve for you, but I must obey the voice of Kho, just as all mortals, even queens, must obey."

Hadon dropped to one knee and kissed the back of her hand. Then he arose and seized her soft white shoulders and pressed her warm breasts to his and kissed her upon the lips. There was a gasp and a murmur from the crowd and a strangled roar from Minruth. But she responded warmly, and then she freed herself, smiling, though the tears were still in her eyes.

"Any other man would have died on the spot, unless I had said he might take me in his arms," she said. "But I know that you are the man I love, and that you are worthy of me. So hasten hence and hasten back, Hadon. I will be waiting."

"The Voice said nothing about his coming back!" Minruth shouted, but Hadon turned and strode away. At that moment, he felt happy.

8

His buoyancy did not last long. By the time he had reached the docks, he was scowling and his face was red. He did not respond to the crowds who cheered him and threw petals at him or tried to break through the guards to touch him. He almost did not see or hear them. He was turned inward and backward to the room which held the throne and the woman out of whom he had been cheated.

He realized that his thoughts were blasphemous. Though Kho Herself had decreed that he should go out on this quest, he felt that he had been cheated. And there was nothing he could do about it. He was as powerless as the lowest of slaves, as the poorest of the poor, he, the winner of the Great Games, a hero!

Burning with the fire that freezes, numb with anger, he boarded the unireme waiting for him. He was scarcely aware of the people to whom he was introduced—the captain, the ship's priestess, and some of his fellow passengers. They must have been awed by his expression and his bearing, because they got away from him as swiftly as they could. And while he paced back and forth on the narrow foredeck, he was not approached by anyone.

The galley was pulled along swiftly by the oarsmen and headed northward and slightly eastward. It passed the fortress on the western tip of Mohasi island soon was going through the broad strait between the naval-base island of Sigady and the two-pronged peninsular, the Python's Head, which projected from the mainland. The fortresses on each ran up their flags in salute to the ship which bore the hero of the Games. At another time, Hadon would have swelled with exultation. Now he felt that he was being mocked, though he had a residue of common sense which told him that this was not really so.

Then, as the hours passed and great Resu began his descent, the galley went northwestward along the cliffs of the western side of the Gulf of Gahete. When night fell, the ship was still deep in the narrow gulf. The air cooled, and with it Hadon. The stars shone brightly, and after a while Lahla, goddess of the moon, Kho's fairest daughter, showered her grace upon all who would appreciate it. She was so bright that Hadon could see smoke rising from Khowot, the Voice of Kho, a cone rising toward the sky. The smoke was a series of broken and strangely shaped clouds, illuminated by inter-mittent flashes of fire. He tried to read the shapes as if they were parts of a syllabary, but he could make nothing of them. Was Kho sending him a message which he was too uncercep-tive to understand?

After a while, the first mate approached him and asked him if he cared to dine with the captain and the priestess. Hadon, suddenly aware that he was hungry, said that he would be pleased.

The roof of the captain's cabin had been removed to let in the moonlight and the cooling air. The interior was bright with pine torches set in brackets on the bulkheads, and the odor of resin was so strong that Hadon almost could not smell the food. A table was set within the narrow cabin for six people and the ever-present unseen guest, dread Sisisken. Hadon stood by his oak chair while the priestess prayed to Kho and Piqabes, Kho's green-eyed daughter, to bless the food and those about to partake of it. Hadon sat down then and ate voraciously, as if he were gobbling up those he hated—Minruth and those vague forces that had brought him to this sorry position. But the hate disappeared in the savory okra soup, the tender juicy buffalo steak, the fillets of horned fish, the emmer bread, the black olives, the cabbage, the delicacy of fried termites, and the papyrus piths. And he indulged himself with one beaker of mead, made from the far-famed honey of the bees of the city of Qoqoda. Afterward he sat at the table talking and chewing on a soft twig to cleanse his teeth.

Three of his tablemates, he found, were to accompany him on the expedition. Tadoku was his second-in-command. He was middle-sized, very lean, about forty, a *numatenu*, and a major in the Vth Army, which meant he was a native of Dythbeth. His body and face were scarred from a hundred fights, and his skull near the right temple was slightly indented where a stone from a Klemqaba sling had almost killed him. He was, Hadon judged, a tough and shrewd man. And, no doubt, he could give Hadon many points on the wielding of a *tenu*.

The second was Hinokly, whom he had seen and heard in the palace. Hinokly was to be his guide through the Wild Lands. Judging from his moroseness, he was not pleased with the task.

The third was the expedition's bard, Kebiwabes. He was about thirty and was dressed in the bard's white linen robe, which concealed somewhat a short slim body. His head was large, his hair a glossy brown, his nose snub, his mouth full and broad, his eyes large and russet-brown and merry. Near him, on a peg on the bulkhead, hung his seven-stringed lyre. It was made of boxwood, and the strings were from the small intestine of the sheep. One of the projecting upper ends was carved with the figure of the goddess of the moon, who was also the patroness of music and poetry. Kebiwabes also seemed to be under the influence of Besbesbes, goddess of bees and mead, judging by the many beakers he drank. As the evening progressed, his russet eyes became blood-red, and his voice thickened as if honey had been poured down his throat. And he became indiscreet, talking openly of things better said in privacy if they must be said.

"When we land in Mukha, Hadon, you will be given command of as sorry a body of soldiers as ever disgraced the army. Misfits, goldbrickers, troublemakers, loonies, thieves, and cowards. All, except for the *numatenu* here, Tadoku, men whom Minruth should have discharged or hanged long ago. Men whom he will be glad to get rid of. Men who will ensure that your expedition is a failure. Why the great soldier Tadoku was assigned to you, I do not know. Is there something of which I am not aware, Tadoku? Have you, like me, offended Minruth in some way?"

"I was chosen by Awineth herself and assigned over the protests of Minruth," Tadoku said.

"That's one good thing, perhaps the only good thing, to happen," the bard said. "Does Awineth know what kind of personnel poor Hadon here has to command?"

"I am not that much in her confidence," Tadoku said, glaring at him.

80

"Well, I was chosen as the bard for this lousy expedition because I composed and sang a satirical song about Minruth," Kebiwabes said. "Minruth did not dare to touch me, because bards are sacred. But he was able to honor me—honor!—by appointing me to your bard. In effect, it's an exile from which, most likely, I will not return. But I don't care. I have always wanted to see the wonders of the Wild Lands. Perhaps they will inspire me to compose a great epic, *The Song of Hadon*, and my name will rank with those of the divine bards, Hala, she who composed *The Song of Gahete*, and Kwamim, she who composed *The Song of Kethna*. Then all will have to admit that a man can create music and poetry as well as a woman."

"Neither of those were drunks," Tadoku said.

Kebiwabes laughed and said, "Mead is the blood of Besbesbes, and if I take enough in, perhaps I will sweat out the effluvia of divinity. In any event, once we are deep into the Wild Lands, there will be no more mead. Willy-nilly, I must be sober. But then I will become drunk on moonlight, on the silver liquor which Lahla pours so freely."

He drank deeply, belched, and said, "If I live that long."

Hadon concealed his dismay. He spoke to Hinokly, who was languidly stirring a spoon in his cold soup.

"And you, Hinokly, do you take as dark a view?"

"Of all the good men who went out into the Wild Lands, I was the least fitted to survive," he said. "I am a scribe, small and weak and unused to hardships and terrors. The others were tall strong men of the stuff of heroes. Minruth himself picked them for the qualities those who go into the Wild Lands must have. Yet I alone did not die. I alone came back. So I will say only that we are in the hands of Kho. Success and failure and the names of those who will die and those who will not are already written in the rolls that no man may read."

"Which is to say that we can't know the future and must act as if the goddesses were on our side," Tadoku said briskly. "As for myself, I pray to Kho and to Resu, who besides being god of the sun and of the rain, is also god of war."

The priestess said sharply, "And what about Bhukla, the goddess of war! War was originally her domain, and Resu usurped it. At least, he did so in the minds of some, but we priestesses know that Bhukla was the first, and the soldier who neglects her will find sorrow."

"I pray to her, of course, priestess, since she is now the goddess of the *tenu*," Tadoku said. "Every *numatenu* prays to her in the morning and before going to bed, and she presides when the swords of the *numatenu* are being made. But, as I was going to say, I rely not only on the gods and the goddesses. I trust in myself, in my hard-won skill with the sword.

"Tell me," he said, turning to Hadon, "what do you know of military service?"

"Not much," Hadon said, "which is why I am glad that you are my lieutenant. As a child, I used to hang around the parade grounds and watch the soldiers drill, and I learned something of procedure and discipline when I worked in the kitchens and as a water boy in the fort near Opar. And I learned some things from my father."

"Then you're not a raw recruit, and your task will be easier," Tadoku said. "You must have picked up much about the politicking and the passing of the buck which are, if not the backbone of the army, the ribs. And you must know that having good cooks is very important. Most laymen think only of the glory of the battle when they think of the army. But having good cooks and good doctors and an incorruptible but foxy supply sergeant are things that occupy an officer's mind more than leading men into fray."

"As I understand it," Kebiwabes said, "you are a poor man. Or were."

"And what is that to you?" Hadon said angrily.

"Much," the bard said. "I am interested in the character of the man who will be leading us into unknown dangers. I have observed that the rich are always corrupted, and the poor are corrupted too, though in a different way. Money and power change a man as surely as if the hands of terrible Khuklaqo, the Shapeless Shaper, had seized him. However, the rich man attempts to disguise it from himself—he becomes arrogant, and he acts as if dread Sisisken were not always around the corner. He becomes hard but not strong, brittle as a badly cast tool.

"On the other hand, poverty is a demon with an odor of its own. The rich stink of money, and the poor stink of its lack.

82

The middle classes stink of both. But a poor man may rise above his poverty, whereas a rich man seldom, if ever, rises above his wealth."

"I don't think I understand you," Hadon said.

"It doesn't matter. You are young yet, but you have wits, and if you live long enough, you will understand. Though understanding, as usual, will have as its companion sorrow. Suffice it that I have faith in you. Lahla has given me the ability to hear a man's vibrations as if he were a lyre plucked by her fingers. In your case, the seven strings of the soul make a sweet music. But the song will not always be a merry one."

Kebiwabes arose and said, "I must go to sleep."

The priestess said, "I had hoped that you would sing for us."

"The sweet mead would come forth as sour music," he said. "Tomorrow I will sing for you. But not until evening. Good night, all."

Tadoku stared after the staggering bard and said, "There goes one of the misfits and troublemakers."

"But he seems to be more troubled with himself than by things outside him," the priestess said. "He has never been violent. He uses only his voice to express his discontent and to criticize things amiss in this world."

"That kind is the worst kind of troublemaker," Tadoku said. "He speaks, and many act out his words."

"I rather like him," Hadon said. "Major, would you do me the honor of sword-exercising with me tomorrow?"

"Gladly," Tadoku said.

Hadon dreamed that night, not of the beautiful Awineth, as might have been expected, but of his mother. He kept running after her, and she, though standing with arms open to receive him, moved always backward and finally was lost in the shadows. He awoke sobbing and wondering if Sisisken had sent him a message that his mother was dead. After breakfast he wrote a long letter to his family. But the letter would have to be posted in Mukha, and it would be many a month—if ever—before it arrived in distant Opar.

Kebiwabes, up earlier than Hadon had expected, saw him writing the last paragraphs on the roll. He approached him as Hadon sealed the letter and said, "You can write? I am impressed. I myself have some facility with the syllabary, but I am afraid to become too literate."

Hadon was surprised. "Why is that?"

"Writing is the enemy of memory," Kebiwabes said. "Look at me. I am a bard who must memorize, and has memorized, thousands of lines. I carry the words of a hundred songs in my head. I began to learn these when I was three, and my lifelong labor of learning these has been hard. But I know them well; they are stamped onto my heart.

"If, however, I depended upon the written word, my heart would grow weak. I would soon find myself halting, searching for the line, and would have to go to a roll to find the lost words. I fear that when all become lettered, which is what the priestess would like, bards will have as short a memory as everybody else."

"Perhaps," Hadon said. "But if the great Awines had not invented the syllabary, science and commerce would not have progressed so swiftly. And the empire of Khokarsa would not be so wide-flung."

"That might be just as well," the bard said. When he was questioned about the meaning of this, he did not reply but said, "Tadoku asked me to tell you that he will meet you at midmorning on the foredeck for an exercise. At the moment he is busy dictating to Hinokly letters to the palace. He seems upset by my words last night."

"You remember them?" Hadon said.

The bard laughed and said, "I am not always as drunk as I seem. He was disturbed because I knew more about the type of men he will command than he did. Apparently no one had told him."

"And how did you find out?" Hadon said.

"Next to the queen's bedchamber, the best place to find out secrets is the tavern. Especially if the palace servants do their drinking there."

"I have a lot to learn," Hadon said.

"Admitting that means that you can learn," Kebiwabes said.

At midmorning Tadoku entered the cabin and saluted Hadon. Hadon returned it with the right arm held out straight before him, the thumb and little finger touching tips, the three longest fingers spread out.

"Officially, you will not take command until we reach Mukha," Tadoku said. "But we might as well get accustomed to our roles before then. And if there is any advice I can give you, anything I can teach you, I am yours."

"Sit down," Hadon said. "First, I would like a frank answer. Do you, an experienced officer and a famed *numatenu*, resent serving under a green youth?"

"Under different circumstances, I might," Tadoku said. "But this is an unusual situation. Besides, you aren't a know-it-all. And, to be frank, if I serve you well, my career may be advanced. After all, you may be king someday."

"You say that as if you don't believe I'll ever sit on the throne."

"Our chances of survival are not high," Tadoku said cheerfully. "And if you will allow me to continue to be frank, if we should get back, our chances of survival may be even less."

Hadon was startled. He considered Tadoku's statement and then said, "You think that our king would dare to kill us?"

"It's a long voyage from Mukha to the island," Tadoku said. "And much can happen aboard a galley. Especially if it is manned by those faithful to Minruth."

"But we will be, or anyway should be, under the protection of Sahhindar."

"If there is a Gray-Eyed God in the Wild Lands and if Hinokly did see him," Tadoku said. "Hinokly may be telling the truth. On the other hand, he may have made up the story to save his neck. Or Minruth may have put him up to it to get rid of you."

Hadon had another mild shock. He said, "But the Voice of Kho? Surely She would not be deceived, nor would She deceive us?"

"She would not be deceived," Tadoku said. "But She may have said what She did in order to carry out plans of Her own. Besides, the oracular priestess always says something which may be interpreted in more than one way. Only after the event can mortals know what She truly meant."

Tadoku paused, and then, as if words came hard, said, "Moreover, priests and priestesses are men and women, and men and women are corruptible."

Disbelief choked Hadon. He said, "You can't mean that Minruth might have bribed the oracle? The voice of the Voice of Kho? That couldn't be! Kho Herself would strike the woman dead!"

"Yes, but Kho may have allowed this so that She could carry out her plans, as I said before. However, I don't really believe that the priestess would lie for the sake of money. She would be too terrified. I just suggested that because one should consider all possibilities, no matter how farfetched they seem."

"You are cynical!" Hadon said.

"I have a sharp eye, and I have been close to the great ones of the empire for a long time," Tadoku said. "In any event I have checked out the personnel of the vessel. It's a merchant ship, you know, basically a mail-carrier. That is odd. Why weren't you put on a naval vessel, since you're such a precious cargo? Why weren't we given a naval escort? What if a pirate ship were to attack us? It's true that pirates haven't been in the waters north of the island for two hundred years. But that doesn't mean that they might not appear again. And what if the pirate vessel were in the employ of Minruth?

"Not that I consider that likely. Such a thing would be too raw for anybody to digest, and the rage of Awineth, as everybody but you seems to know, is awful. Minruth would be the first to die, unless he ordered his troops into action at once. And then he would likely be defeated. On the other hand, Minruth is called the Mad for good reasons, and you cannot expect him always to act as a rational man would.

"However, assuming that he does use good sense, he will take no action until, or if, you return. In the meantime—which will be a long one—much can happen in Khokarsa."

Hadon, instead of being depressed, became angry. When he and Tadoku practiced with wooden swords, he attacked Tadoku as if he meant to kill him. But Tadoku gave him a beating that soon cooled him down, and the points Tadoku gained were thereafter much less. Finally, panting and sweating, the two ceased. A sailor emptied buckets of cool seawater over them, and they sat down to discuss the exercise.

"You have the makings of a great swordsman," Tadoku said. "You will be one in five years if you get enough experience. And if you live that long. Bhukla is fickle, and I have seen better men than myself go to her sister Sisisken. A man has an off-day, and a lesser swordsman kills him. Or he may have problems which he cannot thrust out of his mind during the fighting. Or something has happened to break his spirit, and he may unconsciously wish to die. Or chance, a foot slipping in blood, the sun in his eyes, a fly landing on his nose, weakening caused by the onslaught of a cold or an ill-digested meal—all these and much more may cause the death of even the greatest swordsman.

"However, the chief killers are booze and too much food and the loss of youth. You can do something about the first two, but over the last, no man has control. A man should know when to quit, when to hang up the iron *tenu* and wear only the honorary copper *tenu*. Pride may prevent him from doing this, and then Sisisken, who loathes pride and arrogance, will chop him down."

"And when will you hang up your *tenu*?" Hadon said.

Tadoku grinned and said, "I don't expect to find any great swordsmen, or any swordsmen at all, in fact, out in the Wild Lands. The savages have only stone or wooden weapons—the ax, the spear, and the club. And the sling and the bow, which are not to be sneered at, but swords wielded by the greatest are no good against arrows, so why worry about them? After we get back—if we get back—then I may start wearing the copper. In the meantime, I serve my queen."

They discussed the relative merits of the sword, the ax, and the club.

"At close range, the axman is at a disadvantage," Tadoku said. "But beware the skilled thrower of the ax. As for the club, if it is brassbound, it can be dangerous. However, the only club I would fear would be that in the hands of the monster Kwasin. I saw him once, when he was on his way to the Western Lands, just after he had been exiled. He is as tall as a giraffe and as strong as a gorilla, and when he is fighting, as berserk as a rhinoceros in a rut. He is strangely quick for such a giant, and he seems to know all the tricks of a swordsman. But it is force he depends upon, force that only the heroes of old had. I doubt that even the giant hero Klamsweth could have stood up to him."

"I know," Hadon said. "Kwasin is my cousin."

"I'm well aware of that," Tadoku said testily. "I didn't want to bring it up, since I thought you might not like to talk about it. No relatives of his that I have so far met ever wanted to admit that they were related."

"I'm not fond of him," Hadon said. "But I feel no shame because of his crime. I didn't commit it, and besides, he's not of my totem."

"That's a sensible attitude," Tadoku said. "The more I know you, the less I resent serving under you."

"Ah, then you do resent me!" Hadon said.

Tadoku merely grinned.

9

The galley slowly rounded the curve that took the cone of Khowot out of sight. At midday it was free of the mouth of the Gulf of Gahete. As the cliffs dwindled, Khowot became visible again. At dusk it could still be seen, but it was sinking into the horizon. Clouds of smoke were still rising from it, great black masses, and Hadon wondered if it were about to erupt again. The last serious explosion had half-destroyed the city of Khokarsa two hundred and fifty years ago. It would be ironic if he completed his mission only to find that Awineth and Minruth had perished under gas, smoke, and lava.

Since the wind was from the northwest, the galley was unable to use its sails. It could beat against the wind only to a limited extent, and in this case it had to depend entirely upon the oars. Once again Hadon asked for permission to row at least twice a day. The captain reluctantly said yes. Tadoku was at first upset. It was not fitting that a hero should work side by side with common fellows. But on seeing that the rowers were very pleased because Hadon was working with them, he changed his mind.

"You're shrewder than I thought," he said to Hadon. "It is well to become popular with the lower classes. As long as you preserve your dignity, of course, and don't become a clown to please them. The rowers will boast about this in the ports, and the story will spread throughout the empire faster than mail can be delivered."

Hadon did not disillusion him. He had only wanted to keep in shape, but if others thought he was intelligent enough to have done this for a political motive, let them think so.

Days of hard rowing passed, and the city of Mukha rose from the round of the sea. At noon the galley pulled past the opening of the massive stone breakwaters and docked. Tadoku hurried into the city to warn the rulers that they were to make no fuss about the appearance of Hadon. The orders were that the expedition was to be organized as quickly as possible and marched off northward into the Wild Lands. But such was not to be. Hadon waited in the camp northwest of Mukha for a week before the first contingent of his force rowed into the harbor.

"Break your back hurrying so you can sit on your ass,' Tadoku growled. "The old army motto."

At the end of another ten days (the Khokarsan week was ten days), the last shipload marched off to the shrilling of bagpipes, the throoming of bullroarers, and the clanging of bronze gongs. These were the Klemqaba assigned to the expedition, and Hadon's heart, already low, sank even further. The wild Klemqaba were recruited from the coast northwest of the Strait of Keth and from the even wilder tribes of the mountainous interior. They were short, broad fellows, half-neanderthaloid, half-human, tattooed in blue and green all over, wearing only codpieces of polished buffalo horn which projected in a semicomic, semisinister fashion. They carried small round shields and heavy bronze axes and slings of goat hide and pouches of stones for the slings. Their standard was a carved figure of Kho as the Goat-Headed Mother on the end of a long pole bearing on its length dried phalluses of famous enemies slain in combat. Their breaths stank of *s"okoko*,* *the water of life*, a liquor made in the high mountains, a harsh peaty-flavored drink which only they could down with ease.

* Khokarsan had two syllables for water. -*kem*- meant any relatively unconfined liquid or jellied mass, hence, -*kemu*-, *water-great* or *sea*. -*s"o*- referred to liquids, jellies, or gases in containers.

89

"The best fighting men in the empire," Tadoku said. "Stronger than we are, and without fear, able to eat food which would kill us off, meat a week rotten, vegetables fit only for garbage, and they never complain as long as they're in action. But they're hell to discipline when there's no fighting. And the fact that they're entitled to bring their women along causes discontent among the other troops."

"I don't see why," Hadon murmured. The women were a squat, ugly lot, most of them stronger than the average human soldier, wild-haired, slack-breasted, clad in animal-skin loincloths, some pregnant, others nursing babies. Like the men, they were tattooed from head to foot.

"Why would a soldier, or anyone, desire such women?"

"After a long time without women of any kind, they begin to look good," Tadoku said.

"Couldn't we at least make those with babies stay behind?" Hadon said.

"If they have to make a choice they'll kill the babies," Tadoku said.

Tadoku started to add something but swore instead. He gestured at a group of twenty soldiers in the rear guard. These were bearded and tattooed red and black and carried kite-shaped shields, and their standard was the figurine of a bear-headed woman.

"Minruth is doing his best to screw us up!" Tadoku groaned. "You never, just simply never, put the Klemklakor with the Klemqaba!"

Hadon asked for an explanation and was told that not all the tribes of these people were of the Goat Totem. A few belonged to the ancient Bear Totem, and these were sworn enemies of the Klemqaba.

Hadon had never seen a bear, though he had seen drawings and statues of them. At one time the mountains north of the Kemu had been heavily populated by the small brown bear and the giant russet cave bear, huger than, as the saying went, a lion and a half. But there had been no validated reports of the russet bear for two centuries, and the brown bears had been hunted close to extinction. Nevertheless, their totems were still in existence. In fact, Kwasin was a member of the *Klakordeth* or Thunder Bear Totem. Which made him, though not a blood brother, since he was all-human, a spiritual brother of the hybrids.

"If you must give an order to the two totems," Tadoku said, "make sure that an officer of one is not to transmit it directly to the other. The officer just won't do it."

"How can we maintain discipline then?"

"That's just one of the many problems this fouled-up outfit presents us with," Tadoku said.

Hadon looked thoughtful. During the week in camp, he had learned all he could about the army procedure, and he had considered carefully the welfare of the expedition. He had been given two hundred and fifty men and women, far too large a force. He desired only fifty. A larger body would cause very slow marching and be difficult to feed. When they were about halfway on their outward journey, they would run out of supplies, and from then on they'd have to depend on their hunters. He had a plan to weed out all but fifty before they got to the last outpost of civilization.

That night he had to settle five quarrels and numerous complaints. He stopped a brawl between the Klemqaba and the Klemklakor only by threatening to smash the *s"okoko* containers if peace was not restored at once. The officers retorted that, since they were mercenaries, they would quit if he carried out his threat. He told them that that was fine with him. They could return home in disgrace, and they would miss out on fighting the wild savages.

Tadoku turned pale when he heard Hadon, but he said nothing. Later, after the two totems had sworn not to fight among themselves for at least ten days, Tadoku commented.

"That was a narrow escape. If the totems had said to hell with you, we would have had a battle which would have cut us down to less than fifty. And I'm afraid that less than half of that would have been human. Though the humans are nothing to brag about."

"It worked," Hadon said. "Now, I want some officers and enlisted men to spread stories about the horrors waiting for us in the Wild Lands. I want the weak-livered ones among us to desert. Give the guards orders to ignore anyone they see sneaking away. Even if they're carrying stolen supplies. Be sure to pick good men as guards, because we don't want the guards deserting too, and leaving us wide open for attack."

91

Tadoku saluted and hurried off, though he evidently did not like this unconventional breach of discipline.

By the morning of the third day, Tadoku reported that thirty-five men had stolen away in the night. He was surprised, because he had thought that they would lose a hundred. None of the AWOL's were Klemqaba or Klemklakor, which was to be expected.

"The road ends tomorrow at the outpost," Hadon said. "We've been making only about ten miles a day because we have to match our pace with the oxen-drawn wagons. Also, we'll be stopping every two miles to mark our trail. Once we get to the rough country, we'll be reduced to about five miles a day, if that. We're going to lose the oxen, eventually; they can't survive long in the Wild Lands. So we're going to have another test. Announce tonight that the wagons will be abandoned. Slaughter the oxen for a feast, and tell everybody to drink everything except what they think they can carry. Move the Klemklakor about a half-mile away so they won't be fighting the Klemqaba. Station your best men around the camp, and if things get out of hand, they're to interfere only if I give the order."

"May I ask you what the object of this is?" Tadoku said.

"Tomorrow, before breakfast, I will tell them that they are not to eat until they get to the outpost fort. They must pack up and run for the fort. The first fifty only will be allowed to continue into the Wild Lands. The rest will either be sent back to the fort at Mukha or paid off."

"The Goat and Bear people won't stand for that," Tadoku said.

"If they want to argue with us, they'll have to catch us first," Hadon said. "And when we get to the fort, we'll have the garrison to back us up. I intend to eliminate as many problems right now. It's going to be tough enough when we get to the Wild Lands."

"The women will abandon their babies," Tadoku said. "The hyenas, the jackals, and the vultures will be eating them before the sun has quartered the sky."

"Very well. We'll cheat a little. There are five babies. Pick seven of your best men, fellows you know are trustworthy, and hide them outside the camp. They can follow and pick up the babies, and the mothers can claim them later. Let's hope none of the mothers will be among the first fifty. Oh, yes, we have to have Hinokly and the bard and the doctor, so tell them to start marching at midnight. With that head-start, they should be all right."

"They march in the night?" Tadoku said. "This is leopard and lion country. They might not get to the fort."

"We need Hinokly as a guide and Kebiwabes for morale," Hadon said. "Very well. Pick six good men to escort them."

"I don't think I have that many," Tadoku said, and he groaned.

"Do the best you can," Hadon said.

There was an uproar when Tadoku announced Hadon's orders. Hadon immediately told them that he wanted only men and women who had the stuff of heroes on this expedition. Anybody who would confess that he didn't have it should step forward, and he would be sent back to the fort at Mukha. There would be no official penalties attached, though he could not control those who might jeer at them.

Not a single one of the Goat and Bear people moved. Ten of the humans shamefacedly crossed the line that a sergeant had drawn in the dirt.

"Very well," Hadon said. "Tonight the rest of you may feast and drink all you wish. But don't look to replenish your supply of liquor at the fort."

He dismissed them. The oxen were killed and the clay bottles and goatskin containers of beer, mead, and *s"okoko* were opened. Hadon retired to his tent, which he would use no more after that night. It would be left with all tents and burdensome baggage.

From now on all would be sleeping in their bags under the open skies. Tadoku was scandalized when he learned that all officers, including Hadon, would have to carry their own bags, armor, and weapons.

"It just isn't done! It puts us on a footing with the common soldier!'

"Except for a leather helmet and cuirass, I won't be wearing any armor," Hadon said. "Nor will anybody. We don't need bronze armor against the stone weapons of the savages, and we'll be much more mobile without them."

"But armor is expensive!"

"There's a cave up in the hills," Hadon said. "One of the

scouts located it for me. The armor will be cached there, and we'll pick it up on the way back. If it's stolen, I'll pay for the loss. As king, I will be able to do that. Everyone will be given a receipt now, collectible in Khokarsa. Oh, by the way, what about the priestess for this expedition? Are we supposed to pick up one at the fort?"

"There is nothing about a priestess in our orders, as you well know," Tadoku said. "Either it's an oversight, which doesn't seem likely, or Minruth is sending us out without a spiritual guide."

"We'll get one at the fort anyway," Hadon said. "If they have only one, they can get another from Mukha."

"And suppose the priestess doesn't want to go with us?"

"I'll tell her we'll take a priest of Resu instead. If she's conscientious, she won't allow that."

"Then we will have a mutiny."

"Perhaps you and I and Hinokly and Kebiwabes and the doctor may be the only ones left," Hadon said, smiling. But he wondered if he was predicting accurately.

Hadon left his tent at midnight. Taps had been ignored, at his orders. He wanted the self-indulgent to eliminate themselves for the race in the morning, and apparently there were many doing just that. The shouting, singing, and laughing were almost as loud as they had been two hours ago, and eight men and one woman had been carried off bleeding and stunned to the medical tent, where the drunken doctor, Onomi, treated them. Hadon walked away from the camp toward the site of the Klemklakor. When the din had become low, he listened for noise from the Bear people. But all was silent. He smiled. They had chosen to quit drinking early and go to bed so they would be in shape tomorrow. Only a desire to beat out their hereditary enemies, the Goat people, could have induced them to refrain from gulping their beloved *s"okoko* to the last drop. And they must have a strong leader, otherwise they would never have been able to practice such self-disipline.

At dawn, the drums and trumpets of reveille got most of the camp to its feet, though here and there a sleeper snored heavily. Hadon gave them a little while to drink water and to eliminate, and then he lined them up across the broad plain.

"When the bugle blows, the race is on!" he cried out.

A few minutes later, he gave them the signal, and two hundred and five men and women, uttering savage cries or hoarse croaks, ran forward. Rather, some did. Most staggered or shambled.

Hadon took the lead and never gave it up. He swung along easily, trotting, and when he had covered the ten miles, felt that he could go on another ten. The fort was a massive earthworks construction with several stone towers flying the flags of Khokarsa and of the Mukha queendom. The commander had not expected the force so soon, and there was a delay until he could be summoned from the little wooden temple in one corner of the court. He came cursing and red-faced. Hadon found out later that he and the priestess had been busy at something or other in the privacy of her quarters, and he resented being disturbed. But when he saw Hadon, he forced a smile and greeted him as enthusiastically as he could under the circumstances.

Hadon explained what had happened after he had recovered his breath. The colonel laughed and detailed soldiers to set up two posts and to mark the first fifty to arrive. Hadon talked with Hinokly, the bard, and the doctor, who had made an uneventful journey, though they had heard the roars of hunting lions nearby. After a while, the first ten straggled in, tough old Tadoku and three commissioned officers among them. These were, as Hadon had expected, human soldiers who had abstained from drinking. The Goat and Bear people were very powerful, but long-distance running was not their speciality. Their short legs and massive physiques handicapped them.

Nevertheless, the next group held about twenty of the Bear people and one Klemqaba sergeant. Two more humans walked in, and then a mixed group of humans and Bear and Goat people.

Hadon counted fifty, excluding himself, the bard, the scribe, and the doctor. He ordered the fort's soldiers out to line up along the road.

"Take their weapons away from them. They will be too tired to resist. Give them food and water after they've rested and send them back at once. Without their weapons. These

95

will be shipped back after they've reported to the Mukha commander."

"I suggest that they be sent back under an armed escort," the colonel said. "Otherwise, they might just become outlaws, and we've enough problems with these."

"As you wish." Hadon said. "We need a priestess. Do you think yours would do us the favor of accompanying us?"

The colonel turned pale and said, "She wouldn't want to leave—"

"You," Hadon finished for him, grinning. "We'll see. Please conduct me to her so I may make my request."

On being introduced to the priestess, Phekly, Hadon could understand why the colonel did not want to lose her. She was a beautiful young woman with glossy black hair and large black eyes and a superb figure. And it became evident that she and the colonel were in love.

"I'd have to get authorization from the Mother at Mukha," she said. "That would delay you for many days. However, I have no intention of going with you into the Wild Lands unless the Mother orders me to do so. Which I doubt very much, since she is also my physical mother. I could appoint our priest of Resu as a temporary priestess of Kho—there is precedent for that—but unfortunately he is very sick with a fever. Besides, he is a drunkard and a coward."

"I bow to your wishes, priestess," Hadon said. "Even though they leave us without spiritual guidance and protection."

"You could wait until a priestess could come up from Mukha," she said.

"I have orders from the queen not to delay," he said.

He withdrew, leaving a troubled woman behind him—evidently her conscience was hurting her—and he went out of the fort again. Presently he saw a squat, powerful Klemqaba woman, holding her baby, trotting stubbornly toward him. The spiral tattoos on her forehead indicated that she was a priestess, and, seeing these, Hadon was struck with an idea. He didn't like it, but expediency overrode prejudice now.

"Is she the last?" Hadon asked Tadoku.

"Probably she's the last who will show," Tadoku said, checking the count with Hinokly.

"Appoint her as our priestess," Hadon said.

Tadoku and Hinokly gasped, and Tadoku said, "Sir?"

"I spoke clearly enough," Hadon said. "Yes, I know that no Klemqaba priestess has ever presided over rites attended by the Klemkho. But she is a priestess of Kho, and there is no written law that says she can't conduct rites for humans. Besides, she is tough, otherwise she would have given up long ago. And I like it that she did not abandon her baby. She has a strong character."

"The men won't like it, sir," Tadoku said.

"I don't ask them to like it," he said. "I doubt that they will insult her, even though she is a Klemqaba. But my orders are that any man who does so will be executed."

Kebiwabes, who had been standing nearby, said, "This is a queer expedition, Hadon. Sent out to find a god, and vicared by a Goat woman. But I have more confidence in its success than I had when I boarded the galley at Khokarsa. In my opinion, Hadon, you have the makings of a king. And in you I may have the makings of a great epic."

"Let us hope so," Hadon said. Hadon looked at Tadoku, who was talking to the woman, and he called for his second in command, a man from Qethruth named Mokwaten.

"Let everybody rest for an hour, then feed them. As soon as they have eaten, we will resume the march."

Mokwaten said nothing, of course, but the bard groaned and said, "That march last night wore me out."

"Be glad you didn't have to run today," Hadon said. "We stop at dusk, and you can get a long night's sleep then."

10

It took many days to pass the western flanks of the great Saasares mountains. Their slopes were covered with wild olive trees on the lower levels, oak higher up, and then fir and pine. Far off, whiteness glittered, ice and snow which did not melt even in summer.

"A thousand years ago, the tops of the mountains and the high valleys were filled with rivers of ice," the bard said. "But the climate has been getting drier and warmer, and the ice rivers have melted away."

"The ice rivers still exist in the great mountains along the shore of the world-ringing sea to the north," Hinokly said. "We did not go very high into the mountains there, but we went far enough to see those cold and brooding masses. Then we turned eastward and walked along the foothills until we came to a river fed by the melting snows of the mountains. We made dugouts and voyaged down that river to the Ringing Sea."

"And that is where you encountered Sahhindar?" Hadon said.

"Yes. But he said that we were mistaken about the sea being on the edge of the world. It is only another sea, and there are islands in it, and on the other side is more land. He said that there is no edge to the world. It is"—he hesitated —"round. Shaped like an olive."

"But that's crazy!" Tadoku said.

"I thought it improbable," Hinokly said. "However, I was not about to argue with a god."

"Tell me more of Sahhindar," Hadon said. "And this beautiful witch from the sea, this Lalila, and her child, and the one-eyed manling, and the great ax made from a fallen star."

"He is somewhat taller than you, Hadon, and has bigger bones, and is somewhat more muscular, though not much more. But I have seen him lift a boulder that four men could not lift, and I have seen him outrun a charging elephant. His body is scarred from the knife and the claw and the tusk. Perhaps he bears a hundred scars in all. The most prominent is on his forehead, however, which he said was the result of his scalp being torn open by one of those half-men, the *nukaar*. He has large dark eyes, and—"

"Wait," Hadon said. "If he is a god, why does he not heal the scars? And can a god be wounded?"

"You may ask him if you ever meet him," Hinokly said. "I did not question him; I only answered him. And he has long straight black hair, and he wears only a loincloth of antelope hide and a belt with a leather scabbard holding a large iron knife. He carries on his back a quiver of arrows and a bow. The strong men could not bend that bow. The tips of the arrows, however, are of flint."

"Did he say he was indeed the son of Kho, Sahhindar?"

"We addressed him as such, and he did not correct us. But he carries the bow and he looks as Sahhindar is described to us by the priestesses and priests. And he has companions that only deities would have."

"You mean the violet-eyed woman and the others?"

"No, I mean the great lion, and the elephant on whose back he rode, and the monkey that sat on his shoulder. They obeyed him as if he were their mother, and I swear that he talked to them. The elephant stayed away from us, but the lion walked among us, and we were very nervous."

"Then he never said that he was a god?"

"Never. Actually, he did not talk much to us except to find out where we were from and where we were going, and to charge us to bring the woman and her party safely to Khokarsa and to treat them well. Oh, yes, he spoke our tongue, of course, but strangely. He said that it had changed somewhat since he had last been in Khokarsa."

Hadon felt his skin prickle. "If he was in Khokarsa that long ago, then he must truly be Sahhindar. But why did he not come back with you?"

"I wish he had, since we would not then have suffered such misfortunes. On the other hand, he terrified me when he was around, and I was glad when he left. Anyway, he said he had business elsewhere, and I did not ask him what it was. He was lifted by the elephant onto its back, and he rode off on it with the lion walking beside them and the monkey screeching between the elephant's ears.

"I cannot tell you much about him, but if we should find the woman, we should learn more from her. Apparently Sahhindar had brought her and the others across the Kemuqoqanqo, the Ringing Sea, from lands beyond, and he talked much to them. I did not get a chance to talk to her, because it was shortly after Sahhindar had left us that we were attacked by the savages. The rest you know."

Hadon knew the rest and was not comforted by it. Hinokly had made a map on the way north, but on the journey back he had lost all his papyrus rolls. He was leading the expedition by memory now. That was not good, because they had a vast area to get lost in.

The days and nights passed, one much like the other. The savannas rolled away as far as the eye could see, waist-high tawny grass with short bushy trees here and there and an occasional waterhole or small lake around which grew taller trees. The animal life became more numerous and at length awesome in its number. There were times when the party had to halt and wait for hundreds of thousands, perhaps a million antelopes of many kinds as they ran before them, scared of something behind them and chasing the horizon in front of them. The earth shook and drummed, and dust rose high and then settled, streaking them with brown dirt. They saw many prides of *ruwodeth* (lion), lone or paired cheetahs, leopards, packs of the white-and-black hunting dogs, hyenas, jackals, herds of many *qampo*, (elephants), the huge white *bok'ul''-ikadeth* (rhinoceros), the tower-necked *c'ad''eneske* (giraffe), the *q''ok'odakwa* (ostrich), the *bom'odemu* (warthog), the *bog''ugu* (giant wild pig), and the terrible *baq''oq''u* (wild buffalo). There were many *akarwadamo* (monkeys) in the trees near the waterholes and the rain lakes and also the *akarwadamowu* (baboons). And everywhere there were birds.

There was no lack of meat, if it could be killed. But fifty-six people had to be fed, and hunters had to go out every other day. Individually, they were not very successful, so Hadon arranged for all to take part. Some would lie in ambush while others, jumping up and shouting and waving their spears, initiated a stampede. Then the ambushers would throw their spears or cast their stones from slings at the passing gazelle, antelope, or buffalo. Twice they also flushed out prides of lions which had been stalking the same prey, and one man was severely mauled. He died two days later, and they heaped stones over him and erected over the pile a wooden pole with a tiny figurine of Kho at its end. The priestess, Mumona, chanted the burial rites over him, and the throat of a hare was cut and its blood was poured over the cairn.

"An ill omen," Hinokly said. "The first man to die on our expedition was killed by a lion under the same circumstances. Let us hope that this expedition does not follow in the footsteps of the first."

"That is up to Kho," Hadon said. "Don't spread such talk among the men. They're frightened enough as it is."

Hadon was not scared, but he was worried. Even if the three people he was seeking were still alive, which was doubtful, how could they be found in this great wilderness? He could see his party years from now, reduced to a very few, getting old and weak, wandering here and there, knowing their quest was hopeless. Minruth would not wait for more than two years, if he waited that long. Even if Hadon did complete his mission, he might find that Minruth had talked his daughter into marrying him. Or perhaps Awineth, wearying, had decreed another Great Games and taken a husband.

On the thirtieth day after leaving the outpost, they saw their first savages. These consisted of a dozen men, women, and children, who fled as soon as they caught sight of the Khokarsans. They were short, slim, and dark-haired, wore skins around the loins, and were painted with red-and-black designs. The men were bearded. Some had bows, which made Hadon so curious that he almost sent some men out after the savages. He had seen bows only in drawings and sculpture, and he would have liked to try one. But even in the Wild Lands the taboo against bows held. It would be dangerous even to touch one.

The next day they saw the peaks of some mountains. Hinokly said that he recognized them; they were on the right path. They should go along the foothills of these, keeping northward, until they rounded them. After traveling eastward, they would come to a river that originated somewhere up in the mountains.

"That river eventually joins another which flows southward from the even greater mountains to the north. The two form a broad river which flows into the Ringing Sea. But it will be about three months before we get there. Having to gather plants, hunt animals, and heap trail-mark cairns will slow us down considerably, even though we are going faster because we're not handicapped by oxen."

Hadon stopped and said, "Something's happened! That scout is running as if a lion were after him!"

Hinokly looked in the direction in which Hadon's finger was pointing. Coming from the west was Nagota, one of the better scouts and hunters, a citizen of Bawaku. He was running with all his strength now, though not going swiftly, since he had been obviously running for some time. He almost fell when he got to Hadon, and it was a minute before he got breath enough to gasp out his message.

Hadon could see no cause for alarm. If any danger threatened, it had to be at least half a mile away. He had told Tadoku to draw the party up in a battle formation. They assembled in a center of spear and ax men with two wings of javelin and sling men. Kebiwabes, who had been singing, walked toward them with his lyre in hand. As a bard, he would not be taking part in any fighting unless the situation became desperate.

The scout said, "Sir, there's a giant out there, about a mile away by now, I suppose. He's running toward us, and about a half-mile behind him is an army of savages."

Hadon asked him a few questions and found out in detail what had happened. The scout had been on top of a hill about fifty feet high when he had seen the man on the horizon. He had waited until the man came closer, since one man did not represent an immediate threat. Then he had changed his mind. This man, this giant, rather, looked as if he could take on a whole corps. He was about seven feet high and as muscular as a gorilla. He wore a lionskin kilt, and he was bearded. The beard had made the scout think he was a savage, but when he saw the brass bands around the huge club he was carrying, he was not so sure.

Hadon swore and said, "As if I didn't have enough troubles!"

"What is the matter?" Tadoku said.

"My cousin, Kwasin, is coming! With a pack of savages on his heels!"

"But he was in the Western Lands!" Tadoku said. "What is he doing so far north?"

"We'll soon find out," Hadon said. "Or we will if we can fight off the savages. Scout, how many were there?"

"About fifty."

"And how are they armed?"

"They have no shields. They carry spears, knives, axes, bolas, and bows."

Hadon wondered what had brought so many of them together. Usually, according to Hinokly, their bands seldom numbered over a dozen. But occasionally they assembled for a big hunt or a tribal ceremony. Kwasin must have stumbled across them during one of these events.

Hadon ordered his force to run to a round hill topped by three trees a quarter of a mile away. They could make a better stand there. He waited, and presently he saw a tiny figure come from a clump of trees near a waterhole. Then he went to the hill, where Tadoku had arranged the men in two circles, one within the other.

Shortly thereafter, the first of the savages ran out from behind the trees. He was gaining on the giant, which was no wonder. Hadon though that Kwasin must have had a long head start; otherwise, the heavy man could not have been so far ahead of his chasers. Hadon signaled, and two slingers raced toward him. He picked his leather cuirass and helmet from the ground, where he had set them, and donned them. The helmet was conical, with a neck guard and nose flap, and the cuirass was fitted with a leather apron to guard his genitals. He drew his *tenu* from the scabbard and slashed through the air to warm up his arms.

Kwasin came near enough to recognize Hadon, and his eyes opened even wider. He said nothing because he was out of breath; he puffed like a bull buffalo cornered by lions. Sweat matted his long hair and beard and coated him with a silvery shine. Hadon gestured at the hill, and Kwasin trotted on by him.

By then the first group of savages, about twelve, were a quarter of a mile away. They were tall, and their hair and beards were dyed scarlet, and their dark-white bodies were painted with red, black, and green swirls and X's, and slivers of bone were stuck through their septums.

The first group stopped then, and one of them turned and called out to those streaming behind them. There was a roar, and the rest ran up and lined up before the man who had spoken. Thirty of them carried quivers and short, thick wooden bows. They drew arrows from the quivers and fitted the shafts to the strings. However, they did not fire, since they were about 1,250 feet away and so out of range. But Hadon's slingers could cast their missiles over a fourth of a mile, and at his orders they each loosed, in rapid succession, four biconical lead missiles. Only after three of their men had fallen did the savages realize what was going on. Then, yelling, they charged, and Hadon and his two slingers ran back to the hill and up it. The spearmen opened their shields to let them in, and Hadon joined Kwasin, Tadoku, the bard, the priestess, the scribe, and the doctor. The savages, however, had retreated.

Tadoku ordered the outer ring of spearmen to kneel so the slingers behind them could have a clear field. Kebiwabes started to sing a war song while playing on his lyre, but Tadoku ordered him to cease. He wanted the officers' commands to be clearly heard. The baby started crying then, and the priestess shushed it by giving it the breast.

Kwasin was not breathing so heavily now. He grinned at Hadon and said, "Greetings, cousin! We meet unexpectedly and in strange circumstances in a strange place! What are you doing here?" His voice was deep and booming, a lion's.

"Explanations will have to wait until after we settle with the savages," Hadon said.

Kwasin took another drink of water from a clay canteen. Then he wiped his huge hairy hand over his lips, and his strong white teeth and black eyes glittered in a smile.

"I would not have run like a jackal," he roared, "even though they be fifty strong! But they have arrows! Now the situation is different! As soon as they have exhausted their supply of shafts, I will charge them. And you will be troubled no more!"

Except for Hadon, all stared. Hadon was accustomed to his bragging, if it was bragging. He wasn't sure that Kwasin could not do just what he said he could do.

One of the savages must have been carrying a drum, since a booming came from somewhere in the mob. The savages yelled and screamed and started dancing, with the exception of ten archers. These circled the hill and slowly started up it. A slinger, at Tadoku's order, loosed a missile at one of them. The man had time to duck, and he yelled a warning at the others. They retreated a few steps.

The pounding of the drum increased its tempo, and with a yell the savages quit dancing and began running toward the hill. They came in a disorganized mob, some of them tripping over others. In their lead was a tall fellow with a sunburst of yellow painted on his forehead and five ostrich feathers sticking out of his hair.

"That's their leader!" thundered Kwasin. "Here, you, give me your sling!" He tore a sling from the grasp of a startled man and squeezed his other hand. The slinger yelled with pain; Kwasin caught the falling bicone with his left hand.

Hadon almost struck Kwasin with his sword. "You don't give orders or interfere with discipline!" he shouted. "I am the commander, and if you stay here, you will obey me!"

Kwasin looked startled; then he grinned. "You, my cousin the stripling?" he said. "In command? Kho, how things have changed! Well, cousin, I owe you my life, so far, so I will obey you like a good soldier during this battle—if I like your orders. But grant me this one indulgence!"

Holding the two ends of the sling, he whirled it around and above his head and then loosed it with a *ha*! The missile sped true, so far that the slingers gave a low cry of amazement. The chief of the savages suddenly fell backward. The others stopped, piled up, and crowded around him; in a minute they cried out a mourning. They withdrew then, leaving the corpse on its back while their new leader took over.

This time, ten archers advanced while the rest, brandishing spears and axes, trailed behind them. Halfway up the hill, the archers stopped and aimed their bows. There was a twang, and the arrows flew upward. At the same time, the slingers, at Tadoku's orders, loosed their missiles.

The archers were at a disadvantage in having to shoot uphill. Most of the arrows went too high or too low, but one plunged through a shield of wood and leather and through an arm. Another struck a slinger through the throat. The archers retreated, dragging two corpses and two wounded with them. They went just far enough to be beyond effective range of the slingers. There was a roar, and the spearmen and axmen surged forward up the hill past the archers, who then followed them. These fired over the heads of their fellows, but the arrows went at too high an angle to hit the Khokarsans.

Kwasin suddenly gave a yell and leaped over the two rows of the kneelers, landed, and ran down the hill waving his huge club. Hadon gasped; that jump would have done credit to a lion. Then, seeing that those in the forefront of the enemy turned and ran into those behind, Hadon shouted an order. The soldiers stood up and began to form into a wedge shape. Hadon waited impatiently until they had arranged themselves into a ragged V, and he gave the command to charge. He was at the head, as was his duty, his sword held in two hands. Ahead and below, Kwasin smashed into a knot of men, and they and he went over and were rolling in a tangle down the hill. But he was up again and swinging the club as if it were a wand, smashing spears out of the way, cracking skulls, shattering arms.

The savages broke and ran, and Hadon was the only one of his force besides Kwasin to spill their blood. He overtook a squat man pumping his short legs furiously and with a stroke sent his head rolling from his shoulders. The body continued running, blood spurting a foot high from its neck, and then it fell forward.

The savages ran until they were near the clump of trees. There they regained their wind and talked for some time. Hadon ordered his men to retreat to the top of the hill. The wounded would be treated while he decided what to do next. He had considered charging them while they were still disorganized, but he was afraid that his men might get carried away and break ranks in pursuit. If they did, they might get cut off.

Hinokly said, "I think that if we'd let them take their dead, they'd go away. They can't take many casualties; they need every able-bodied man for hunting, and the survivors won't like having to take care of the dead men's families. From what I know of these savages, they would just as soon go home with the corpses and brag to their women what great fighters they are and how they slaughtered us."

"What will they have to show their wives as trophies?" Tadoku said.

"We'll have to give them our dead, too. Part of them, anyway. If these are like the others I've seen, they'll want the heads and the prepuces."

"The ghosts of our dead would never forgive us!" Hadon said.

"Well, you can bury them and march off. But these savages will dig them up after we've left and take what they want," Hinokly said. "Of course, then the ghosts will be angry at the savages, not us."

Four of his men were dead and six wounded, three severely. The enemy had discharged about half of their arrows, but they still had enough left to inflict heavy casualties. However, they were undisciplined. If Hinokly was right, they would be glad to retreat with honor. On the other hand, they knew the country, and they might be able to arrange an ambush later on. Or they might dog them, trying to pick them off one by one. It would be better to smash them now and utterly discourage thoughts of further attack. It would be worth it, even if he sustained more casualties.

Hadon went to Kwasin, who was sitting on the slope with the dead around him and blowing like a hippopotamus. He was terrible-looking, splashed with blood, though none of it seemed to be his own.

"Do you feel up to leading another charge?" Hadon said, knowing that his words would sting Kwasin.

"Up to it, cousin?" Kwasin rumbled. "I was just planning on charging them all by myself, as soon as I recovered my wind!"

"In which case you would bristle with arrows," Hadon said. And a good idea that is, he thought.

Kwasin heaved himself up and said, "I am ready. I will eat them up; my club will pound them into bread."

"It is better to let men see deeds than hear words," Hadon said. He called Tadoku to him. After a short consultation, Tadoku arranged the men into battle order. With ten slingers in each wing and twenty-four spearmen in the center, they advanced on the enemy. Hadon and Kwasin were about ten feet ahead of the spearmen.

The savages lined up two deep with the archers in the rear

107

and the spear and ax men kneeling in the front. When his force was just out of arrow range, Hadon ordered the center to stop while the wings advanced. Some of the savages, becoming nervous, loosed ineffectual arrows. The slingers kept on coming, and then they stopped and cast their stones. Two savages fell, and the archers began firing. Three of his slingers fell, at which Hadon gave the order to charge. The slingers dropped their slings, unslung their little round shields, pulled out short, heavy leaf-shaped swords or axes, and ran yelling forward. A few more arrows whistled around the Khokarsans, but none struck.

Their chief shouted at them, apparently urging them to hold. But the sudden exhaustion of their arrows and the glinting of the sun on the bronze swords and spearheads seemed to unnerve them. Or perhaps it was the sight of the bloody giant Kwasin roaring and waving his club. Before he could get to them, they turned and ran. All, that is, except their chief. He ran desperately at Kwasin and hurled his spear, but Kwasin struck it aside in its flight and was on the chief. The chief pulled his flint knife from his leather belt, but he must have known that he had no chance. He seemed to stand as paralyzed as a sheep about to have its throat cut, and his head broke apart under the brassbound club. Hadon was disappointed. He had hoped that they would hold, and thus be so badly hurt that they would from then on leave his men alone.

From the speed with which they were retreating, however, it seemed that they intended to run forever.

Kwasin leaned on his club, panting, and then sat down on the grass in a puddle of blood, bone, and brains.

"I feel as if I could sleep and eat for a week!" he muttered.

Hadon gestured to Tadoku and told him to bring four slingers and four spearmen. Then he stood over Kwasin, his sword raised in both hands. He said, "Cousin, I must have your oath by Kho and Sisisken that you will obey me from now on as if you were the least of my men. This is a military organization, and no one may accompany us who does not acknowledge me as the chief. Either give your word or die! I will not let you go, since I know how vindictive you are! You would get revenge later!"

Kwasin's face became even redder, and he stared as if he

could not believe what he was hearing. He started to get to his feet, but when Hadon raised the sword higher, Kwasin sank back.

"You would take off my head?"

"This sword has sheared through the neck of a lion," Hadon said. "And thick as your neck is, a lion's is thicker."

"This isn't fair!" Kwasin said. "You can see how tired I am! My muscles quiver as if they were jelly, and I am slow with fatigue! Another time, and I would knock your legs out from under you with my club and break your back with my bare hands!"

"This is not another time," Hadon said. "Give me your word now, or you will speak no more."

"My ghost will haunt you and bring you, too, down to the queen of Sisisken," Kwasin said.

'I'll take that chance. Quickly now! Karken hungers for Kwasin."

"What?" Kwasin said.

"Karken, my father's sword."

Suddenly Kwasin lay flat on his back and laughed. It was weak laughter, because he was so tired. But it was evident that he thought the joke was on him and he was willing to laugh at himself. Hadon watched him warily, because Kwasin might be trying to gain an advantage. Kwasin sat back up and said, "You're the only man who ever stood up to me, Hadon, and lived to brag about it. And you wouldn't be doing that if you were not shrewd as a fox and know that I am too fatigued to lift my club. Very well, I swear by mighty Kho Herself that I will obey you until you die or until we get back to civilization. After that, my oath no longer holds."

"You heard him," Hadon said to Todaku.

He lowered the sword and walked away. A moment later, he looked back. Kwasin, still sitting, was wiping off the club on the grass.

Hadon ordered the force to fill their canteens and water-bags from the waterhole and then to bathe in it. He cleaned off his sword and saw to the wounded, among whom were three savages.

That evening they buried the dead and cut the throats of two of the wounded savages, draining the blood into a leather helmet so that the ghosts might drink from it. In the morning one of the wounded soldiers had died, and he was buried and the surviving savage was sacrificed over his grave. That left two walking wounded and three whose recovery, if any, would take weeks. One was a Klemqaba whose sergeant obligingly put him out of his pain after being forgiven for shedding his blood. The remaining two, humans, were placed in litters made out of poles, and the expedition resumed its march.

Days passed with a feeling of smallness, isolation, and pointlessness growing larger each day. The mountains on the right, the unending savanna on the left, were the same. Mountains, trees, and lion-yellow grass were always there in the burning sun, and when the eyes were closed for sleep, they were still there behind the lids. Again and again, Hadon wondered what he would do when he reached the shores of the Ringing Sea. Which way to go, east or west, or turn south-ward? Where in this vast land could the three he sought be? For all he knew, he might pass by their bones and never see them. They could be hidden in the grass, behind a bush, in a hollow. Or they might be alive but only a few miles away, perhaps lying behind some bushes and afraid to call to them.

One of the wounded died one night, and for no reason that the doctor could determine. He had been well enough to walk and had even been joking when he lay down to sleep. And in the morning he was dead.

A hunter died of a snakebite; another, of an insect bite. A third just disappeared, and though Hadon sent out searchers, they could find no trace. One evening a Klemqaba and a Klemklakor quarreled. The latter was killed and the former was badly wounded. For one tense moment the Bear and the Goat people were about to fall on each other. Hadon shouted that he would massacre them all if any on either side used his weapon. This would have been a laughable threat, since the tattoed soldiers outnumbered the others. But Kwasin was looming behind Hadon and shaking his great club, and the chiefs of the two groups harshly ordered their men to lay down their arms. Hadon conducted a court-martial and found that the survivor had been the offender. Fortunately, he did not have to execute him. He died that night.

As for Kwasin, he was an endless irritant. His bragging and boasting got on Hadon's nerves, and though he obeyed Hadon's orders, he jeered at him. Hadon remonstrated with him for this, but Kwasin merely said, "I did not swear to keep my mouth shut."

Kwasin did have some interesting stories, however. After he had been sentenced to exile, he had been shipped to the city of Towina, which lies southwest of the island of Khokarsa on the shore of the Kemu. From there Kwasin had been escorted deep inland to the last outpost. He had wandered into the Western Lands, his club on his shoulder, stalking wonder and terror as if he were an ogre. At least, that was the way it was if he were to be believed.

"At first there were only the savannas, endless leagues over which great herds of antelopes and elephants roamed. And over which hundreds of prides of lions and packs of wild dogs and the lightning-streak cheetah hunted. I have a mighty body to feed, as you no doubt observed, and I would starve on meat that would make two men fat. How was I to kill the fleet and wary antelope, I, with my great body which can be so easily detected and with only a club and a knife to hunt with?

"And then I saw how the hyena and the jackal follow the lions and how these beasts, thought to be so cowardly, would dash in behind a lion, sometimes in front, snatch a piece of meat, and dash away. And I also observed packs of wild dogs worry a lion eating a carcass and sometimes drive him off. So I said to myself, very well, I will let the lion do the killing for me and then take his meat away from him. And so I did. I would walk up to the carcass and its killer, or its killers, since lions usually work in prides, and I would run them off. Or if they attacked, as they often did, I would stun them with my club or break their legs. Then I would cut off enough meat from the kill to last me several days and leave the rest for the lion. Or if I had killed the lion, I would eat him."

Hadon noticed Kebiwabes taking this in. Doubtless the bard was thinking of composing another epic, *The Song of the Wanderings of Kwasin*. Hadon felt jealous, though he also felt that jealousy was unworthy of him.

"Every once in a while, I would see a small group of blacks, and then I would stalk them and swoop in, smashing them, and would run off with a woman. I am as lusty as a sea otter or a hare, as you well know, Hadon, and where one man may be satisfied with one woman or indeed unable to satisfy one woman, I need a dozen. The black women are ugly and do not bathe often, but one must be philosophical and thank Kho for what is available."

"And did you then kill these women?" Hadon said.

"Only with a surfeit of love!" Kwasin said, and he guffawed. "No, I let them go, though few were able to rise and walk away at once. And some begged me in their tongue, which I did not understand, of course, but the expressions were eloquent, some, I say, were obviously begging me to keep them. No, I did not kill them. I wanted them to bear my sons and daughters, since the breed needs improving, and eventually, who knows, all the blacks of the Western Lands may be my descendants.

"By the way, I see you have only one woman with you, and she is an ugly Klemqaba. Where is the priestess?"

"She *is* the priestess," Hadon said. "Don't force yourself on her, or you may be doubly cursed by Kho. Besides which, I would regard that as a serious, that is, fatal, breach of discipline."

"And if I should humbly ask her?" Kwasin said, sneering.

"She may accept you as a husband. By now she is married to half the men and all the Goat and Bear people."

Kwasin haw-hawed and said, "Once I have been with her, she will divorce the others. Well, I am glad we are in the Wild Lands, where the savages are white and not so squat, and some of the women, under the stink and the dirt and the paint, may even be good-looking. But surely, Hadon, you are not married to this half-ape?"

"Of course not," Hadon said stiffly.

Kwasin laughed again and said, "To continue! Then I came to the jungles, where there were no lions to hunt for me. The leopardess is queen there, and it is not easy to find her in that thick tangle. I thought I would starve, but then I came across a great river—"

"The Bohikly?" Kebiwabes said. "The river discovered by the expedition of Nankar in six-eighty-five A.T.?"

Kwasin stared and said, "Do not presume on your sacred status as a bard and interrupt me, Kebiwabes. Only Hadon may do that, since I have sworn an oath of obedience. However, I do not mind intelligent questions. Anyway, I found thousands of crocodiles along that river, and so I took to dashing out of the jungle and overhauling them before they could get into the water and cracking their thick skulls with my club. They make good eating. Occasionally I found a tiny settlement of blacks along the river, though mostly in the northern regions. Apparently they haven't worked their way down to its mouth yet. Then I would ravage among them and ravish their women. Some of them I kept so they could teach me to find plant life, since I was weary of meat only.

"Eventually I came to the headwaters of the Bohikly and wandered westward. And then I was stopped by the Ringing Sea. I thought of making a dugout and venturing out westward, hoping to come to the edge of the world itself. But, I thought, what if the sea extends for a thousand miles? How could I survive? So I did not venture out. Besides, Kho might not wish a mortal, even such as I, to look over the edge into the abyss. Who knows what secrets She hides down there?"

Kwasin then had thought of roaming along the shore of the Ringing Sea and perhaps circumambulating it. He could not decide which way to start, north or south, so he sacrificed a red river hog to Kho and asked Her to choose his way. He waited, and after a while a white *kagaga* (raven) swooped over him and flew northward. And so he had set out in that direction, keeping to the shoreline.

"But after a year, I became convinced that I could walk forever and still I would not come to the place from which I started. Besides, I grew lonely. I saw only three settlements of blacks along the shore, and I lusted for women. I did take several of the women I abducted along with me, but one died of a fever and one I had to kill because she tried to knife me, and two escaped.

"Then I came to a great mountain range which ran northward and eastward along the beaches. I followed that, and behold, one day I saw across the sea a great rocky mountain.* The Ringing Sea was *not* a sea which ran around the edge of the world. There were other lands beyond that land."

"Or perhaps," Hinokly said, "the mountain was only an island in the Ringing Sea."

"I said I didn't like to be interrupted, scribe," Kwasin said. "So I considered crossing the waters to that rocky mountain, but the current is swift there, though the waters are narrow. I walked on, and after many months came to a place where the mountains cease—at least for a while. Here a great river ran into the sea—"

"Probably the river we found," Hinokly said.

"Scribes have big tongues and thin skulls," Kwasin said, glaring. "Anyway, I had become weary of the sea, so I turned inland and made a dugout and paddled up the river. Now I was in the land of white savages, and the women were more pleasing, though they smelled as bad as the blacks. However, after I dunked them in the river and got them to comb out their hair and wash off the paint, they were acceptable. Some of them would have attracted attention in Khokarsa, they were so comely. And so I improved the stock along that river.

"Then I came to the mountains from which the river flowed, and I set out wandering the savannas southward. I thought that perhaps I might return to Khokarsa. Kho might have forgiven me by now. I had done enough penance for what was, after all, only a drunken prank."

"Raping a holy priestess of Kho and smashing the skulls of her guards was only a prank?" Hadon said.

"That priestess was a teasing bitch," Kwasin said. "She
* Gibraltar.

114

urged me on, and then, when I had bared myself, became terrified, though I suppose I shouldn't blame her for that. And I was only defending myself when I killed the guards. You have to admit that there were extenuating circumstances. Otherwise, why was I not castrated and flung to the hogs? Why was I punished with exile only, though Kho knows that was a horrible punishment?"

"You escaped execution because the oracle said that you should not be killed," Tadoku said. "No one except Kho knows why you were let off so easily after such a grave crime. But Her Voice must be obeyed."

"I thought I would go to an outpost or perhaps even Mukha itself and ask if my exile was over," Kwasin said. "After all, the oracle had said that I would not have to wander forever."

"Perhaps she meant by that that death would put an end to your exile," the scribe said. "The Voice of Kho speaks words that have more than one interpretation."

"But a club on the skull of a gabby scribe has only one interpretation,' Kwasin said. "Do not arouse me, Hinokly."

And so the giant had walked around the mountains and then gone south. Then he had come across an assembly of the tribes in this area. They were, he supposed, holding some yearly religious rite. He did not know, but he did know that there were many good-looking women there. When he had his chance, he had seized one and run off with her. But the savages had tracked him, and he had to run.

"Only because they had arrows," he said. "Otherwise I would have scattered them as a lion scatters a herd of gazelles."

"Of course," Hadon said, and he laughed. Kwasin scowled and clutched his club.

"Can you retrace your route to the river that empties into the sea?" Hadon asked.

"With my eyes closed!" Kwasin bellowed.

"Good! Now we have two guides, you and Hinokly. Surely we cannot get lost now."

But they could. The mountains here were not one formidable range but many small ranges and isolated mountains and valleys. Hinokly confessed that he did not know where they were. Kwasin refused to confess, but it was evident that he was as confused as Hinokly. After they had wandered for three weeks, often backtracking, Hadon decided that they should go west until they were clear of the mountains. Then they would march north for a week before turning eastward. And in another three weeks, they came across their first river. Both Hinokly and Kwasin declared that this was the river up which they had come.

"There must be still another farther eastward," Hinokly said. "This stream and the other originate in these mountains and run parallel, I suppose, northeastward until they run into a larger river. That one must originate in the great range which runs inland along the Ringing Sea. The three rivers become one, which flows into the sea."

"Are we near to the place where you lost the witch, the baby, and the manling?" Hadon said.

"No, that was below the confluence of this river and the one from the northern mountains. It was somewhere between that confluence and the confluence of the river east of this."

They felled trees, chopped off the branches, shaped the exterior and interior into dugouts, and shaped planks into paddles. Each dugout could hold seven, a lucky number, and there were seven dugouts, some of them undermanned. Hadon put the giant Kwasin in a vessel with two others. This was designated the scout boat, since Kwasin wanted to lead them. Also, the sight of the monster might discourage the savages from attacking. They were vulnerable now, especially to arrows, because the river was lined with a broad and thick jungle. They encountered hippopotami and crocodiles, and elephants often came down to bathe and drink. Birds by the hundreds of thousands lived along or on the river, and the trees screeched and vibrated with monkeys. Now and then they glimpsed the small antelope which made the jungle its home, and the leopard which hunted them, monkeys, and river pigs. The slingers killed monkeys and birds, and the spearmen slew crocodiles, hippos, and pigs. For the first time since leaving the outpost, they had more than enough meat. The river also contained many kinds of fish, which gladdened the Khokarsans.

Unfortunately, the day before they arrived at the confluence, a wounded hippo upset a dugout, and he and two bulls had killed five men before anything could be done. One man was pulled out of the water; the other swam to a mud-bank only to be seized by a monstrous crocodile and carried off into the river.

Afterward, the priestess cast her omen bones, and reading them, declared that they had offended the godling of the river. They sacrificed two pigs, a boar and a sow, which they had captured during a hunt, and the next day went smoothly. Near evening they came out onto the broad river that ran down to the sea.

Hinokly, sitting behind Hadon, said, "I last saw the three about twenty miles from here. But I won't be able to recognize the exact spot. There were no distinguishing landmarks around."

"In any case, they wouldn't be likely to stay there even if they survived," Hadon said. "But we'll explore the area around there. If they died, their bones might still be there."

The next day, what with traveling with the current and a steady paddling, they reached the place where Hinokly thought the attack had occurred. Hadon ordered the dugouts to put into a marshy spot that contained several small islands. They camped on one, huddling around fires the smoke of which was supposed to keep the mosquitoes off. But it didn't.

"Some of us got sick with swamp fever," Hinokly said. "Five died, and when the savages attacked, many were too weak to fight. You can expect to lose some men before we get to the sea. Fortunately, there are not many mosquitoes on the beaches."

"What do mosquitoes have to do with swamp fever?" Hadon said.

"In fifteen-thirty-nine A.T.," Hinokly said, "the priestess-doctor Heliqo observed that in areas where swamps and standing water were drained off, the mosquito population decreased. And the incidence of the fever dropped in proportion. Also, where there were no mosquitoes, there was no swamp fever. That was fifty years ago, and she was scoffed at then. But lately the doctors say that she was probably right."

"That's nice to know," Hadon said. "But in the meantime, about all we can do is pray to Qawo, our lady of healing, and M'agogobabi, the mosquito demon, that we be spared.

"Or," he added, "the next best thing is to get out of here

and go to where there are none of the little devils. I can't imagine those three staying here, and if they did, they are surely dead. The fever might not kill them, but they would be too weak to hunt, and the leopards would get them."

Despite this reasoning, he knew that they had to search the region. They started the next morning, wading through the marshes until they got to higher ground, walking a half-mile, and plunging back through the marsh to the river banks. As they went, they shouted the names of Lalila and Paga. Though the noise would attract the savages, they had to call out. Otherwise, the ones they sought might be very close and yet not know their saviors were nearby. Also, so much din might scare away both savages and the large predators. At least, Hadon hoped that it would.

By the end of the second day he knew that this method of search was hopeless and stupid. If they were alive, they would not stay here. They would either have gone back to the seashore or gone south toward Khokarsa. The best thing was to proceed to the sea first and find out what they could there. If there was no sign of them, they would go south again.

That morning, many of the party became sick. Hinokly and the doctor shook their heads and said, "Swamp fever."

Hadon moved them to the higher land, since there were too many sick men to paddle the boats on down the river. He found a place on top of a hill about sixty feet high that had a spring of good water. They settled down to battle out the chills, the fever, and the sweatings. He fell sick the third day and experienced once again the coldness, the heat, the sweatings, and the delirium that had several times afflicted him in his youth. The few left standing, including Kwasin, who claimed immunity from the demon, had to take care of the others and hunt for food. The priestess, Mumona, was also spared, and the chief burden of nursing fell on her. The doctor died the sixth day; several days later most of the humans and some of the Goat and Bear people were dead.

On the twelfth day Hadon felt well enough to take short walks around the camp. On the fourteenth day, he went into the wilderness to set traps for hares. He also brought down a monkey with a stone from his sling, a welcome addition to the pot. When he returned, he was greeted with a loud cry from Mumona. Her baby had just died.

"She'll soon enough have another," Kwasin said unsympathetically. "Though no one will know who its father is."

Kwasin was angry at the priestess because she had refused to lie with him. Under other circumstances he might have brained her, since he could not see why she would reject a man who was not only the strongest man in the empire but the handsomest.

Hadon went to comfort her. He had grown fond of her during the sickness, and he admired her uncomplaining attitude and the skill with which she treated the men. She could not cure them, but she had eased their chills and fevers as best she knew how.

The expedition, only thirty strong now, paddled away from the place of death a few days later. Of the humans, only Hadon, Tadoku, Kwasin, the bard, the scribe, and a young private from Miklemres had survived, and most of these were weak.

They traveled uneventfully, getting stronger each day, until they reached the falls of which Hinokly had warned them. Here the river went through a narrow rocky valley and fell about sixty feet in thunder and steam. They got off the boats as soon as they heard the roar and portaged the dugouts, with much difficulty, down the steep slopes beside the cataract. A mile below, they camped for the night. The next morning, as they set out, three arrows shot from the dense brush nearby. And a Klemqaba was dead of a shaft through his neck.

Though burning to get revenge, Hadon gave the order to move to the center of the river out of range and go on. To have plunged into the jungle against an unknown number of enemies would have meant only the loss of more men.

Twelve days later they came out of one of the mouths of the river and gazed awe-struck at the Ringing Sea.

12

There were, Hadon found, about a hundred and fifty savages, mostly consisting of groups of a dozen to a score, living along a twenty-mile stretch of the shore. These might have the information he needed, and dead people could not give it. He ordered that his men should not attack unless attacked. Leaving the force, he walked alone into the nearest encampment. This was a dozen small cone-shaped huts of poles covered with hides. The people fled as he approached them, gathering on a little hill near the camp and shaking their spears at him. He walked boldly up to them, his hands held to indicate his desire for peace. Presently, one of the slim, dark, hawk-nosed men, holding his stone-tipped spear before him, walked slowly toward him. He jabbered away in a harsh tongue which Hadon did not, of course, understand. He stood his ground, continuing to make peaceful gestures, and then, slowly, held out a rosary of tiny emeralds, a gift to Hadon from the priestess at the outpost fort. It was an expensive gift, but he hoped that it would be worth it. Though the man would not take it, probably because he thought that it might contain an evil magic, his wife could not restrain herself. She came forward and gingerly took it and then put it around her neck.

It took several days before their suspicions melted and he could bring in the Klemqaba woman, the bard, and the scribe. Kebiwabes charmed them with his singing. The scribe drew some pictures for them, and Hadon passed out some copper coins. They had no idea of the meaning of money, but they found ways to use the coins as ornaments. Hadon, meanwhile, was learning the language. It had a number of back-of-the-mouth and throat sounds that he found difficult to master. But he had a throat that could change shape like mercury, and he was soon speaking it well enough so that the savages no longer broke up in merriment at his abominable pronunciation.

Hadon permitted his force to move in within half a mile a

few days later. They had orders that they were not to molest the women on pain of instant death. Kwasin complained about this; he was all for spearing the men and using the women.

"You are worse than the savages," Hadon said. "No, I need these people. Perhaps they might be able to tell me something of the people we are seeking."

"And after you find out?" Kwasin said. "Then do we take the women? There is a little one with big eyes and conical breasts whom I cannot stop thinking about night and day."

Hadon spat to show his disgust and said, "That would be the basest treachery. No, you will not. If we find out that the men are not jealous of their wives, and if a woman says yes, then you may vent yourself. As for that woman you spoke of, I think she likes me but fears you."

Kwasin roared with frustration and banged the end of his club into the ground. Hadon, grinning, walked away. Nevertheless, he was worried that some of his men might try to sneak around and take the women into the bushes.

At the end of three weeks, Hadon felt qualified to ask about Lalila. He talked to the chief and found at once, to his delight, that these people knew of her. Moreover, they knew of Sahhindar.

"We first met them two winters ago," the chief said. "They came into the village, the violet-eyed yellow-haired woman, her child, the one-eyed manling, and he whom you call Sahhindar. My grandfather and his grandfather knew him, and they would have worshipped him as a god, since he lives unchanged through time, as a god lives. But he forbade any to worship him, saying that he was subject to death and was no true god. I had seen him when I was a child, and I remembered him. He stayed with us for a while, helping us to hunt and to fish, and telling us many wonderful tales. Then he and his people, who he said came from across the great water, moved on. They were going southward, he said.

"I thought that I might never see him again, since he usually appears only once or twice in a generation. But only four moons ago the woman, the child, and the manling reappeared. Sahhindar was not with them. The woman said that Sahhindar had entrusted them to a party of men from the far south, who also live on the shores of a great sea. They were attacked and separated from these men, and they found their way back to us. I asked them to stay with us, but they said that they would go after Sahhindar. He had gone along the coast toward the rising sun, and he may be anywhere in this world by now, for all anybody knows."

"Was he with a lion and a monkey and an ...?" Hadon hesitated, at a loss for a word. He described an elephant as best he could, but the chief was confused. Apparently he knew of lions and monkeys, but he had neither seen nor heard of elephants.

"No, he was with none of these beasts," he said. "If he had been, I would have said so."

That night the Khokarsans and the savages feasted on two hippos, and the next day the visitors set out. The woman with the big eyes and conical breasts threw her arms around Hadon and cried. He regretted that he had to leave so soon, but he promised himself that if it were at all possible he would return this way. The band set out eastward, with two men keeping an eye on Kwasin. Hadon feared that the giant would try to sneak back to the savages, and so ruin all the goodwill that had been so patiently built up. There was little to keep Kwasin from deserting them, of course, but if he did, he would not be permitted to rejoin them. Kwasin showed no signs of doing so. The loneliness of his wanderings was still with him. He did not want to be where he would have no one to talk to.

"Kho is with us," Hadon said to Kebiwabes. "We should overtake them. The chief said that they will not turn southward for many, many days' journeys. There are vast and rugged mountain ranges between the shore and the inland savannas, and to reach the savannas they have to go around the mountains. We will march as swiftly as possible and overtake them before they get to the far end of the mountains."

"If Kho is willing," the bard said. "I weary of this wilderness. I would see fair Khokarsa gleaming white in the sun and go into its streets, crowded and noisy though they be. I would drink again in the taverns and in the halls of the noble, and sing songs that the people will love and my colleagues will find it hard to fault. And the women ... ah, the women! Slim and fair-skinned and smelling sweetly of perfumes and speaking with soft voices of love."

"Yes, but if you had not come with us, you would not have the seeds of a great epic germinating in your heart," Hadon said. "That is, if you can make something out of what has happened. To me it has not been poetry, but vexation, hardship, solving trivial and important problems every hour of the day, sickness, wounds, and worries at night that keep me awake."

"That is the stuff of great poetry," Kebiwabes said. "The voice and the lyre change all that into glory and beauty. Men and women will weep with sorrow or exclaim with joy at my words and music, and you, the harassed, bone-tired, mosquito-bitten, worrying man will be transformed into the brave hero whose only cares are great issues and whose lusts become great loves. The song will not mention your dysenteries, your fever, the bags under your eyes from sleeplessness, the fleas you scratch, your uncertainties, nor the way you cursed once when you stumbled on a stone and hurt your big toe. And that skirmish with the savages will become a battle in which thousands participate and the faceless of the ranks are slaughtered by the heroes, and the heroes indulge in long-winded dialogues during the battle before they clash for glory.

"And yet in a sense, what I sing will be as true as if it actually happened."

"Let us hope that you have the genius to work this transmutation," Hadon said.

"That is what worries me," the bard said and he looked sorrowful. But a moment later he was grinning as he sang for the delight of all the bawdy song of Corporal Phallic.

Meanwhile, as they marched, Hinokly, the scribe, was making a map of the country. "Two previous expeditions have gone as far as the sea along approximately the same route we took," he said to Hadon. "But none have gone east along the coast from the river that empties into the Ringing Sea. We are the first Khokarsans to come this way."

Two months later, after encountering a few dozen small tribes who had either fled inland or took to their boats, they had come to what seemed the end of this range of mountains. Ahead lay flat savannas. They had found no sign of Lalila and the others.

"We could go ahead," Hadon said during a conference with Tadoku and the scribe. "But I think that it is likely that the three went southward after the mountains ceased. If they did not find Sahhindar, they would decide to try again for Khokarsa. And if they did find the Gray-Eyed God, he would have directed them southward. Or perhaps he himself is guiding them southward."

Hinokly, who had been looking at the map, said, "I would guess that we are directly north of the city of Miklemres. I may be wrong, of course, but if we go south now, we should come to the Saasares massif. In either event going west or east on the north side of the Saares, we shall round it and come to Mukha or Qethruth. Or we might hit the pass through the Saasares. Of course, there may be other mountains between us and the Saasares, and if we go around these, we might get lost again."

"We have the stars and the sun and the great Kho to guide us," Hadon said. "We will march south."

First he let the troops camp by the seashore for a few days so they could catch fish and swim and sleep. On the day before they were to leave, he went out by himself, climbing around the hills, meditating, fingering his rosary, now and then sitting down to gaze upon the beach and the great rolling sea, the waves of which were higher and heavier than those of his native seas. At midafternoon he sat down on top of a cubical hill of rock, leaned against an oak, and looked down toward the shore. Directly below, the beach ran to the sea. On his right a ridge of hills thrust like a stone finger into the waters. Below it huge boulders were scattered in the sea, which was shallow at that point. They formed a natural breakwater against which the waves flew apart in foam and spray or shot through the spaces between. Hadon watched the sea and the white birds that wheeled above it, dropping now and then to clutch a fish. The sun shone brightly; the breeze was mild and cooling; before he knew it, he was asleep.

Sometime later he jerked awake, his heart hammering. How foolish he had been! He was alone in dangerous country, and though he had seen no savages for a week, that did not mean that there were none. Also, there were antelope and gazelles in this area, and where they were, leopards were. He vaguely remembered a dream that had come as he struggled up from sleep, something to do with Awineth. Had she not spoken to him, warned him of something? Of what?

He shook his head, scanned the countryside around, but could see nothing but birds and a small foxlike creature with huge pointed ears slinking from one bush to another. And then he heard, faintly and far off, a barking that was not quite like a dog's. He rose and looked to his right, and presently he saw the round black heads of those flippered creatures which the Khokarsans had called sea dogs* when they first saw them on the shore of the Ringing Sea. These were putting out to sea to dive for fish, and they had come from behind the wall of boulders below the hills to his right.

He decided to go down to the boulder breakwater and spy upon these beasts. The natives at the village near the mouth of the river said that they were the companions and the guardians of their sea goddess. If a man could catch one and keep her from slipping out of her oily coat, he could learn the secrets of the sea and be forever free of hunger. Once, they said, in the far past a hero of their village had seized one, and she had left her skin behind, but he had swum after her and caught her, and she had turned into a beautiful sea woman. She had taken him down with her to her home at the bottom of the sea, where he lived forever, eating and making love. She was the daughter of the goddess, and she loved the mortal, and if a man could emulate that hero, he, too, could become immortal. But he must never again go on the beach, or he would suddenly become very old and very sad, because he would have lost all.

Hadon had no desire to live deep in the cold waters forever. He did hope that the sea dogs might shed their skins if they thought no man was around. He would then see the daughters of the goddess in their naked beauty. Or would he be so enchanted by the glory that he would forget Awineth and the throne, which after all were only temporal delights, and try to lay his hands upon one of them?

His own people had a story of the hero who saw Lahhindar, the Gray-Eyed Archer Goddess, as she bathed. He had been torn apart by her hyenas for the blasphemy. It was dangerous to spy upon goddesses.

Nevertheless, Hadon went down the hill and across the beach and presently was wading through the sea. He crouched

* Seals.

125

low, bracing himself against the waves, and peered around the side of the boulder that was twice his height. At first he saw only the surging waters inside the ring of boulders and a sea dog sitting on top of a boulder near the center of the circle. Then he heard voices, and his blood seemed to run backward, and he grew faint. Was he indeed about to witness the dangerous beauty of goddesses unclothed?

He hesitated, but his curiosity was far too great for him to walk off as any discreet and wise man would.

He inched around the side of the boulder, keeping his chest close to it. Finally he had a clear view of the arena of water. To his right, on a narrow beach, was a little bearded man with a big head, and beside him was a naked child of about three. Her hair was yellow, and her skin was the whitest he had ever seen.

He knew then that he had found those so long sought. Or, at least, two of them. The Goddess had directed him to them; it must have been her voice, not Awineth's, he had heard in the dream.

But where was Lalila, the White Witch from the Sea, the Risen-from-the-Sea?

Suddenly the waters roiled before him, only a few feet away, and a woman burst from the green. She stood up, smiling, and her wet hair was long and yellow, her oval face was beautiful, more beautiful than that of any woman he had ever seen, and her eyes were large and of a strange color, like those of the violets that grew on the mountains above Opar.

Hadon gasped with more than the shock of recognition. Then he was trying to assure her that she was in no danger, because she was screaming, and those eyes were full of fear.

13

Hadon thought of trying to grab her so that he could tell her that he was no enemy. Instead, he let her go. He waded after her as she swam swiftly toward the manling and the child. The two were standing up now and shouting, and the manling was brandishing a long-handled iron ax that looked too heavy for him even to lift. Hadon held his hands out to show that he was peaceful. The woman, halfway toward her companions, stopped swimming and stood up, the sea just below the superb breasts. She was not smiling, but neither did she look fearful now. And when Hadon and she got onto the beach, she spoke to him in a heavily accented Khokarsan. The manling, though no longer shouting, held the ax ready if Hadon should make a threatening move.

"You frightened me," she said in a lovely voice. "But then I realized that you had to be a man from the inland sea, because of your leather helmet and armor and the great sword that you carry in the scabbard on your back. But how . . .?"

"It is a long story," Hadon said. "Let us sit down here, and I will tell you as much as I can before we go to my camp."

Lalila and Paga dressed themselves first. The manling put on a long kilt of gray fur, and the woman put on a short kilt and a poncho of the same material. Then she combed her dripping hair with a notched mussel shell. Hadon observed them closely during this dressing. How beautiful she was, how white-skinned! And she was tall, perhaps five feet six inches. She did indeed look like a goddess.

The manling was as Hinokly had described. His legs, though thick and powerful, were no longer than those of an eight-year-old child's. His torso was, however, that of an average-sized man. His shoulders and long arms were heavy with muscle, and his chest was deep and broad. His hair was brown, flecked with gray, a tumbled mass on top of a huge head. The right eye was filmed over, the result, according to Hinokly, of its striking a stone when his mother had thrown him into the bushes shortly after his birth. His nose was flat, his mouth full and broad, his face scarred. Despite its ugliness, it had a strange attractiveness. When he smiled, he became almost beautiful.

According to Hinokly, he had been born far to the north, in a land beyond the Ringing Sea, a land largely covered by moving rivers of ice. When his father, returning from a sea-dog hunt, had found out that he had been thrown away and left to die, he had gone looking for his bones. Weeks had passed since his mother had cast him away, yet the father had found him alive and healthy except for the shattered eye and the scarred face. A wolf bitch had found him and suckled him. It was said that Paga sometimes went into the forest and talked to the wolves. It was also said that he sometimes became a wolf at night and ran with his mother and her pups. Hadon hoped that this was not true. Wereleopards, were-eagles, and werehyenas were burned alive in Khokarsa. Hadon had never seen a wolf, of course, but Hinokly had mentioned one as described to him by Lalila, and Hadon supposed that the fur these two wore was that of the wolf.

The two, now dressed, sat down. The child, reassured by her mother, paddled around in the sea close to them. Hadon told them his story as briefly as possible, stopping now and then to define a sentence unit they did not know. When he had finished, he said, "We would probably have missed you, but Kho Herself sent me to you. And Sahhindar? Have you seen him?"

"We have been looking for him," Lalila said. "When we left him to go with the men from the south, he said that he was making a pilgrimage far to the southwest, to the sea that runs on the extreme edge of the world beyond the mountains southwest of the city of Mikawuru. He was visiting again the place where he would be born in the far future. I did not understand his words, and he did not explain. He did say that he was not a god, that he could die, and that he had traveled backward in time but now had to travel forward, as all mortals do."

"I do not understand that," Hadon said. "But is it true that it was he who brought in plants which until then had not grown around the two seas and gave them to the Khoklem, and showed them—my ancestors—how to cultivate them, how to domesticate animals, and how to make bronze?"

"Yes, he did," Paga said in a voice as deep as Kwasin's. "It was also he who once came to Lalila's ancestors and showed them how to domesticate goats and sheep and how to weave and dye."

"But it was all in vain," Lalila said. "The man whom you call Sahhindar told me that he knew it would be in vain. My people are dead now, and their knowledge is lost and will not be regained for many thousands of years."

Lalila paused, looked strangely at Hadon, as if she might not say what was in her heart, and then said, "Just as his gifts to your ancestors were in vain."

Hadon felt a slight shock, and he said, "What does that mean?"

"I do not know," Lalila said. "But once he spoke idly of Khokarsa as if it had long been dead, buried, and forgotten. Except for the city of Opar. He said that it had been built long before he was born and that it was still standing when he was born. But it had been rebuilt many times.

"And he said also that he would teach the savages no more new things, that they must proceed at their own pace. Time would defeat him, no matter how many people he raised from savagery."

"Perhaps he may visit Khokarsa again, and then we will learn more," Hadon said. "In the meantime, we must proceed on our own. Let us walk back to the camp, which is several miles from here, and you can tell me your story."

Lalila called the child Abeth in, and she put on her a cloak of antelope skin that, Lalila said, Sahhindar had made for her. They walked along the beach silently for a while, the woman and Hadon matching their pace to the short legs of the child and the manling. Paga spoke first. He was, he said, born in a very small tribe of people so isolated that they thought they were the only people in the world. They lived by hunting and fishing, their chief prey being the sea dogs and an occasional stranded whale, a creature like a monster fish, but warm-blooded. Paga, cast out a second time, had been rescued by a man named Wi and had voluntarily become his slave. The tribe was dominated by a cruel giant who had slain Wi's daughter, and so Wi had challenged him for the chieftainship. Paga it was who had found a stone fallen from the sky, a stone made of iron and some other metal that was even harder than iron. He had crudely fashioned it into an ax for Wi, and Wi had slain the giant with it and become the chief.

"And then Wi's problems, instead of being solved, were greatly increased," Paga said. "Once he had been the slave of the chief. Then he became the slave of the people. And he had much trouble with his wife, who loved him but could not endure me, as most women cannot. And she was jealous because Wi loved me and would not drive me out into the wilderness again. She could not understand that Wi was both wise and good-hearted and that he loved me, not as a man loves a woman but as one who needed his protection and who, in turn, could counsel him wisely. He did not believe the people when they said that I was a worker of evil and that I took a wolf's shape at night.

"And then, one day, a dugout floated onto the shore, and Wi found in it a woman near death. This woman, Lalila. And the troubles he had had before he found her became trivial."

"True," Lalila said. "Though I am not a troublemaker in my heart, my presence seems to cause trouble. To make a long story short, Wi nursed me back to life and protected me. We fell in love, though for a long time Wi would not marry me because of a law he had originated, which restricted one wife to one man. And he did not have the heart—"

"The guts," Paga said.

"The heart to cast out his wife. In the end, the great river of ice whose front loomed over the village moved and wiped out most of the tribe. Some of us—Wi, Wi's son, Wi's wife, his brother, his brother's wife, Paga, and I—were left alive but afloat on a mountain of ice. It began to melt, and we had to get off in our boat, which was only a small hollowed-out log. Wi, seeing that if he got in, his weight would sink the boat, shoved it out with the rest of us in it. The fog blew in then, and we could barely see Wi. But Paga dived into the cold sea and swam to the remnant of the ice mountain. If he had to die, he wanted to die with Wi. Besides, he could not see leaving Wi to die all alone. To die with your loved ones around you is bad, but to die alone is terrible.

"I did not know what to do. I loved Wi and wished to die with him. Life was not worth living without him. Or so, at least, I thought at the moment. But Wi's son was with me, and he needed a protector. Then I considered that he had his mother and Wi's brother and sister-in-law. And with one fewer, their chances of survival would be greater. So I swam to the ice mountain too.

"There we waited for the cold or the sea to take us, but presently the fog cleared. The others were not in sight, and we never saw them again. But there was land a mile or two away, and then we saw several uprooted trees drifting by. We swam to one, and Wi chopped off the branches on top and rolled it over and chopped off those on the other side. Using some branches as paddles, we got the log to the shore. We almost died doing it, because our legs were in the icy waters. But we did not die."

"And then," Paga said, "we wandered along the shore looking for the others. As Lalila says, we never saw them again. Finally we turned inland for Lalila's homeland. We found the lake over which her people lived in huts on piles. But the huts were empty, and the bones of their owners lay in the lake or along the shore. We did not know what had caused their deaths. We thought that a pestilence of some kind had struck many, and the others had fled. We waited for three moons for some to return, but they never did. Lalila's child by Wi was born. Then a band of tall yellow-haired men came, and we fled into the mountains. They pursued us until we were trapped in a cave, trapped by the bear in the cave and the men without. Wi slew the bear, a creature twice as large as a lion, but he was clawed badly across the back. Then he turned and fought the yellow-hairs while I thrust with a spear from behind him, between his legs. Seven men he slew with the ax before a spear went through his throat.

"All seemed over, but then came cries from the men still outside. Those within ran out, only to be felled by arrows that came so fast that it seemed three men were firing. The remaining yellow-hairs fled, and presently a tall man with black hair and gray eyes came out from behind a boulder. It was Sahhindar, who had visited the village again, seen our tracks, and followed us."

"We buried Wi, and with him my heart," Lalila said. "Then

131

we told our story, and Sahhindar said that he would take us to a land where we could live in comfort, a land such as we had never dreamed of. When we encountered a Khokarsan expedition, Sahhindar entrusted us to their care. The rest you know."

"Not all of it," Hadon said. "When the expedition was attacked, how did you escape the savages after your boat overturned?"

"We swam to the opposite shore," Paga said, "though the weight of the ax almost drowned me. It was tied to my wrist, and I couldn't get the knot loose. But Lalila helped me support the ax. We carried it between us, each swimming with one hand. The child could swim almost at birth, and so we did not have to worry about her. By the time we reached shore, the river was alive with crocodiles attracted by the uproar. That was fortunate for us, since five savages had remained behind to go after us. But they did not dare attempt the river. And so we decided to go northward, in the direction they would not expect us to take. As I said, we also decided to seek out Sahhindar and tell him what had happened."

Hadon said, "I wonder why Sahhindar did not accompany you all the way to Khokarsa? Surely he knew that there were many dangers between the Ringing Sea and the Kemu?"

"I think that he was on a mission of his own when he rescued us," Paga said. "He deferred it to see us to safety. When we met the Khokarsans, he thought he could entrust us to them. He was eager to get going."

"Perhaps he would not have left us if he had known that I was bearing his child," Lalila said. "But then I did not know it myself. Of course, that did not matter in the end, since I lost it two moons after it was conceived."

"You carried the seed of a god in your womb?" Hadon said. He felt awe at the same time that, for some unknown reason, he felt sick. Or was the reason so hidden? Was it because he felt jealous?

"He says he is no god, but certainly he is as close to being a god as a mortal can get," she said. "However, I am not unique. He says that half the population of the lands north of the Ringing Sea and half the population of Khokarsa must be descended from him. After all, he has been roaming about for two thousand years."

"I myself can trace my descent to Sahhindar," Hadon said. "Though to tell the truth, I have often wondered if the genealogy was not just something that my ancestors made up. But apparently not."

"Lalila is also a descendant of Sahhindar, a great-granddaughter, I believe," Paga said. He chuckled and said, "In fact, Sahhindar once commented that he was a descendant of himself. Though what he meant by this, I do not know."

They came into sight of the camp then and were quickly challenged by a sentry. Hadon went through the ridiculous rigmarole of identifying himself, and escorted the three to his headquarters, a tiny hut made of poles covered by leafy branches. There he told Tadoku to summon all to be informed that the first phase of their mission was completed. He had no intention of looking also for Sahhindar. If Minruth demanded to know where he was, he would be given the general location. Let him send someone else to look for him.

14

Kwasin was the one who gave the most trouble, as was to be expected. All the males adored Lalila, but though they might wish to lie with her, they would not have dared suggest it by words or touch. Hadon had ordered that she was to be treated as a priestess even if she were a savage. The order was not necessary, since word spread quickly through the small camp that she was indeed a priestess of the moon. This was not true. However, her mother had been one and Lalila in due course would have succeeded her. Moreover, her name, which meant *moon of change* in Khokarsan, reinforced the belief that she was a holy one. And her titles, the White Witch from the Sea and the Risen-from-the-Sea, were enough to scare off even the randiest. The latter was also, by another coincidence, a title of Adeneth, goddess of sexual passion and of madness.

Kwasin was the only one not scared, of course. On first seeing her, he exclaimed with wonder, fell on his knees, seized her hand, and kissed it. Hadon watched him in alarm, because there was no telling what the giant would kiss next. He put his hand on the hilt of his sword, ready to draw it and lop off Kwasin's head if he should insult her. Kwasin rose to his feet and bellowed that he had never seen a woman so lovely or so radiant, that she was indeed like the goddess of the moon, fair and remote and holy. He would bash in the skull of anyone who dared even hint of violating her. Hadon hated him for that. To tell the truth—and he did so in his heart—he desired her mightily. And he suspected that Kwasin, if he managed to be alone with her, would not find her untouchable. At least, not as far as he was concerned.

And what of Awineth, the young and beautiful queen who was waiting for him by a throne that would be his? Ah, yes, what of dark-haired, dark-eyed, shapely Awineth? She was far off, pale and tenuous as a ghost seen at dawn. Which was not a very realistic attitude, Hadon told himself. She represented glory and power, and to give these up by giving her up was madness. Besides, Awineth would regard such an act as an unforgivable insult. She could reject him if she wished, but for him to reject her would probably result in ... what? Exile? Or death on the spot? The latter, most probably.

It was truly insane to consider such a thing. Unthinkable. But he was thinking it, and so was mad. And knowing this, he still was happy. Why was he happy? Lalila had not given the slightest sign of any tender feeling towards him.

They had a long way to go, and who knew what might happen before they arrived at the border of the empire?

Kebiwabes, the bard, also seemed struck by the madness which the full moon or a beautiful woman sometimes sends. He began composing the *Song of the Moon of Change*, the *Pwamwotlalila*, and at the end of the second week of their journey southward sang it. It was not an epic, but a lyric modeled in the spirit and after the structure of the songs that the priestesses of the temples of the moon, the *Wootla*, the Voices of the Moon, sang at the beginning of the annual orgiastic rites in the ancient days. These rites had been suppressed for five centuries, though they were still practiced secretly in the countryside and in the mountain areas. Hadon, listening, felt arousal of spirit and flesh. Kwasin stripped and danced the ancient Dance of the Mating Bear, causing Lalila to turn away in embarrassment. Mad Kwasin danced on, his eyes glazed, seemingly unaware that she had walked away into the darkness.

Hadon followed her to apologize and found her and the manling standing by a great boulder in the moonlight.

"I could not stop him," he said. "To have interfered would be insulting the goddess of the moon, since her spirit has seized him."

"Do not apologize," she said. "My people have—had—similar dances, and I have witnessed them without being offended. But in this case the dance was not impersonal. It was obviously directed at me, and it made me very uncomfortable. I fear that monster; he has been touched by the moon; there is no telling what he may do when he is possessed. And from what you and the bard have told me, Kwasin is no respecter of chastity or holiness when he is seized."

"True," Hadon said, "but he knows that the next time he transgresses, he may die. If men do not strike him down, Kho may. And he also wishes to have his exile terminated, which will not happen if he offends her again. So, though he is possessed, he is still trying to control himself. I will give him that, and I am not one to give him much."

"He is also possessed of a stature and strength which all men should desire," Paga said. "But I do not. Both Kwasin and I are misshapelings. He has been given too much and I too little. But whereas the deities have made me small, have cut off my legs, they have given me an intelligence to compensate. Him they have given too much of the body and so have deprived him of his wits. I have a keen nose, Hadon, and I smell misfortune and evil sweating from that great body. Tell me, is it true that you lived with him for a while when you were both young?"

"That was my misfortune," Hadon said. "We both resided with our uncle in a cave high above the Sea of Opar for a few years. Kwasin had to have someone to bully, and since he dared not insult my uncle, who would have kicked him

135

off the cliff into the sea, he bullied me. I am good-natured, and I put up with it for a while, trying to get him to be more agreeable, trying to get him to become a friend. Eventually I lost my temper and attacked him. It was humiliating, because he beat me severely and laughed at me while he was doing it. I am strong, but I am a weakling compared to Kwasin, as, indeed, all men are.

"My uncle did not say a word to Kwasin about this, but he did arrange a series of athletic contests for us with malice aforethought. Whoever lost would be beaten by him, and my uncle saw to it that the games were to Kwasin's disadvantage. We ran the quarter-mile and the half-mile, and though Kwasin, huge as he is, can keep pace with me for fifty yards, he lags far behind in the longer runs. So my uncle beat Kwasin severely when he lost. Kwasin was probably strong enough even then to strike my uncle down, but he was afraid of him. I think my uncle was the only man Kwasin ever feared. Perhaps because he was even madder.

"My uncle also had us exercise with wooden swords. Though I took some very hard, near-crippling blows, my skill overcame Kwasin's brute force, and I bruised and stunned him often. At last he caught on to what was happening and said he wanted no more of the races and the wooden swords. My uncle smiled and said that that was all right with him. But he might renew them if he thought it was wise. Kwasin ceased to bully me, except in subtle ways, and he has never forgiven me. He considers that I defeated him, a thing which he cannot forget. He must always have the upper hand, always be the dominant. Now I am his commander, and he hates me even more."

"Yet he sometimes jests with you, and even seems to like you," Lalila said.

"Kwasin is two people in one. He is one of those unfortunates whom Kho has given two souls. Too often, the evil soul is the ruling one."

The child, sitting nearby, complained that she was tired. Lalila took her to their little lean-to to sing her to sleep. Hadon listened to her voice, as silvery and as soft as the light of the moon, and he was consumed with a fire as hot as the sun's, as if the moon had summoned the sun to rise before its time.

Paga, watching him, said, "It seems the fate of some to be

driven mad and of others to drive people mad. Lalila, unfortunately for her, is of the latter. She is not evil, but she brings evil. Or rather, she brings out the evil in people. Her beauty is a curse to her and to the men who desire her and to the women who are jealous of her. It is sad, because she desires only peace and joy; she has no wish for power over others."

"Then she should live in a cave far from all men," Hadon said.

"But she loves to be with people," Paga said. "And perhaps deep within her there is a desire to have power over men. Who knows?"

"Only the Goddess knows," Hadon said.

"I do not believe in gods or goddesses," Paga said. "They exist only in the minds of men and women who created them so they can blame someone outside themselves for the things they themselves bring down on their heads."

Paga, carrying the ax on his shoulder, waddled away while Hadon stared after him. But no thunder and lightning, no heavings of the earth followed. The moon shone serenely, the jackals yapped, the hyenas laughed, in the distance a lion roared. All was as before.

They continued southward. Ten days later they came to a river the headwaters of which were somewhere in the mountains to the northwest. Paga felled trees with his keen-edged iron ax, and they chopped off the branches with their bronze axes. With fire and ax, they shaped the logs into dugouts and made planks for seats. These were fitted into grooves in the interior and secured with wooden pins. They put their supplies, armor, and weapons underneath the seats, and using paddles they had fashioned from long blocks of wood, they set out.

The current was swift here, and Hadon hoped that it would remain so for hundreds of miles. It was pleasant not to have to paddle hard, to allow the stream to do most of the work. Moreover, getting food was easy. The river was full of fish, and ducks and geese thronged its surface and the banks. The fish were easily caught on hooks, or speared, and the vast numbers of crocodiles and hippopotami ensured that they would not suffer for lack of meat, though the taking was dangerous. The jungle alongside the river harbored many types of antelope. Several types of berries and nuts and a variety of green cabbage provided plant food.

Moreover, Hadon had a chance to talk to Lalila, since she sat directly behind him. As the days drifted by, Awineth receded even more in his mind and heart and Lalila became ever more glowing. Sometimes he suffered from the sharp points of the trident of conscience, but he could not control the workings of his love for Lalila.

Hadon regarded the finding of the river as a good omen. On the tenth day of travel, however, he changed his mind. The muddy shore, which had sloped gradually from the river, suddenly became steep and rocky, and the narrowed river became stronger. As the hours passed, the stream sank deeper into the rock, and at noon the tops of the cliffs on both sides were twenty-five feet above them. The current was too swift to paddle back up the river. The sky, which had been bright, became black. A strong wind whooped above them, and a half-hour later rain fell. It was so thick that Hadon sometimes wondered if a river high in the sky had not fallen on them. He set Paga and Abeth to bailing with the leather helmets, while he, Lalila, and the two soldiers in the stern steered with their paddles.

Lightning cracked above them, fiercely illuminating the darkness and frightening them. The flashes showed them that they were now perhaps fifty feet below the tops of the cliffs. Hadon did not need the lightning to know that the water was becoming rougher. The river had become even more narrow, and they were beginning to encounter huge boulders.

Then they rounded a curve and were in the grip of rapids.

There was nothing to do but pray to Kho and the unknown river godling and to ride it out. Their boats were tossed up and down, turned around, the sides sometimes striking the perpendicular walls of the canyon. Once, during a flash, Hadon glanced back. He saw the third vessel behind him spin, its stern smashing into the side of a great rock near the wall. When he looked during the next flash, the boat and its occupants had disappeared in the foam. Lalila's face was white and strained. Paga looked pale too, but he grinned at Hadon, his large teeth like gold insets in a curved alabaster skull.

That was Hadon's last look behind. The rest of the transit, he was too busy trying to keep the boat straight, trying to steer it past the threatening rocks, shoving his paddle at times against the canyon wall to keep the boat from colliding.

No use. The dugout rode up, up, up a white-headed wave, leaned far to the left as it scraped against the wall, and turned over. He heard Lalila shriek as he pitched into the maelstrom. Something struck his shoulder heavily—either the boat or a rock—and his head came above the surface briefly. He went under again as if the river godling had seized him by the ankles. He scraped against stones, fought upward, heard a roar louder than that of the rapids, and was cast outward and down. Half in water, half in spray, he fell, struck solid water, was plunged deep, scraped again on the rocky bottom, fought upward, and suddenly was in relatively smooth water. But the current was still strong, and he had to fight hard to get to the shore.

He dragged himself up a gentle slope of grass-covered earth and sat panting. Then he saw Lalila and the child clinging to the bottom of an upturned dugout, and he swam out to help them. Lalila, gasping, said, "Get Abeth! I can make it!"

The child seemed in even less danger than her mother. She swam strongly to the shore, and Hadon, hearing a cry through the thunder of the cataract, turned. For a minute the large brown head of Paga was above the surface. Hadon dived toward it, and by accident or the grace of Kho, his hands touched Paga. He felt blindly around, touched him again, felt along his arm, felt the thong attached to the wrist and knew that at the other end was the reason why the manling had been dragged down. The ax. The wonder of it was that Paga had been able to swim up even once.

Hadon seized Paga's long hair and swam heavily upward. Reaching the surface, he pulled the manling on up. The current carried them past Lalila and the child, who were crawling out onto shore. Hadon, his one hand under Paga's chin, towed him in to land about fifty yards down. Paga's head kept going under, but he did not struggle against Hadon, and suddenly Hadon was able to stand up. He lifted Paga above the water and walked backward to the shore. There he placed the manling face-down, his one arm outstretched, the ax still in the water. Paga coughed and wheezed, and water ran from his mouth and nose, but he would live.

As suddenly as it had come, the rain left.

Several boats, upside down or rightside up, floated by.

Tadoku, the scribe, and the bard swam by, and Hadon plunged into the water to help them. Tadoku made it by himself, but the scribe and the bard might not have gotten to safety without Hadon's aid. All three were battered, bruised, and bleeding.

Hadon waded out again, waist-deep, and grabbed the Klemqaba priestess and pulled her in. Some more dugouts floated by, one with the Klemqaba sergeant and a Klemklakor private clinging to it. Five more men succeeded in getting ashore; they said that their two boats had stayed unhurt until they had gone over the falls. Their fellows must have drowned after striking the bottom at the foot of the falls.

Hadon thought that that was to be expected. The cataract was about fifty feet high.

He dived in again and pulled a man ashore, but the fellow was dead. That one seemed to be the last they would see. The others were either whirling around in the turmoil below the falls or had been carried along under the surface past them. Of the fifty-six who had left the outpost above Mukha, only twelve were alive. Except for Paga's ax and the knives they wore in their scabbards, they were weaponless.

"I did not think that even the river godling could defeat Kwasin," the bard said. "Surely he could not have drowned. That is too commonplace a death for such a hero. If he is to die, it must be with the corpses of his enemies piled high around him, himself and his club bloody, and Sisisken hovering above him, waiting to take his ghost off to the garden reserved for the greatest of heroes."

Paga, who was now standing, though weakly, snorted with disbelief.

"He is, though a giant, only a man," he said, "and a river is no respecter of men."

He looked upward at Hadon and said, with a strange smile, "I am your slave now, Hadon. You have saved my life. Once Wi saved my life, and I became, as is the custom of our people, his property."

"You are not among your people now," Hadon said.

Paga spat and said, "That is true. Nor do my people exist anymore. I alone survive, I, Paga, the ugly one-eyed manling, the rejected. But I choose to observe the custom, Hadon, and I am yours. Though I hope that I bring you more luck than I

140

brought Wi. However, I am also Lalila's, which might become embarrassing if I should have to choose between you two."

"If I had my way, she and I would become one," Hadon said.

The statement surprised him, but it seemed to surprise Lalila even more. She gasped and looked with an undecipherable expression at him.

"So that is the way it is," Paga said. "It is to be expected, however."

Lalila did not speak. Hadon, feeling foolish, turned away. At that moment the others shouted. Hadon looked toward where they were pointing and saw the massive dark head of Kwasin appear out of the boiling water and spray below the cataract. He swam slowly toward them, and when he stood up in the shallows, blood from a deep gash streamed from his side.

Kwasin paid it no attention. His face was twisted and black with fury. "I lost my club!" he roared. "My precious club! It fell from my hand when I was forced to cling to a rock! Then I dived for it, but the river was too strong even for such as I, and I was swept away! Where is the godling of the river? I would seize him and choke him until he gave it back to me!"

"Brave words," Paga said, sneering.

Kwasin stared at the manling and then said, "I may step on you and press you into the mud as if you were a loathsome lizard, ugly one. Do not anger me, for I am eager to kill someone. Someone must pay for my loss!"

Paga got to his feet and began untying the knot that bound the thong to his wrist.

"This was almost the death of me," he said. "It was the death of Wi. I do not think that those yellow-haired men would have chased us so eagerly if it had not been the desire to get this ax, though perhaps they were equally eager to get Lalila. In any event, I am convinced that the Ax of Victory, as I sometimes call it, brings victory for a while to its owner, and then death."

He finished the untying and held the ax out to Kwasin.

"Here, giant, is a gift from a dwarf. Take it and use it well. Wi, some days before he died, told me that I should have it if he died. I told him I did not want it as my property. I

141

would carry it only until I came across someone who deserved to wield it. You are that one, since I doubt that there is on earth a mightier. But I warn you. Its luck lasts only a short time."

Kwasin took the haft in his right hand and swung the ax.

"Ha, that is a mighty weapon! With it I could crush battalions!"

"And no doubt will," Paga said. "But he who loves killing must in the end be killed."

"What do I care for your savage superstitions!" Kwasin bellowed. "However, I thank you, manling, though you must not expect me to love you for it!"

"Gifts don't bring love to giver or taker, giant," Paga said. "Besides, I love Lalila and Abeth, and, I believe, Hadon. I don't have any more love to go around. As for your love, you love only yourself."

"Careful, manling, or you will become the first victim of your own gift!'

"The elephant trumpets when he sees a mouse," Paga said.

The ax was indeed a curious one, one which Hadon might have coveted if he had not been a swordsman. Its head was massive, so heavy that only a very strong man could use it effectively. It was crudely fashioned from a lump of iron and some other metal, but it had a sharp edge. The handle, according to Paga, had been made from the solid lower leg bone of some kind of antelope* that was found only in the northern part of the lands beyond the Ringing Sea. This beast was twice as big as an eland. It did not have horns but had some kind of bony growth from its head which spread out into many points. Paga had dug it out of a bog, where it had been so long that it had half-turned to stone. He had worked out a deep slot at one end for receipt of the neck of the ax, and he had bound it with strips from the hide of a creature something like the giant antelope but smaller.† After the haft and the ax had been lashed together with these, he had knotted the ends and poured the resin of heated amber over the lashings. The bone haft was also lashed with strips of hide. At the other end of the bone, which was as hard as elephant ivory,

---

* The giant Irish elk.
† The reindeer.

142

was a knob, the knuckle joint. Paga had rubbed this down to make a smooth sphere.

"Have you forgotten that you are wounded?" Hadon said to Kwasin.

Kwasin looked down in amazement at his side and said, "I must attend to it," and he hurried off to see what the Klemqaba woman could do for him.

They stayed the rest of the day below the rapids, fashioning spears for those who had lost them. They found some quartzlike rocks which Paga chipped for them into points, he being the only one who knew this art. Hadon watched him closely, since he might someday again be in a situation requiring the working of stone into weapons.

Finally he decided that watching wasn't enough. He asked Paga to teach him, and after painfully banging and bloodying his fingers, he managed to knock off a "mother," as Paga called it, a section of rock from which he had to knock off the "daughters." These he ruined, but on his second round of attempts, he worked a spearhead that Paga said was satisfactory though not praiseworthy.

"But this knowledge may save your life someday," Paga said.

He did not sleep well that night, because of the pains in his side where he had struck the rocks of the rapids and because of a swelled thumb from the stone-working. When he finally did sleep, he dreamed that Awineth came to him, first reproaching him for unfaithfulness and then warning him of great danger. He awoke with all asleep around him except for two guards under a tree nearby. A ghostly owl floated over them, making him wonder if it was an omen sent by Kho. But what good were omens if he did not know what they meant?

Nevertheless, he kept awakening the rest of the night, each time thinking that something dreadful had happened. Once he saw Lalila sit up and look at him. The moon was bright, and she was near enough so that he could see that same unreadable expression. For a moment he thought about talking to her, but she lay back down, and he drifted off again.

15

They rose stiffly at dawn. An hour's gathering in the jungle brought in enough berries and nuts to fill their bellies, and they set out again. They had not gone more than two miles when Hadon saw two dugouts caught against a fallen tree by the other shore. One was turned over; the other was upright. Unfortunately, there were crocodiles nearby. As the river was a quarter of a mile broad at this point, Hadon did not believe that it was wise to swim to the boats. Yet there might be weapons in them, secured under the seats. Also, he had a faint hope that one of them carried his sword.

"If we can get the boats, Kwasin can chop us another out of a tree, and we'll have swift transportation again," Hadon said. "So we'll create a diversion. We'll give the saurians some tempting food a little downstream."

That was easier said than done. They spread out into the jungle to hunt an animal whose carcass would be large enough to attract the great reptiles. Lalila, the child, and Paga stayed behind, guarded by two soldiers.

Near dusk, hungry, tired, and frustrated, the hunters reassembled on the shore. No one had caught anything large, though two had stoned three monkeys. But there, drawn up on the mud, was a dugout with Paga grinning beside it.

Hadon asked Paga how he had done it, though he knew before the manling told his tale. He cursed himself for his lack of wits. Paga had walked upstream until he came to a place where there did not seem to be any crocodiles. He had swum across, walked back down, and with a branch managed to paddle one of the dugouts back. He had been carried downstream about a mile, but then he had walked back in the shallows, shoving the boat ahead of him.

Paga leaned into the boat and drew out something that brought a cry of joy from Hadon. It was Karken, his sword.

"I seem to be a dispenser of weapons," Paga said.

Kwasin said, "You are not as useless as your size would indicate, manling."

"The sea dog seems clumsy on the land, but in the ocean he is swift and graceful," Paga said. "My ocean is my intelligence, giant. You would drown there."

"If you had not given me this ax, little one, I would crack open your ocean."

"So much for gratitude," Paga said.

"Kwasin, put your ax and your arm to use and spare us your tongue," Hadon said. "Fashion some paddles, so we may cross to the other boat. And after that, chop down a tree so we may fashion out of it another dugout."

"The ax is getting dull," Kwasin said. "Nor am I a carpenter."

But he obeyed, and when Hadon and Tadoku paddled across, they heard behind them the lusty blows of his ax against the trunk of a tree.

Three days later they set out once again. This time Hadon determined that if they came to a canyon, they would retreat upstream at once and walk along its side. The river, however, wandered back and forth across a land only slightly higher than itself. Except for the flies in the day and the mosquitoes at night, their life was almost idyllic. Even the giant Kwasin lapsed into a decent human being for a while, though Hadon was afraid that the strain would eventually result in an explosion of temper. Kwasin had, however, talked the Klemqaba woman into marrying him, and this seemed to pacify him somewhat. Her other husbands were not happy about it. They complained that he had ruined her for them. Hadon paid them no attention. What the woman did with her mates was up to her, as long as it did not interfere with discipline.

At the end of fifteen days they came to a large lake alive with many thousands of ducks, geese, herons, cranes, pink flamingos, and a giant blue-and-black flamingo unknown to Khokarsa.

They paddled across the lake to the other side, searched along its shore, and concluded that it had no outlet. Reluctantly they abandoned their dugouts and set out on foot. And then, after weeks of walking through the lion-yellow grass, they saw the first peaks of a vast mountain range, some of which were snow-capped.

"According to my calculations, that should be the Saasares," Hinokly said. "If we can find the pass that leads to Miklemres, we can proceed south, and our journey is ended. If we can't, we'll have to go eastward until we can round their end and then go south to Qethruth."

"I never thought we'd get this far," Kebiwabes said. "How far have we gone, Hinokly?"

"It's a year and one month since we left Mukha," the scribe said. "If we find the pass, it shouldn't take more than two months to get to Miklemres. Less, if we can find the pass at once."

And in a year much can happen in Khokarsa, Hadon thought. Has Awineth given me up for dead and chosen another husband?

Unsurprisingly, he found himself hoping that she had. He would be free to ask Lalila if she would accept him as her mate. It was not easy to give up the desire for the throne, but she would be worth it. However, so far she had given no indication other than a warm friendliness that she was thinking favorably of him. He would have asked her how she felt long ago if he had not been the queen's affianced. What if Lalila said yes and when he got to Khokarsa he found that Awineth was still waiting for him? She might—no, *would*—have him and Lalila killed. Well, *he* would die, but surely Awineth would not dare touch one who was under the protection of Sahhindar.

When they came to the foothills, Mumona, the Klemqaba woman, drew out the carved goat's teeth from the pouch dangling from her belt. She chanted while whirling widdershins and then cast the teeth into the ashes of their campfire. After studying the pattern they formed, she announced that they should go west. After a few days' journey, they would come across the military outpost that guarded the entrance to the pass. And, sure enough, after walking for five days, they saw its walls and sentinal towers, built of oak logs.

The sentinels saw them long before the had toiled up the slope of the great hill to it, and the wanderers could hear drums and brazen trumpets far off. Presently a troop of soldiers, their bronze armor and spearheads bright in the sun, trotted toward them. Hadon explained to the officer who they were, and a runner was sent to speed the news to the commandant. Thus they entered with a fanfare of trumpets and were greeted warmly. They were bathed in warm water and animal-fat soap and anointed with olive oil. Hadon, Tadoku, Kwasin, the scribe, the bard, and the three from the far north were invited to eat with the commandant and the fort's priestess. The others were sent to the barracks to eat with the soldiers, but Hadon insisted that Mumona must sit with them.

"But she is a Klemqaba!" Major Bohami said.

"She is also our priestess," Hadon said. "Without her, we would have no spiritual guidance. And she has been of great help in taking care of the physical needs of my men. Without her, I myself might have died of swamp fever."

"What do you say, Mineqo?" the major said.

The fort's priestess was of ancient stock, as were many who came from the northern shores of the Kemu. She was tall, blond, blue-eyed, and beautiful despite a hawkish nose and thin lips. She wore a bonnet of the tail feathers of eagles, indicating that she was a priestess of W"uwos, goddess of the red-headed female eagle. Around her neck was a chain of eagle bones from which hung a tiny figure of W"uwos carved from an eagle's leg bone. Around her waist was a belt of eagle skin, and below that a kilt of skin covered with eagle feathers. On a stand near her was a giant eagless, chained, glaring at the party as if she would like to eat them. But she was not hungry; she was fed living hares and snakes.

"If she is a priestess and has done all that Hadon says, then she will sit with us," Mineqo said. "But if she eats disgustingly, as I understand the Klemqaba do, then she will leave."

"I have trained her not to blow her nose or relieve herself while eating with others," Hadon said.

The Klemqaba was summoned and sat quietly through the meal, saying nothing unless she was addressed, which was not often. The meal was delicious. Hadon forgot his usual abstinence and ate of tender partridge stuffed with emmer bread, sweet pomegranates, domestic buffalo steaks covered with hare gravy, *mowometh* berries (the sweetest thing in the world), okra soup in which duck giblets floated, and fried termite queens, a rare delicacy. He also indulged too much in the mead, which was cooled with ice brought down from the mountains. This was the first time in his life that he had

147

experienced iced drinks, though if he became king he could have such every day.

Kwasin ate three times as much as the others, gobbling, smacking, and grunting, and when he finished, belched loudly. The priestess frowned and said, "Hadon, your bear-man has cruder manners than the Klemqaba."

Kwasin stared, his face becoming red, and said, "Priestess, if you were not a holy woman I would eat you too. You look good enough to eat."

"He has been out in the Wild Lands a long time," Hadon said hastily. "I am sure that he did not mean to offend you. Isn't that so, Kwasin?"

"I have been gone a long time," Kwasin said. "And I would not offend the first beautiful woman I've seen, Lalila excepted, since I began my wanderings so many years ago."

"Kwasin? Kwasin?" the priestess said. "Now, where have I heard that name before?"

"What?" Kwasin bellowed, spraying mead down his beard. "You haven't heard of Kwasin? Have you been in the sticks all your life?"

"I was born here," Mineqo said icily. "I have been to Miklemres twice, once for five years to attend the College of the Priestesses and once to attend the coronation of the high priestess of that city. But no, savage, I have never heard of you."

"I thought you knew," Major Bohami murmured.

She turned to him fiercely and said, "Knew what?"

"This is the giant that ravished the priestess of Kho in Dythbeth and killed her guards," he said weakly. "Instead of being castrated and flung to the pigs, he was exiled. The Voice of Kho Herself decreed that sentence."

"Why didn't you tell me?" she said.

"I was busy arranging for the comforts of Hadon and his people. And I thought you knew. It is not up to me to advise you on what to do."

"And you are the man whose child I carry," she said. "I hope it isn't as stupid as you!"

The major reddened but said nothing. Kwasin gulped down a beaker of mead, belched again, and said, "O Priestess, do not get angry. It is true that I was exiled, but the Voice of Kho also said that I would return someday. She did not say when, so I have come back to plead forgiveness from Her. I have suffered more than enough; my sin should be expiated by now."

The priestess rose from her chair and said, "That is for Kho to decide! But you have been forbidden to step inside this land, and this fort is in the boundary of the empire!"

She pointed a finger at the doorway and shouted, "Out!"

Kwasin heaved himself up and gripped the edge of the table with his massive fingers. "Out, you say? Out to where?"

"Out of this fort!" she cried. "You may sleep by the gate for all I care, like an outcast dog, but you will not stay in this land! Not until the Voice of Kho has been notified that you are knocking at the gate and not until She says—if indeed She will—that you may enter!"

For a moment Hadon thought that Kwasin intended to upset the table. He moved his chair back, at the same time whispering to Lalila and her child to get out of the way. Paga, he noticed, had already done so. But Kwasin, quivering, his eyes black lava, managed to control himself.

He said, "It is only because I do not wish to offend mighty Kho again that I do not ravage through this fort, slaying everyone. I will go, Priestess, but I won't hang around here like a jackal waiting for scraps. It will take months to get a message from the Voice of Kho, and I am impatient! I will go on into the land, and woe to him who dares to get in my way! I will go to the mountain of Kho myself and there throw myself on Her mercy!"

"If you attempt to enter without Her permission, you will be slain!" the priestess said.

"I'll take that chance," Kwasin said, and he turned and walked out. Hadon followed him in time to see him come out of his room with the great ax. Kwasin said, "Ho, cousin, do you mean to stop me?"

"Why should I?" Hadon said. "No, I am not trying to get in your way. But though you have offended me and been as troublesome as a fly up my nostril, I would not see you commit suicide. I beg you to do as the priestess says. Stay here until Kho bids you come or bids you depart."

"Kho is a woman and no doubt has changed Her mind about me by now," Kwasin said. "No, I am going to Her and demand that She say yes or no Herself. I'm not going to wait.

As for my being killed before I get there, that is nonsense. I don't intend to march through the land where everyone will see me. I will steal through the country like a fox, steal a boat when I get to the Kemu, and sail to the island. And then I will go softly and at night up the mountain and face the oracle, the Voice."

"And if Kho is still adamant?"

"Then I just might ravish the oracle and knock the temple down with this ax," Kwasin said. "If I die, I will not do so meekly."

"Sometimes I think you mean it when you say fantastic things like that," Hadon said.

"Of course I do," Kwasin said. He strode out of the room, which suddenly became much larger.

Hadon returned to the dining room. Lalila said, "What does he mean to do?"

"He is indeed mad," Hadon said. "Kho has taken his senses away, and I am afraid that She will take his life soon."

"Perhaps he would be better off if She did," Paga said. "He is a miserable creature, full of arrogance and hate. But if such were to be struck down, this world would have only a few people left in it. Which would be a blessing."

"Let us not talk of him," Mineqo said. "Sit down, Lalila, my dear, and we shall talk of you. Before that elephantine buffoon interrupted us, you were telling me that you were a priestess of the moon among your own people."

"Not I," Lalila said. "My mother was. I would have been if my tribe had not perished."

"And what other goddesses do you worship?"

"Many. We also worship many gods. But the two greatest deities are the moon and the sun. They are twin sisters, daughters of the sky, who gave over her empire to them after the first humans were created by her."

"Ah!" Mineqo said. "Among us the sun is the god Resu, though in the ancient times Resu was Bikeda, a goddess. She is still worshiped as such in some of the rural and mountainous areas. Just so was Bhukla once the chief deity of war but was dislodged by Resu and became the goddess of the sword. All this came about because the Klemsaasa, the Eagle people, conquered Khokarsa when she was weakened by earthquake and plague. They strove to make Resu greater than Kho

150

but did not succeed. But the priests of Resu have not given up the struggle, even though they tempt the wrath of Kho."

"I do not understand," Lalila said. "How can the deeds of mortals cause changes in the heavens?"

"That is a deep question, and the answer is deep. It was all explained to me when I was in the college, but it would take me an hour to explain to you. First, I would have to define the technical terms, and that might cause more confusion than ever. However, you may be enlightened when you get to the city of Khokarsa. Since you are a priestess of the moon, even though from an alien people, Awineth may decide that you can be initiated into the priesshood."

"Sahhindar suggested that I might benefit if I did become a priestess," Lalila said.

"Sahhindar!" Mineqo said. "The Archer God came to *you* in a dream?"

"No dream," Lalila said. "Sahhindar talked with me and walked with me in the flesh, as a man, as real and solid as Hadon. It was he who sent Paga, Abeth, and me here. He put us under his protection."

"Is this true?" the priestess said, turning to Hadon and Hinokly.

"True, Mineqo," Hinokly said. "I was there when the Gray-Eyed God charged our expedition to return to Khokarsa and see that she was given both safety and respect there. Evidently you had not heard of this."

"But why didn't you tell me this before? I thought that your expedition was only a scientific survey team."

"There was too little time, O Priestess," Hinokly said.

Mineqo looked bewildered. "I do not understand this at all. Sahhindar was exiled by Kho because he disobeyed Her. The priests of Resu claim that Sahhindar is therefore the ally of Resu."

"He is no god, Mineqo," Lalila said, "though godlike. He told me himself that he is only a mortal. He says that he was a traveler in time, that he had been born in the future, over eleven thousand years from now, and that he traveled backward by use of a . . . ."

She hesitated and then said, "We do not have a word for the thing which transported him. He used a word from his own language to name it . . . a . . . mashina, I believe he said."

"And what is this ... masina," Mineqo said, unable to utter the -sh- sound.

"Something like a boat which carries a device that pushes it through time, as a boat is pushed by wooden blades."

"Pardon, Priestess," Hadon said. "Lalila has never seen a boat with sails. A more apt analogy would be that time is like a wind which pushes the time boat's sails."

"But Sahhindar was the one who taught the Khoklem how to domesticate plants and animals, how to make bricks, how to make bronze, how to add and subtract and multiply," Mineqo said. "That was two thousand years ago. Do men live that long?"

"Sahhindar said that there are a few people of the far future who have an elixir which keeps them from aging," Hinokly said. "But I myself heard him disclaim his godhood."

"Do they know that at the palace?" Mineqo said.

"They do," Hinokly said. "I imagine that that revelation has caused a storm of controversy among the colleges."

"Such things are beyond me," Mineqo said. "I have lived too long in this isolated post to remember all the philosophy I was taught as a young girl. Let the colleges decide what this means. I will send all of you with an escort to the chief priestess at Miklemres, and she can decide what to do with you."

"That is *my* province!" Major Bohami said. "I am the military commander here, Mineqo, and I say who is to come and to go. At present, we are short-handed, and I cannot spare more than a couple of guides."

"I have heard you boast that you and five men could disperse any attack by the barbarians," Mineqo said. "And the last trouble we had with them was when I was a little girl. The Klemklakor are too few around here to be a danger, but what if they attack this party deep in the mountains? You know that they often try to ambush our supply trains."

It was evident that the major felt that he had to protest his sovereignty, yet wanted a way to agree with the priestess. He said, "Since you put it that way, I agree that there is sense in what you say. But I will issue the orders, and I do so only because our guests are so important. The wishes of the king and queen and of Sahhindar make it imperative that I give them all the protection that we can spare."

Hadon said, "We would like to leave shortly after dawn."

"That shall be done," Mineqo and Bohami said at the same time.

Bohami glared at her, and she spoke in a low voice, "You will sleep alone tonight, Bohami, unless you apologize."

"So be it," Bohami said. "I don't like your undercutting my authority. You should consult with me in private and leave the public issuing of orders to me."

Hadon was embarrassed and so bade them good night as quickly as he could.

16

The party, accompanied by twelve soldiers, climbed up the narrow cliff-girdling path. Toward noon they put on the thick mountain-leopard furs provided them. The snows hung above them, making them uneasy. The soldiers said that more than one patrol and supply train had been buried in avalanches. In fact, the fort was beginning to run short of goods from Miklemres because the last train had been wiped out. The avalanche may have been an accident or it may have been triggered off by the wild tribes of the Bear Totem. These, the soldiers said, were the descendants of the mountaineers who had stayed behind when the Klemsaasa invaded Khokarsa with their rebellious Miklemres allies and conquered the devastated capital. Since the Klemklakor had been at war with the Mountain Eagle Totem then, they had not taken part. Escaped criminals and runaway slaves had added to their numbers during the one thousand and eleven years that had passed since the Klemsaasa had left the Saasares ranges. It was said that the Klemklakor were so numerous now that they needed only a leader to unite them to become a dangerous threat to the Miklemres queendom. So far, they were so busy fighting among themselves that the Khokarsans had been able to control them.

"Klemklakor is a generic term for them," Tadoku said, "Actually, though the Bear people are in the majority, there are a dozen totems in these mountains, most of them descended from refugees. But all are enemies of the Khokarsans. If we should have another Time of Troubles, they would sweep down on Miklemres like locusts. United, they would be a formidable enough force. Being heretics, they use the bow and arrow, and this makes them triply dangerous."

The trail wound down again. By the morning of the second day they were warm enough to shed their furs. Two days later they put them on again. On the fifth day they saw a bear only a quarter of a mile away. Hadon became excited because he had never seen this legendary creature in the flesh.

"If you think it is big, you should see a *klakoru*, a cave bear," Hinokly said. "Rumours have it that there are still a few in the highest ranges. Those who have seen them say that they are as big as elephants, though no doubt that is an exaggeration."

At noon of the seventh day they were proceeding down a trail halfway up the slope of a mountain. Suddenly the earth trembled and the mountain roared. They looked up and saw a dozen gigantic boulders bounding toward them, followed by a mass of smaller stones and snow. There was no place to run, though some did run. The rest, Hadon among them, jumped below the trail into a depression and flattened themselves out against the earth. Within a minute the first of the boulders soared over them, striking a few feet past them. Others followed them, rumbling and banging, one smashing a fleeing soldier, and then it became quiet, the only sound that of the boulders still leaping and rolling far below.

They got up cautiously while snow powder and dust fell on them. The mass behind the boulders had slid to a stop a few yards above the trail. Kho had protected them.

The incident, however, was not over. Far above were the yells of men in a desperate fight. Hadon saw tiny figures emerging from a stand of firs. They scattered in two directions along the slopes, and presently they had run into the trees to the north and the south. After a while a familiar figure emerged. It came slowly down the slope, skirted the loose mass directly above the party, and walked toward them on the trail. It was Kwasin, gigantic in bearskins, covered with blood, and carrying his bloody ax on his shoulder. One hand held two severed heads by their beards.

He flung the heads at the feet of Hadon and roared, "Behold the ambusher of the ambushers, cousin! I spied them long before they saw me, and I crept up on them. I wasn't in time to prevent their rolling down boulders at you, but shortly thereafter I launched my own avalanche! Myself! Though they were a score, I attacked them and slew half a dozen before they decided that I must be a werebear! Then I clothed myself in furs they no longer needed and cut off some trophies. You may thank me now, cousin, for saving your life, though if the beautiful Lalila had not been with you I might not have interfered!"

"In which case, Lalila may thank you, but I won't," Hadon said. "And what now?"

"I will go with you to Khokarsa and protect you!"

"After we reach Miklemres, it is you who will need the protection," Hadon said. "Are you depending upon my status as the king-to-be to get you to the capital safely?"

"You see through me!" Kwasin said, and he laughed.

"Then you will have to obey my orders again."

"So be it! But when we reach the capital, cousin, and Awineth compares you to me, she may change her mind and take me as her husband. How would you like that, little one?"

Better than you could guess, Hadon thought, but he did not reply.

Two months of slow up-and-down travel passed. Four times they were lucky enough to escape hunting or raiding bands of Bear people. Their scouts saw the barbarians and warned the party in time to permit hiding or flight. And then, at noon one day, they came around a trail, and the plains of Miklemres spread out below. Their joy was quickly smothered, however, when they saw heavy smoke rising from two places along the river. The next day they cautiously approached the first site. Seeing no one living, they entered into the charred area. Many mutilated corpses lay in the ashes. The sergeant from the fort poked around and confirmed what they all knew.

"The Bear people. There must have been at least three hundred."

"There aren't many women and children," Hadon said.

"Oh, they took the women as wives, and the children will be adopted into the tribe and will grow up to be as bloodthirsty as their foster fathers."

He shook his head and said, "They are getting arrogant. The last time this happened, about ten years ago, we sent up large punitive expeditions which cleared the mountains for many miles roundabout. General D"otipoeth collected three thousand heads and brought in five hundred prisoners, men, women, and children, to be hanged along this road as a warning. At the last minute the chief priestess reprieved the children."

They proceeded quietly with scouts far ahead and that evening came to the ruins of the second village. There they found the same ruin and carnage. They went without incident through this country of grapevines, beehives, and emmer fields until they encountered the third village. This was as large as the first two together and was protected by a log fort containing three hundred soldiers. The commandant, Abisila, a tall gangling redhead, came out to greet them. Grimly he asked them to identify themselves. Hadon gave their names. The commandant looked even grimmer and said, "I thought so. There is no mistaking you and that bearded monster. Hadon of Opar and Kwasin of Dythbeth, I arrest you in the name of Minruth, king of kings!"

17

Resistance was useless. They were surrounded by fifty men pointing spears at them. Hadon finally said coolly, "And what is the charge?"

"That I do not know," Absila said.

"But that is illegal?" the scribe said. "The law clearly states that when a man is arrested he must be informed also of the charge!"

"Haven't you heard?" Abisila said. "No, I suppose you haven't. There is a new law in the land!"

"Why?" Hadon said, but the commandant would not answer. He gestured at his men to take the weapons of the prisoners. Hadon withdrew his sword to hand it to Abisila but hesitated. Should he instead chop off the commandant's arm and try to break out? But if he did, he would quickly be run through. And—a stronger motive for surrendering peacefully—Lalila and the child might be harmed in the melee.

Kwasin, as usual, did not think of the consequences. He roared, and his ax flashed by Hadon and sheared off Abisila's arm. He turned then and leaped at the ring of spears, cut through or knocked aside a half-dozen spearheads, and in a few seconds had cut off two heads and an arm. There was shouting and confusion as the soldiers milled around, too closely packed to get at Kwasin and many not knowing what was happening. Kwasin picked up a headless corpse with his left hand and cast it at the outer ring and knocked down three men. Then, his ax flashing out to one side and shearing a spear, he had broken through.

For several seconds no one pursued. The second in command restored some order, and ten men ran after the giant, who had disappeared in the nearby village. The others surrounded Hadon's party with their spears again. Hadon handed the sword to the captain and said, "I warn you that the woman, her child, and the manling are under the protection of Sahhindar."

The captain turned even paler and stammered a question. Hadon explained as best he could, and the result was that Lalila and her two companions were taken to the quarters of the dead commandant. Tadoku, Hinokly, Kebiwabes, and Hadon were locked inside a large room behind bronze bars. Tadoku protested. He was told that though he was not under official arrest, he was to be treated as a prisoner until his case was judged at Khokarsa. The scribe declared that this was illegal, but the captain merely walked away.

And so, three weeks later, all except Kwasin were on a galley headed for the city of Khokarsa. Hadon, though

157

chained, was allowed to walk the deck during the day. The captain and the priest were permitted to talk to him, and from them he learned much of the situation. Minruth, becoming impatient, had demanded that Awineth forget Hadon and marry him. She had refused, and her father had confined her in her apartments. The king's troops had then seized the city. Those military and naval units loyal to Awineth had been disarmed or slain. The Temple of Kho on the slopes of the volcano had been occupied and the priestesses there put in prison.

The men who did that must have been brave, Hadon thought. Even the most fanatical devotee of Resu would have feared the wrath of Kho. But Minruth had promised them great rewards. Power and wealth were more important than even fear of the deities to some men. Minruth had picked these to carry out this outrageous mission. He had not, however, dared to violate the oracular priestess, the Voice of Kho Herself.

There had been, of course, a mass uprising. The poor and many of the middle and upper classes had swarmed out to avenge the blasphemy. But the undisciplined mob did not stand a chance against catapults of liquid fire. The troops of Resu cast hundreds of bundles of the incendiary composition on the people in the jammed streets and burned them alive. The residential and commercial areas around the Inner City burned to the ground, killing thousands and leaving the heart of the city, except for the Inner City, in ashes.

The key centers of the other cities of the island had been simultaneously seized and the mobs there dealt with in a similar fashion. Only Dythbeth, always a thorn in the side of Khokarsa, had revolted successfully. Minruth's armed forces had been massacred. But Minruth had it blockaded now, and it was said that the citizens were eating rats and dogs to stay alive. They could not hold out for more than another week.

Part of the navy had stayed loyal to Awineth and Kho. After some strong fighting, those ships that could get away had fled to Towina, Bawaku, and Qethruth. These cities, like most in the empire, had seized the opportunity to declare independence. The empire was aflame with revolution. Minruth did not care. He would reconquer.

"Mighty Resu will defeat the mortals who persist in placing

158

Kho above her natural master, Resu!" the priest cried.

Hadon felt like kicking the gaunt, blazing-eyed priest into the sea. The captain, though a follower of Resu, winced. Evidently he had not shed all fear of Kho. Nor was he accustomed to be without a priestess. A priest on a ship without a priestess was supposed to be bad luck. Piqabes, the green-eyed Our Lady of Kemu, did not favor such vessels.

The captain told Hadon of the rumblings and shakings of the earth below the city of Khokarsa and the clouds of smoke and the sea of burning lava that had issued from the volcano.

"Awineth is said to have declared that Kho Herself was going to destroy the city," the captain said. "Many of us wet down our legs when we heard that rumour. But Minruth said that that was not so. Resu was locked in combat with Kho deep within the mountain, and he would eventually overthrow Her. Then She would take the lower throne and become his slave."

"And Minruth was right!" the priest blared. "Otherwise, why would the lava have destroyed the sacred grove and inundated the temple, knocking it down and burning all the priestesses within it? Would Kho, if She were all-powerful, have permitted this? No, Resu did it, and She was powerless to prevent it!"

"The grove and the temple are destroyed?" Hadon said. "Those ancient holy places?"

"Destroyed forever!" the priest shouted. "Minruth has promised that he will build a new temple there, dedicated to Resu!"

"And what of the oracular priestess? Was she killed by the lava?"

The priest gaped at Hadon and then said, as if it pained him, "She seems to have escaped into the wild lands back of the volcano. But Minruth's men are searching for her. When they find her, they will bring her back in chains! Once the populace sees her in Minruth's power, they will know that Resu is all powerful!"

"If they find her," Hadon said, "I hope that this struggle does not cause Kho to destroy all the land and those within it."

"Resu will triumph, and things will be as they should have been long ago!" the priest said.

"What of Lalila?" Hadon said. "What does Minruth plan for her? After all, she is under the aegis of Sahhindar. The Gray-Eyed God said that he would avenge her if she were harmed in any way."

This last was not true, but Hadon did not mind lying if he could help Lalila.

"How would I know?" the priest said. "Minruth does not confide in me. When she stands before him, then she will be dealt with as justice requires."

Or as Minruth requires, Hadon thought. The dispenser of the law is the interpreter of the law.

The days and nights passed steadily but slowly. Once again Hadon, desiring to stay in shape, asked to be allowed to pull an oar. The captain was scandalized but after a brief argument gave his permission. Hadon wore handcuffs when he worked and was forbidden to speak to the other oarsmen. The captain wanted no subversive talk spread among the sailors.

At long last the northwest coast of the island rose from the horizon. The galley followed the coastline, which was flat farmland for many miles at first. Then a mountain range, the Saasawabeth, arose. Hadon overheard the captain and the priest talking of guerrillas holed up in it and of the expedition against them. Apparently the seven mountain ranges of the island were the strongholds of thousands of Kho worshipers.

The Saasawabeth became farmland again, but in a few days they were opposite the Khosaasa. The galley left those behind, though not out of sight, and after a week they were entering the mouth of the Gulf of Gahete. Even from this distance the tip of Khowot could be seen. The smoke issuing from it had, however, been visible after passing the Saasawabeth. The galley pulled steadily down the gulf, the cliffs on its right, the high farmlands on its left. Smoke rose from many of the peasants' huts and barns, burned by the troops of Minruth.

Then mighty Khowot rose from the sea, and after two days its base was in sight. On the fifth day, the higher part of the Tower of Resu came into view. This, the priest said, was no longer dedicated to both Resu and Kho. In fact, he had heard rumors that Minruth intended to name it after himself.

It was said that the king of kings was considering making a certain theory of the College of Priests a fact. This was that the king was, in essence, Resu himself, that a piece of the spirit of Resu inhabited the king's body and so made him holy. He would be the sun god incarnate, and hence worshiped as a god.

"He is indeed mad," Hadon said.

The priest glared at Hadon and said, "That blasphemy will be reported to Minruth!"

"That won't make my case any harder," Hadon said.

The spires and the towers of the city of Khokarsa lifted, though not as soon as Hadon had expected. This was because the city no longer glittered white. Smoke from the volcano had settled on it, and to this had been added layers of smoke from the burning buildings outside the Inner City.

"Thirty thousand people perished during the uprisings and the fires that followed," the priest said. "The scourge of Resu is terrible indeed! Minruth is said to have wept when he heard this, but later he became joyous. He said that it was the will of Resu and so was necessary. The hardhearted must be destroyed in a ritual of purification of the land. The spirit of blasphemy must be stamped flat forever."

"But all those innocents, the children?" Hadon said.

"The sins of the parents descend upon the children, and they must pay too!"

Hadon was too shocked by this insanity to reply.

The galley proceeded through waters that had once been crowded with seagoing merchant vessels and river boats and barges from inland cities and the rural areas. The stench of the charred corpses beneath the ruins struck them full force, choking them. Then the galley passed between the forts of Sigady and Klydon, and then the fort on the western tip of Mohasi island. The ship bore to the southwest and turned south into the entrance of the great canal. It eased gently in between two docks while drums beat. The prisoners were marched off to a customs house. The captain sent a runner with a letter enclosed in a silver box on the end of a golden staff. This would be delivered to the king of kings, who would read therein that the hero Hadon and his party were awaiting the king's disposal.

Hadon looked curiously at the Great Tower, which was

indeed awe-inspiring. Its base was almost half a mile in diameter, and its staggered stories rose to almost five hundred feet. Yet it was only half-built. And it might be a long time before work was resumed on it. Twice before, its building had been halted for long periods during Times of Trouble. And during periods of comparative prosperity and peace, the enormous expense of its construction had taken a large, much-resented portion of tax money.

Two hours passed before the runner appeared at the head of a dog-trotting corps of palace guards. The prisoners were hustled out and marched off behind a blaring band to the citadel. Once again Hadon crossed over the moat and ascended the broad and steep steps to the acropolis, though this time it was from the western end. And he did not come as a conquering hero, victor of the Great Games, husband-to-be of the chief priestess and queen of queens.

They passed through huge bronze gates into the citadel and through broad streets lined by marble temples and government buildings. Some of these were round, or nine-sided, built in ancient times. Others were square, of the style that had come into being about three hundred years ago. The palace itself, the most ancient building, of massive granite blocks overlaid with marble blocks, was nine-sided. Hadon was grieved to see that the statues of Kho and Her daughters, upholding the roof of the great porch, had been defaced. Surely the hands of those who had committed this blasphemy would be withered.

A herald met them at the western doorway, and the prisoners were officially delivered to him. The interior palace guards replaced those who had conducted the prisoners, and two trumpeters replaced the band. They marched through broad stately halls lined with works of art from all over the empire. Then they were in the enormous throne room, glittering with gold, silver, diamonds, emeralds, turquoises, topazes, and rubies. They walked down a long aisle formed of silent courtiers, most of them men. The herald halted before the thrones, thumped the end of his staff on the many-colored mosaic floor of marble and inset diamonds, and cried out the greeting. This time it was Minruth he addressed first. His final phrase, "And remember that death comes to all!" was omitted. Instead the herald shouted, "Mighty Resu, in whom our

162

king of kings is incarnate, rules over all!"

As if that were not shocking enough, Minruth's throne was now on the higher dais, and the fish-eagle which had once stood on the back of Awineth's throne was chained to Minruth's throne. Moreover, judging from its smaller size, it was a male. Minruth, heavily bearded, sat on the throne. This was another change Hadon had noticed among the soldiers and the courtiers. All were unshaven.

Awineth sat on her plain oak throne, clad in a garment that matrons wore after their breasts had begun to sag. From neck to foot, her superb figure was hidden in a voluminous linen robe. She seemed to have aged several years; her eyes were underscored with the blue-black of anxiety and sleepless nights. But her eyes were bright when she looked at Hadon.

There was a long silence afterward, broken only by the coughs of courtiers. Minruth gazed long at Hadon while he chewed his lower lip. Finally he smiled.

"I have heard much about you, Hadon of Opar, since you returned to our land! None of it is good! You unlawfully conducted the exiled Kwasin into the land, and that requires the extreme penalty!"

This was a lie, but he who sits on the throne may twist the truth to suit himself. Hadon thought it useless to protest.

"Kwasin was, however, no longer an exile. The ban imposed by the wife of Resu no longer holds, and I would have welcomed the hero Kwasin if he had forsworn loyalty to Kho. But he broke free from arrest and murdered my soldiers while doing so! Thus, he will die after suitable torture!"

If you can catch him, Hadon thought.

Minruth paused, glared at Hadon, and then looked at Lalila. When he spoke, his voice was gentler.

"I have been informed about this woman, the Witch from the Sea, I believe she is called, among other things. If she is indeed a witch, she will be burned. It does not matter that she might be a good witch! There is no such thing now. All witches are evil, and magic is to be practiced by the priests of Resu alone!"

"Science, you mad fool," Hinokly said, so softly that Hadon could barely hear him. "There is no such thing as magic. Science!"

"But I have been told that her witchery consists only of her

163

beauty, and she cannot be blamed for that! If my interrogators are convinced that she is truly not a practicer of magic, then she will be free and honored. I like what my eyes see, and what the king of kings likes, he takes to his heart. I may honor her by taking her as my wife. You may not know it, Hadon, but men may now have more than one wife."

Awineth stirred and said, "That is not according to our ancient law, Father. We are not barbarian Klemqaba. Nor is it lawful to have forced me to marry you."

"I did not ask you to speak!" Minruth said. "If you speak once more without my permission, you will be conducted to your apartments, and we will hold court without you!"

Awineth looked angry but did not reply.

"The ancient laws are repealed. The new laws rule the land," Minruth said. "Now, there are also the cases of the child and the manling to be judged. The child would be burned with her mother if she were judged a witch, but I do not think that that will be the verdict."

Hadon felt a new shock. He had never heard of such a horrible thing. To burn children for the crimes of the mother was one more evil that would surely bring the wrath of Kho down on Minruth's head! The wonder was that he had not been struck down long ago. But Kho bides Her time.

"The child is as beautiful as her mother, and when the time comes, she may also become my wife."

Hadon ground his teeth and thought of hurling himself at Minruth. Minruth was as mad as a buck hare during mating season. He was fifty-seven now, and though it was said that he was still as virile as a young bull, he could not seriously assume that eleven years from now he could bed Abeth. Or could he?

"And then there is the hairy one-eyed manling. It has been reported that he is a werebeast, that he assumes at night the shape of an animal like a dog, an animal known only in the lands of the far north. Is this true, manling?"

Paga said, "It is true that I was suckled by a four-legged bitch, O King of Kings. The two-legged bitch who bore me cast me out into the bushes to die. She had no heart, but the beast who found me had one full of motherly love, though doubtless she would have eaten me if she had not just lost her cubs. The first milk I tasted was hers. She gave me the only love I have known, excepting that of the hero Wi and of Lalila and her child, though the god Sahhindar was kind to me, and Hadon does not reject me because I am a misshapen manling. I am not a werebeast, O King of Kings, though I am half-beast and proud of it. Often the beasts are more human than the humans. But when the moon is full, I am no more affected by it than you, and perhaps not as much."

"Big words from a little man," Minruth said. "I will not inquire into the meaning of that last statement, since you would lie about it anyway. And you bring up Sahhindar, the Gray-Eyed Archer God. He is a younger brother of mighty Resu and no lover of Kho. Like you, he was abandoned by his mother and raised by the half-apes of the woods. And it was he who gave man plants and taught him how to domesticate them and the beasts, and how to calculate, and how to make bronze. Even the priestesses admit that, though they say that he committed a divine crime by giving us these gifts before Kho had decreed that they should be given.

"It is said that the woman and her child and you have been placed under Sahhindar's protection. Is this indeed so, Lalila?"

"Indeed it is true," Lalila said. "Hinokly can vouch for that."

"But it is also true that Sahhindar has told you that he is no god, that he is only a man, though a strange one? Is this true, Lalila?"

"It is true," Lalila replied.

"Gods often lie to test mortals. But if he should come to this land, he will be interrogated. And if he is an impostor, he will suffer what all mortals must."

"But he is no impostor!" Paga said. "He does not claim to be a god!"

"Strike him with the butt of a spear!" Minruth yelled. "He must learn to unloosen his tongue only when I say he may!"

An officer took a spear from a soldier's hand, and Paga fell to the floor beneath the blow. He groaned once, clamped his teeth, and got to his feet shaking his head.

"The next time, it will be the point, not the butt!" Minruth said. "And now for the scribe, the bard, and Tadoku. They too accompanied Kwasin, and so share in the guilt of the murder of my soldiers. Major, take them with Hadon and the

165

manling to the cells reserved for traitors."

"The queen and Kho forever!" Taroku yelled.

Those were his last words, brave but foolish. Minruth screamed an order, and Tadoku died with three spears through him. Hadon swore that if he ever had the opportunity, he would see to it that Tadoku was buried under a hero's pylon with the sacrifice of the finest bulls. Then he was taken away while Awineth and Lalila wept. He was led with the others to a door that opened onto steps that wound down and down, down a long hall along which torches flared, down more winding stone steps, down another long hall, and down a final spiral staircase. The two upper halls were lined with cells packed with men and women, and sometimes with children. Hadon had heard that the rock beneath the citadel was as tunneled as an ant's nest, that its network of corridors and shafts was equaled only by that beneath the city of Opar. But whereas Opar's had been dug to remove gold, the citadel's was intended for the deposit of criminals. It was also a place of refuge for the tenants of the citadel if invaders should ever take the surface buildings.

They went along a hall carved from granite, past cells, most of which were empty, and halted before the last door at the end. A turnkey unlocked it while the thirty guards held their spears ready. That their escorts were so many indicated that the prisoners must be thought dangerous indeed. But when he saw a giant figure in the darkness at the rear of the room, he knew what generated the fear.

"Welcome, cousin!" a familiar voice boomed. "Come in and enjoy Kwasin's hospitality!"

18

The guards withdrew, and the only light was that which traveled weakly from torches at the far end of the hall.

Kwasin said, "You will be able to see better soon, though not much better. Forgive me if I do not as yet approach you, cousin. I am chained to the walls, chained with iron, not bronze. The first time I was put in a cell, in one on the floor above, I broke the bronze chains and killed four men before they beat me unconscious. I awoke here, locked in iron."

"When did they catch you?" Hadon said.

"They didn't. I got across the river after killing the ten men who ran after me, and I hid in the hills. But I was hungry, so I stole a calf from a peasant's yard. As ill luck would have it, the peasant's daughter attracted my attention. I carried both her and the calf off into the woods, and I satisfied myself with both of them. But the bitch took advantage of me when my back was turned and raised a great bump on my head with my own ax! When I awoke, I was bound, and soldiers were cursing and puffing as they carried me off down the hills. That may be the Ax of Victory, Paga, but it carries bad luck with it."

"Perhaps it does," Paga said. "But in this case, it was stupidity and lust, not an ax, that got you captured."

"Do not think that because I am chained I cannot get at you, manling. I have loosened the bolts from the walls, and I can walk to the door whenever I choose. Are the guards all gone?"

Hadon said, "As far as I can see."

There was a screech of metal pulling loose from stone. His chains clanking, Kwasin began walking about.

Hadon explored the chamber, his eyesight having become adjusted to the dim light, as Kwasin had said it would. It was cut out of granite to form a room thirty feet wide, sixty feet long, and about fifteen feet high. A faint breeze came from a hole in the ceiling.

"The air shaft is large enough to accommodate you, Hadon," Kwasin said. "But getting to it is another matter. Besides, I was told that about ten feet into it is a bronze grille that would stop you if you did get that far."

"We will see about that," Hadon said. He found a dozen old blankets smelling of mildew, a great vase of water, six clay cups, and six chamberpots. And that was all. Kwasin, questioned by Hadon, said that he had been fed only twice a day. During that time, the chamberpots were replaced with empty, though not always clean, pots, and the water supply was replenished.

"They will come with the second meal in a few hours or so," Kwasin said. "I'm not sure of the time, since I've lost all sense of it."

"We might as well see now if we can get one of us into the shaft." Hadon said. "If you will be the base, Kwasin, I will stand on your shoulders as the second story of the human tower. Then Kebiwabes, who is the next tallest, can climb up us."

"But even if I could do that," the bard said, "how do I get up into it? And what about the grille?"

"I will lift you up, throw you if I can, so you can brace against the walls of the shaft," Hadon said. "I want you to find out just what is above. Perhaps the guards were lying when they told Kwasin that there was a grille there."

"But I might fall!"

"Then you will die a day or two sooner. And be thankful, since you will escape the torture."

"I am a bard. My person is sacred."

"Is that why you are in jail?"

Kebiwabes groaned and said, "Very well. But I fear that the songs of a great artist will die before birth in this dismal cell."

"That is up to dread Sisisken," Hadon said. "She is mistress of the underworld, and surely she is unhappy with Minruth and the worshipers of Resu."

Kwasin braced himself below the hole. Hadon backed to the door and then ran forward. Using as a springboard the back of Paga, who was on all fours, he leaped up onto the shoulders of the giant. Kwasin clamped his hands around

Hadon's ankles. Hadon wavered for a moment, then recovered his balance.

"Not so tight, Kwasin," he said. "You are cutting off the blood."

Paga and Hinokly lifted Kebiwabes as high as they could. He took hold of Hadon's waist and began to climb up Hadon's body. Twice Hadon almost fell with him, but he managed to keep his balance until Kebiwabe's legs were around his back. There the bard stuck, unable to go any higher.

"You will fall, Hadon, and I with you."

Kwasin rumbled, "Get on up, bard, or I'll smash your head against the wall."

Kebiwabes groaned and inched on up. With a convulsive effort, he pulled himself up, his legs dangling. Hadon toppled forward, and the two, Kebiwabes yelling, fell heavily on the stone floor.

Hadon got up and said angrily, "I told you to make no sudden moves! Are you hurt?"

"I thought my arm was broken. However, it is only skinned. But badly, badly."

Kwasin growled and seized Paga by the waist and hurled him straight up the shaft. Paga yelled, but he did not fall back. Hadon, looking upward, could barely distinguish him. The manling's back was against one wall and his feet against the other.

"Being small has its uses," Kwasin said. "Though perhaps I could throw even you, Hadon, as far." He guffawed and said, "Of course, if I missed, your head would break open."

Hadon said, "Paga, can you make it?"

"With much loss of skin," Paga said. "This rock is hard."

They waited for what seemed to be an interminable time. Then they heard Paga, apparently swearing in the language of his tribe.

Presently he was back at the mouth of the shaft. Kwasin gave the word, and Paga fell into the giant's arms.

"Ho, hairy baby, you are as bloody as if you had just been born! Did you indeed come from a stony womb?"

"No stonier than that of the woman who gave me birth," Paga said. "Let me down gently, elephant."

"Perhaps you would like to suckle?" Kwasin said, laughing

as he forced the manling's head to his nipple. Paga bit, Kwasin yelled with agony, and Paga fell.

"Do you want to bring the guards?" Hadon said fiercely. "Are you hurt, Paga?"

"Not as much as the elephant," Paga said.

"If we did not need you, I would brain you against the wall!" Kwasin bellowed.

"The fault is yours, giant," Paga said. "You owe me an apology."

"I apologize to no one!"

"Quiet, for the sake of our lives," Hadon said. "Paga, what did you find?"

"The guards did not lie. There is a bronze grille about ten feet up the shaft. It is composed of four bars, melted into each other at the junctions. The bars are about half an inch thick. Their ends are in holes dug into stone. I could bend the bars but could not get them loose from the holes."

"You are too huge to climb the shaft, Kwasin," Hadon said. "Even if we could get you within it. Do you think you could get me inside it?"

"Your legs are too long," Paga said. "You would be folded like a babe in its womb."

"My mother said I was a difficult birth," Hadon said. "Nevertheless, I got out. Kwasin, you must throw me hard enough so that almost my entire body will enter the shaft. Stand below to catch me if I fall."

"Of course I can do it!"

"I hope so," Hadon said. "If it were anyone but you, I would not even let you try it."

He told the giant how he wanted it done. Kwasin crouched, placed his hands palms-up under Hadon, who faced him. He lifted Hadon, who balanced himself, until his hands were even with his knees. Then Kwasin crouched a little, and said, "Here goes, cousin!" and straightened upward with a grunt. Hadon shot out at a slight angle from the perpendicular, drawing up his feet as he did so. He felt as if he had been propelled from a catapult. His shoulder rubbed along the wall, he fell back, but his legs, now against his chest, straightened out a little. And he was lodged in the shaft with his buttocks hanging out of the shaft.

"See, I told you!" Kwasin shouted.

"Quiet, monster, or our work will be undone," Paga said.

The ascent was painful and slow. It was necessary to brace his back against the wall and to shove himself upward a few inches with his legs. The skin quickly wore away from his back. Moreover, the walls were slippery in several places from Paga's blood. He gritted his teeth, and sweating and panting, got to the grille. It was as Paga had described it. He bent his head to look down the shaft and saw Kwasin, a lighter darkness in the darkness of the cell.

"I'm going to hang from the middle of the grille," he called down. "Perhaps I can weaken it by my weight alone. Then I will brace myself again and try to pull one end loose."

"If you fail, I will catch you," Kwasin said.

Hadon gripped the grille in the middle and let his legs go. The bars bent; suddenly they tore loose with a screech. Hadon yelled briefly but clamped his teeth. He had, however, drawn his legs up, and he shoved them out again. A few feet above the mouth of the shaft, he slid to a stop. His back felt as if it were covered with a thousand army ants.

He told Kwasin to get out of the way and worked the grille, which he held perpendicularly, past his body. He let it fall with a clang, and a moment later he dropped into Kwasin's arms.

"No nonsense," Hadon said. "Let me down."

"I have delivered twins," Kwasin said, obeying. "One, very short-legged and hairy; the other, very long-legged and bearing a gift of bronze. Both are ugly indeed."

"Hide the grille under the blankets," Hadon said.

"No, wait a moment," Kwasin said. He picked up the grille and began to bend it. After a few minutes he had a rod, which he swished above his head.

"Here is a weapon for you, Hadon, though a poor one. I will use the bolts at the end of my chains as a scythe."

"We need to know what is at the other end of the shaft," Hadon said. "Paga will go up again, since he is the shortest. But we will wait until after the meal. It wouldn't do for them to find one of their prisoners missing."

He had Hinokly wash his back with water from the vase. When the guards were heard coming, he and Paga sat with their backs against the wall. Kwasin reinserted the bolts in the holes and leaned against them. He complained to the guards

171

about the small portions served. Their officer chuckled and said, "Weak prisoners make good prisoners."

Hadon noted that this time there were only ten spear-men. That "only" was a big "only," however.

Though there was not enough food to satisfy Kwasin, the others had plenty. Its quality was poor, consisting of cold okra soup, stale millet bread, and chunks of tough beef. But they ate with gusto, and Hinokly gave Kwasin a piece of his meat.

"We must keep you strong," he said.

"I wish the others were as thoughtful as you," Kwasin growled. "My belly is bounding toward my backbone like a leopard after an antelope."

"We'll wait an hour for the food to digest," Hadon said. "Then Paga goes up, if he's willing."

"I am not sure my back can stand it."

'I'll go up this time," Hinokly said. "Though I am a skinny old man of thirty-six, I am wiry. But let's see if we can make a poncho from a blanket. That should help keep the skin from scraping off."

Using the end of one of the bronze bars of the grille, Hinokly tore out a hole from the blanket and slipped it over his head.

"The latest fashion in escapee wear," he said.

Once again Kwasin tossed a man through the hole. They sat down to wait, or paced back and forth in the gloom. Several times Hadon looked up the hole, but he could see only a very faint light issuing from someplace far up. He lay down on a blanket after a while but could not sleep. Just as he was about to rise, he heard Hinokly's voice issuing hollowly from the shaft.

"I'm back. Catch me, Kwasin."

Hadon jumped up, and when Hinokly had been set on his feet by Kwasin, he said, "What did you find?"

"About another ten feet above the place where the grille was are two shafts that run horizonally. One is at right angles to the other. Both are big enough for Kwasin to walk upright in. I went down the one to my right and came to another vertical shaft. This, I believe, admits air to the corridor outside our cell. There is a grille it it, but it is only a few inches below the lip of the shaft. You could probably tear it out,

Hadon. I jumped over it and continued. I came to another shaft which ran at right angles to the one I was in. I went down it a little distance and passed over another shaft. This, I believe, leads to the cell across from ours. I continued down it and went past the place where the wall in the corridor below seems to end. I came across another vertical shaft and looked down into another cell. It was lit more brightly than ours, so I concluded it was near torches. I watched and listened for a while, but if the cell was occupied, the men in it were silent.

"Apparently that cell is in a corridor which does not connect to that outside our cell. I went on, feeling in the dark, because I could not see these shafts, of course, unless there was a source of light below. Then I came to the end. There was, however, another vertical shaft there. I listened and heard, from far below, the gurgling of water.

"I suppose that that shaft leads to the underground water supply. You know, don't you, that there is an underground water tunnel connecting the citadel to both gulfs? If the citadel were beseiged, its defenders would not run out of water. Of course, the tunnel is probably guarded, especially now that Minruth fears attack from the worshipers of Kho. The tunnel is supposed to be a little-known secret, but anyone who has delved into the Great Temple archives, as I have, knows of it."

"Was there a ladder in the water shaft?" Hadon said.

"I felt for one, but if there is one, it starts below the reach of my hand. I then went back, retracing my route to where I had turned into this horizontal shaft. I was afraid of getting lost, and carefully memorized my right and left turns. I proceeded down the shaft, that is, I stayed in the same shaft that ended in the water shaft. Twice my foot came to the lips of vertical shafts, and I jumped over these. The light from below got stronger with each one, so I knew I was getting close to the end of the corridor which runs outside our cell. Moreover, two of the cells were occupied, and I noticed when we passed through our corridor that the two cells closest to the bottom of the staircase contained prisoners.

"But the shaft I was in must lead past the staircase. It ran straight for approximately half a mile. And there were a dozen horizontal shafts at right angles to it, each intersecting with a vertical shaft. Then I came to its end. I looked up the vertical shaft there and saw stars. But how could I get up it? It was possible to go down it, since I could lean out against the opposite wall, and then, bracing myself, work down it. But to go upward was impossible. I had no way of getting to a point where I could brace myself.

"I felt upward on the chance there was a ladder. I almost cried out! Above, on the wall nearest me, was a bronze bar! I gripped it with my hand turned inward, swung out, turned, gripped it with my other hand, and reached up and found another bar. I felt uneasy, of course, because I didn't know how long the bars had been set into the stone. They might be corroded, since the shafts are at least a thousand years old. However, it seemed reasonable that they would be replaced from time to time. This shaft must be one of the escape routes arranged for the royal family, in which case the ladder would be inspected from time to time."

"You are intolerably long-winded!" Kwasin said.

"He has to tell it step by step," Hadon said. "We all must know the route by heart before we go blundering around in the dark."

"And how am I to get up this shaft?" Kwasin said. "Do you plan to leave me here?"

"If we do, we'll come back with a rope," Hadon said. "I promise that if it is at all possible, we will get you out."

"On your honor as an Ant man and as my cousin?"

"Yes. Continue, Hinokly."

"I went up and up until I was sure that I was above the underground shafts. Moreover, the solid granite had become marble blocks. There was no mortar between them, but I could feel the divisions with my fingertips. I kept going on. Oh, yes, I heard water far below when I first came to the shaft, and the breeze was stronger and more humid. And at last I came to the opening and stuck my head out. The moon was out by then, so I could see, though not as well as I would have if it were not for the smoke from Khowot.

"I was on the roof and looking eastward. I hung out of the opening as far as I could and determined that the entrance was actually the mouth of one of the many carved heads that adorn the roof."

"But the palace is domed," Hadon said. "Isn't the dome too steep to allow climbing on it?"

"I would say so. What you mean is that if there are entrances to the shaft, they must be from the apartments of the royal family itself. So when I went back down the ladder, I felt on both sides of the ladder. And I found at one place hairline divisions outlining an oblong section in the wall— door-shaped, that is. Moreover, the ladder ceases to be continuous at the upper and lower parts of the hairlines. Obviously the runs are attached to a panel of stone which slides or falls inward to give entrance. But I dared not thump it to test it for hollowness. Now, it seemed reasonable to me that there should be something in the shaft which would permit one in it to activate a mechanism that would cause the section to open. I could find none. So the section can be moved only from the other side. It is a one-way escape route."

"If we had a torch, we could examine it closely," Hadon said. "There may be something that you could not see in the dark."

"We now have torches," Hinokly said. "I'll tell you why in just a minute. I got to the bottom of the ladder, and I swung on the lowest rung back and forth and got my feet onto the lip of the shaft. When I was back in it, I felt downward. My arm could not reach a rung below, but I lowered myself over the edge, and sure enough, my feet touched a rung. So I went downward, down, down, at least two hundred feet, I estimate. When I came to the last rung, I lowered myself with my feet hanging. My toes touched wet stone, and then I was on a stone floor. I groped around. The shaft led downward for about twenty feet at a forty-five-degree angle to the horizontal. And then I was on what seemed a level stone floor that was very near a running stream. I went forward cautiously, but quickly stopped. My outstretched hand had encountered wood. I felt the object and determined it to be a boat. It was long and slim, and the walls were thin. It seemed built for speed. Inside it were seven paddles. But it was like no boat I have ever heard of. A wooden runner curved above it from prow to stern.

"I went past it for about ten feet and came to the water itself. Then I went back and searched on both sides of the boat. And I found seven other boats. Nearby, against the wall, were several large barrels. The tops had bronze handles, so I pulled the tops off and felt within. One contained torches, tinder, flint, and irons. One contained dried meat and hard bread. Another held infantrymen's swords. And the fourth held a long coil of rope."

"Did you bring any of the food back?" Kwasin said.

"Forget your belly," Hadon said. "Where are the torches?"

"I made three trips," Hinokly said. "There's food, a torch and igniting materials, and two swords on the floor of the shaft just above us. And the rope. That was very heavy, but I tied one end around my waist and pulled it along behind me."

"Even in sealed barrels the supplies would get wet in a short time," Hadon said. "They must be replenished from time to time. What is their condition?"

"Good," Hinokly said. "They must have been stocked recently."

"Well done indeed, Hinokly," Hadon said. "Now, there are two things we can do. We can go back up the shaft now, haul this hippopotamus up with the rope, and go to the boats. I would guess that if we went up the water tunnel to the right, we'd go northward and come out on the Gulf of Gahete. That will bring us close to the volcano, and we can escape up along the Road of Kho, around the volcano, and get to the wild lands back of it.

"The second thing is to wait until after breakfast. We'll be more rested then, and the guards won't check on us until about midafternoon when the second meal is brought in. Also, there should be more visibility in the day; the light from the shafts will be brighter. But for all we know, we may be taken out in the morning. So I say that we should leave now."

Hinokly groaned and said, "I am so tired, I don't think I can get back up the shaft. My muscles are quivering, and my back is raw. The blanket quickly wore out."

"Paga can go first and let the rope down. He can hold it while Kebiwabes and I go up. Then we'll haul you and Kwasin up. Provided that he isn't too big to squeeze through."

"Paga, throw down some food first," Kwasin said. "I'm starving."

"Food will add to your weight, elephant, and it might make you too swollen to pass through. Your paunch blows up like a cobra's hood when you eat."

"Get ready, you two," Hadon said. "Every minute will count. And—"

"Kho, what is that?" Kwasin bellowed.

Hadon heard a rumbling, and he felt slightly nauseated. For a few seconds he did not understand what was happening. He seemed to be standing on a bowl of jelly or a raft that was being tossed up and down.

Then he cried, "Earthquake!"

19

It lasted for only eight seconds, though it seemed much longer. They rose from the floor, feeling in the soles of their bare feet dying vibrations deep beneath them. Down the corridor cries for help came from the prisoners, and the panicky voices of guards echoed.

"Quick! Put the bolts back into the wall!" Hadon said to Kwasin.

Kwasin obeyed, none too soon. Running footsteps and a torchlight approached. Two guards stopped before the bars, looked within, and raced away. Kwasin pulled the bolts out, and Hadon told him to throw Paga up the shaft.

They waited impatiently until Paga called down for them to stand clear. The end of a thick rope made of cords of papyrus dropped onto the floor. Hadon tied it around his waist and was tossed upwards. He caught like an olive pit in the throat of the shaft. Paga took up the slack and kept it tight while Hadon inched upward. On reaching the horizontal shaft, he felt around until he located a torch, a flint, a box of tinder, and irons. The torch was pine impregnated with fish fat. He struck sparks from the iron with the flint, and presently the tinder was flaming. He dropped some of it on the head of the torch, which soon was flaming and smoking. Paga untied the rope from Hadon's waist and let it down again. Hadon placed the torch on the floor and helped Paga draw up Hinokly and Kebiwabes.

Kwasin tied the end of the rope under his arms. All four above took hold of the rope, with Hadon and Paga at the edge of the shaft and the scribe and the bard pulling behind them. The giant's three hundred and ten pounds of flesh and thirty pounds of bronze gyves and chains came up slowly. Hadon called down to him to brace himself against the walls and thus ease the weight.

Kwasin said, "That's impossible! The skin on my shoulders is being pulled off; I'm being flayed alive! I can't brace myself!"

"Either the rope will break or our arms will come out of their sockets," Paga said.

"Pull!" Hadon said. "And whatever happens, don't let loose. If another—"

This time there was a crack as of a hippo-hide whip. Then a rumbling, louder than the first, and a shaking, more intense than the first. Kwasin's terror yowled up the shaft. Hadon shouted to the others not to let loose, and they held. In about twelve seconds the stone was quiet, except for a distant rumbling. Hadon ordered the resumption of the hauling. Kwasin, moaning with fright and with the pain of seared skin, moved slowly upward, like a bird being swallowed by a snake.

Hadon and Paga had to take frequent rests, and when they finally unplugged the shaft, they were exhausted.

"You could have been more gentle," Kwasin growled, inspecting the bloody skin on his shoulders.

"We could have left you stuck there, too," Paga said. "I don't think I can lift my arms."

They ate, though Hadon was impatient to get going. He kept looking down the shaft, dreading the appearance of a light. If the guards checked on them again, they would raise an alarm. On the other hand, they might be so panic-stricken that they could not be bothered to search for them. Especially, he thought, since no one would want to enter the shafts at a time when they might cave in.

"Mighty Resu is struggling with the Mother of All," Kebiwabes said. "We are ants under the feet of battling elephants. Let us hope that they do not destroy us during their struggle."

"We are fortunate," Hadon said. "The king's men will be too disorganized to worry about us."

"You call it fortunate to be buried alive?" Kwasin said.

"Quiet!" Hadon said. "I hear voices!"

He looked below and saw lights. A man shouted. The bronze door swung creaking inward, and then a guard was looking up the well. Hadon withdrew his head.

"Rested or not, we must go," he said. "They will have to go after ladders, but that might not take them long. Also, they may have other entrances we don't know about."

Hinokly, holding the torch, led the way. Hadon and Kebiwabes carried the swords; Paga, one end of the rope; Kwasin, the food, which he continued eating. When they were over the shaft leading down to the corridor, Hadon saw a number of guards run past it.

"Their commander is a cool one," he said. "He's sticking to his duty even if the city falls in on him."

He quit talking. The walls and floor were shaking again. But the shock was much less than the first two. After it ceased, they continued to the shaft up which the scribe had climbed. Here Hadon said, "You may go down if you wish and take a boat out at once. But I am going up."

"Why?" Kwasin said.

"He means to look for Lalila," Paga said. "I will go with you, Hadon."

"I will be looking for Awineth, too," Hadon said. "I am duty-bound to do so."

"But not love-bound?" Paga said.

"You are crazy!" Kwasin said. "You would venture into the beehive when there is plenty of honey outside? The world is full of beautiful women, cousin!"

"I don't expect you to understand," Hadon said. "There is nothing to keep you from leaving me."

Kwasin snorted and said, "Nothing except that people, if they heard about it, would say that I was a coward! Lead on, Hadon!"

Hadon tied the end of the rope around the bottom rung. When they came back they could slide down past the mouth of the horizontal shaft to the top rung of the lower ladder. He swung out and pulled himself up rung by rung until his feet were on the lowest rung. Then he climbed swiftly up. The odor of smoke came to him. Looking up, he saw that the stars were no longer visible. Behind him came Paga, and behind Paga came Hinokly, the end of the torch clamped between his teeth. Kwasin came last, with one end of the rope tied to his neck. Halfway up, Kwasin would coil the rope around a rung so that the guards would not see it dangling down the shaft if they came this way. On the way back, they would untie the rope at this end and drop it. Though Kwasin's wrists were connected with a heavy chain, its length enabled him to reach up for one rung while clinging to a lower one. The chains from the iron collar around his neck dragged below him, the bolts now and then catching on the rungs and causing him to swear.

When Hadon saw the oblong of hairlines in the rock, he had Hinokly pass up the torch to him. Hinokly was glad to get rid of it; he muttered that his jaw had been about to break. Hadon examined the face of the section for controls but could find none. He pulled out on the bars and pushed in on them. Nothing happened. They did not seem to be connected to a mechanism within. That, he told himself, was to be expected. The royal family would not wish to arrange it so that an enemy could figure out a way to get in.

Perhaps the wall was thin at this point. Should he thump on it with the hope of attracting someone inside? If it were Minruth's apartment, he would have them at his mercy. Guards might be stationed by the exit to ensure that no one left or entered without royal permission. In fact, Minruth would be sure to have guards here if this were Awineth's apartment, since she would know about it.

Far below, a bellow welled up. The walls quivered, and Hadon hung on with one hand, clutching the torch with the other. When the temblor ceased, he pulled at the bars to determine if they had been loosened, and he found them still firm.

Hadon told the others his conclusions. Paga said, "It is useless to stay here. The guards will soon be at the mouth of this shaft."

Hadon hesitated. Should he knock at the door?

Someone shouted from far below. Hadon looked down and saw torchlight and a soldier leaning out of the mouth of the vertical shaft to look upward.

There was still the exit from the head of the statue on the roof. They could climb down the steep dome with the aid of their rope. Perhaps they could go down that to another carved head, which might be the entrance to another shaft.

Hadon made up his mind. He passed the torch down to Paga, drew out the short leaf-shaped sword from his belt, and thumped its hilt end against the stone. It rang hollowly. He had not been mistaken in thinking that the section was a thin shield leading to rooms beyond.

But what if there wasn't anyone there?

He banged the hilt heavily, again and again.

Kwasin roared, "They're coming up! And I can't reach down! They'll cut my feet off!"

Hadon looked down. Two torches were being held out from the horizontal shaft to light up the lower rungs. Three guards were climbing up, with a fourth hanging on the lower rung. The soldiers wore bronze cuirasses and helmets and carried swords in scabbards. And they were coming swiftly.

Even if Kwasin could hold them off for a while, and that did not seem likely, they could soon be attacked from the secret exit. An intelligent officer would find out where the party was located in respect to the shaft and could send men to go through the exit. That is, he would if he knew about the exit. Perhaps he did not. Minruth and Awineth would not wish many to share their knowledge.

Hadon repeated the heavy thumping. Whether enemies or friends were within, someone should come. If an enemy, he might be taken. At least Hadon would have someone to fight. He wouldn't be clinging helplessly to a rung, waiting to be cut down and to fall to the hard stone far below.

"Pass the torch down to Kwasin," Hadon said to Paga. "He can drop it on the first soldier."

Paga did as ordered, and Hadon beat on the stone again. But the section did not move. There was still time to go up to the end of the shaft. He could fight a rearguard action while the others slid down on the rope over the dome. But was there anyplace they could go to when they reached the end of the rope?

Hinokly said that there was a stone head about fifty feet below the one from which he had looked. The rope should be just long enough to reach it. They would have to leave the rope and climb over the top of the head and let themselves

181

in from above. That is, they would if the head contained an entrance to a shaft.

"Let's go," Hadon said, and then he fell inward with a crash.

20

He was lucky. If a man with a weapon had been standing on the other side, he could have killed him while he sprawled astonished, half on the section, half on the floor. He was up quickly, however, and shouting, "Awineth!" She came to his arms, clinging to him and kissing him passionately while she wept.

Hadon pushed her away and said, "No time for that. What is the situation?"

She looked past him at Paga scrambling down the section. "There are others?" she said. "How did you get out?"

"No time for stories," he said. He was in a small room lit by a bronze lamp. The walls were unpainted, and a rack held swords and spears and axes. The door was open, showing him a much larger room with bright murals of pastoral scenes and a life-size, life-colored marble statue of Adeneth, the goddess of passion, in a corner. At the foot of a great bed a corpse sprawled. His armor showed that he was an officer.

"He was stationed in this room," she said. "There are two guards stationed outside the door of the room beyond my bedroom. He heard the noise you were making. After he had listened a moment, he unlocked the door, came out, locked the door, and started across the room. Meanwhile, I had taken a dagger from my jewel box. I called to him, and when he turned, I stabbed him in the throat. Then I opened the section, though I did not know whom to expect. But I prayed that Kho would intervene, that by some miracle it would be you."

"Where is Lalila?" Hadon said.

"Why do you care?" she said.

"It is my duty to keep her from harm," he said, hoping she would not ask why. "Quickly! Where is she?"

"In an apartment down at the end of the hall," she said. She looked at him strangely and said, "But my father spent the night with her."

"That is to be expected," Hadon said, thought he felt sick. "I don't suppose he would still be with her?"

"With Khowot shaking the earth?"

Hadon moved into the great bedroom to make room for the others. Puffing and cursing, Kwasin climbed out, looked around him, saw the axes, and roared, "Paga, you are strong, though a manling! Cut my chains off with an ax!'

Hadon asked Awineth how the section was closed. She pointed to a large closet just off the little room. He entered and pulled down on a huge lever. The section, attached to chains at its end, rose quickly, presumably pulled by counterweights beyond the wall. There was a cry from the frustrated soldiers below, and then silence.

Kwasin lay face-down on the marble mosaic floor and stretched out his arms.

Paga said, "First your head and then the chain, Kwasin," but he brought down the edge of a warax on the chain that connected the wrists. It took five strokes before the link parted. Paga then chopped off the chains connected to the bolts.

Kwasin heaved up, bellowing, "At last I am free!" and seized the largest ax and sword from the rack. With an ax in his right hand and the *numatenu* sword in his left, he roared, "Now we will cut our way out of the palace!"

"Let's hope we don't have to," Hadon said. "And keep quiet! There are guards a few doors away!"

At that moment the palace cracked and shook again. Through the shafts which led to air vents on the dome, a roar came. It was followed by a number of thuds, as if heavy objects had struck the roof.

When the temblor ceased and the noise had stopped, Hadon said, "Where are Minruth's apartments?"

"Would you slay him?" Awineth said.

"If it is possible."

"Let me do it," she said. "Kho will forgive me for killing my own father."

"Where are his apartments?"

"They are on this floor in the northeast corner on the other side of the building. But he has ten men, all famed *numatenu*, stationed at all times at his door. Besides, he will be on the ground floor or out in the streets trying to calm his people."

"How many guard Lalila and the child?'

"Three, the last I saw."

"Do you know where my ax is?" Kwasin said.

"The ax and Hadon's sword are kept in my father's apartment."

"Such luck!" Kwasin bellowed.

"Ten men guard them," Hadon said. He went into the entrance room and took a *numatenu* sword. It wasn't Karken, the Tree of Death, but it would do.

Hadon told the others what to do. Awineth put the dagger in her belt and chose an infantryman's sword. Hadon said, "You hang back, but if you see anybody in trouble, you may help him."

"I am not a man," she said, "but I have trained with the sword since I was a small child. Bhukla has had many sacrifices from me."

Hadon went into the next room, the others behind him. This was twice as large as the bedroom, being a hundred feet long and forty wide. In its center was a sunken marble bath ringed by statues of the beasts and heroes of the nine-year Great Cycle. Its gold-plated and jeweled door was at the far end, which was a good thing, since it had kept the guards from hearing the noise within. They passed through this, opened the door, and went into another large room. On the left as they stepped into it was the door which gave entrance to the corridor.

Hadon said, "Call to them, Awineth."

Awineth rapped on the door with a heavy golden knocker. A voice came through the thick oak bronze-bound door. "What is it O Queen?"

"Your officer has had a fit, one probably brought on by

the fear of the quake. The Divine One has seized him."

There was a moment of silence, then the soldier said, "Your pardon, O Queen. But we have orders from Minruth himself that no one is to open this door but Major Kethsuh."

"How can he do that when he is jerking and foaming at the mouth?" she said. "But I do not care, even if no one now guards me."

"Do they know of the shaft exit?" Hadon said.

"No."

"Then they won't be worried that you will escape."

The guard outside said, "One of us will summon an officer, O Queen, and he may decide what to do."

Hadon whispered to Awineth. She said, "Just a moment. I think that the major is reviving. I will see if he is capable of staying on duty."

"As you wish, O Queen."

Hadon was relieved. He did not want any more soldiers brought to this end of the palace.

"We won't be able to get any of them in here," he said. "So we'll go out after them."

He unbarred the door, waited a minute to assure himself that the others were in position, and then shoved the door outward. It struck one of the guards; the other was standing back a few paces, facing Hadon. He brought his spear up, but Hadon's sword sheared it and on the return stroke cut half through the man's neck. Paga fell on the soldier on the floor and stabbed him in the eye. Kwasin leaped over the two and charged down the long hall, the bard and the scribe behind him.

There were two soldiers before the door at the end of the hall. One ran, doubtless to get help; the other stood his ground. Kwasin bellowed and hurled the ax, and it rotated, its butt striking the fleeing soldier and knocking him down. Kwasin swerved after the fallen man, leaving Kebiwabes and Hinokly to deal with the lone sentinel. This man began shouting an alarm. The felled man got to his feet and picked up his spear, but Kwasin smashed it aside and split his bronze helmet and his skull. Hadon ran to help the scribe and the bard. Before he arrived, the scribe had cut through the spear and Kebiwabes had chopped down on the man's arm. The soldier staggered back against the door, then slumped down as Kebiwabes cut through his neck.

Hadon burst through the door, causing Lalila, sitting on a chair, to scream. Abeth came running through the door beyond, then halted to stare white-faced at Hadon. A moment later, both were weeping, laughing, and hugging him. Hadon freed himself, looked at her bruised face, and said, "No time for that. Come with me."

He halted. Awineth stood in the door, her large dark-gray eyes bright. "So this is the way it is?" she said.

"She has never said she loved me," Hadon replied.

Kwasin entered, saying, "Let us go after our weapons, Hadon."

"We have five men against ten," Hadon said. "All ten are professional swordsmen, and three of us are unskilled with the sword. The odds are too high against us. Besides, the men in the shaft will have told Minruth what has happened, and he will know at once where we are. We must get away before he sends more men up here."

Kwasin said nothing. He stuck his sword and the handle of his ax in his belt and lifted a long and massive oak table. Holding it vertically before him as if it were a shield, he walked through the door.

Hadon cursed and said, "My duty is to see that the women are gotten out of here. Yet I feel—"

"That you are deserting him?" Paga said. "No such thing. He is deserting us for his own mad reasons. You have no reason to feel that you are a coward, Hadon."

"I know," Hadon said. "But if we were at his side, perhaps ..."

He stopped and then said, "Back to the room!"

"I wish that I could witness that battle," Kebiwabes said. "The last battle of the hero Kwasin! What a scene for my epic!"

"You would have to be alive to sing it," Paga said, "and you won't be if you stay here."

Hadon did not think that Kebiwabes would ever sing of anybody, but he thought it wise not to say so.

He led them back to Awineth's apartments, where they barred the doors behind them as they proceeded to the entrance room. Here he stationed the others behind him

186

while Awineth pulled on the lever. The section could be released slowly or quickly. Awineth disengaged it so that it fell suddenly, and with a crash it hit the floor. A soldier who had been clinging to the rungs on the outside also fell in. Hadon cut his arm off and leaped up the slope of the wall to the entrance. The head of another man appeared. Hadon smote through the helmet and skull. The man fell straight down, dislodging two below him. They fell screaming past the torchlight below and into the darkness.

Cautiously Hadon stuck his head out. But there was no one above him.

Ten men were still on the rungs below. He carried the bloody body of the man he had first struck down and eased it over the side. It struck the top man, and three hurtled together down the shaft. The others began to climb down. Hadon went into the bedroom, seized a heavy chair, brought it back, and dropped it. Three men were knocked off. That left two desperately climbing back down. Paga and Kebiwabes brought in another chair and a heavy marble bust. Hadon dropped the bust, after which the chair was not needed.

"There are still men in the horizontal shaft." Hadon said. "How many, I don't know. I will soon find out."

Hinokly entered the room, saying, "The king's men are beating on the door."

"If we pile heavy tables and some of those statues against the door, we can delay them," Hadon said. "And it would help if we could fire the room. Awineth, have you any flammable materials?"

Awineth did not answer for a moment, because the palace shook and rumbled. More objects struck the dome far above them. When the palace had quit shaking, Awineth said, "There is a charcoal fire always burning before the image of Great Kho in the chapel beyond the reception room. You can set the draperies on fire with that. And perhaps the furniture will catch fire."

Hadon went into the reception room, which was noisy with the crashings of a heavy object against the door. Then there was a pause, and he heard Kwasin's bellow.

"Let me in, you fools! It is I, Kwasin!"

Hadon hurried to draw the massive bar. Kwasin entered, looking disheveled and sweaty, but his expression was triumphant. He carried the Ax of Wi and Karken.

"Here, stripling!" he shouted. "Here is your sword, which you were too timid to go after!"

Hadon shot the bar and said, unbelievingly, "Ten *numatenu* slain, and in so short a time!'

Kwasin put his ax down and began to pile chairs, tables, and statues before the door. "Ten *numatenu*? Ten ghosts! They were all gone! Evidently Minruth had called them to his side. So I broke down the door with my table and went in for my ax. There were two swordsmen inside, making sure, I suppose, that no assassins sneaked into the apartments to surprise the king when he returned. I slew them and then hunted for my ax. I found it, and with it your sword, which I brought along for you, though I should have sent you after it. No thanks to you that we have our beloved weapons! But when I came back, I looked down the great staircase in the northeast corner, and I saw that a horde, an ant stream of men, was swarming up the steps. I ran into a room and dragged out four heavy tables and put them at the head of the stairs with a marble statue of some king or other. When they had rounded the last landing and were coming four abreast up the steps, I raised the oak table above my head and launched it at them. It crushed scores and knocked down many more.

"Then, as the survivors behind came over the table and the pile of corpses, I threw the second table at them. And when the next wave came, I crushed them with the third table. By then they had decided to retreat, but I dropped the statue on more and hastened their flight. I ran down to this room then, only to find that you had locked me out. I was breaking down the door with another table, and cursing you for your lack of foresight, when you opened the door."

"I thank you for the sword," Hadon said.

He helped the others tear down draperies and pile furniture, and he dumped the brazier of coals on several papyrus rolls. These blazed, presently the draperies were afire, and the wooden furniture began to smoke. A moment later, axes crashed against the door. They ran to the entrance room, where Hadon climbed out onto the first rung, with Kwasin behind him.

When he reached the sixth rung above the opening of the

horizontal shaft, Hadon tied the end of the rope to the rung. He then untied the end attached to the bottom rung and hauled it up. Holding his sword in one hand, and the rope in the other, he launched himself down and out. The rope carried him in an arc which brought him within the opening. He released it and swooped in against five startled soldiers. His feet knocked down one torch carrier, and he fell heavily on his back. The pain of the impact on his raw back almost tore a scream from him. But he was up quickly and laying about the others before they could bring their swords into play. Two fell, and two retreated to spread out as far as the tunnel would allow them. Hadon whirled, kicked the torch carrier in the face, knocked him against the wall, and cut his head off. He whirled again, but he did not charge. In a moment Kwasin hurled in, fell forward on his face, cursing and skinning his knees, but he retained his hold on his ax. At sight of him the two soldiers fled.

Hadon and Kwasin picked up the two torches. When Paga came down the rope and was drawn in, Hadon handed him a torch. Kwasin held the other while they went after the soldiers. These had gone into the shaft leading to the shaft above the cell. The last one was just going down a ladder. Kwasin ran bellowing into it, dragged up the ladder as far as it would go, and banged it around. The soldier screamed as he fell.

Kwasin chopped off the ladder level with the floor. Hadon pulled the rest on up until its end hit the ceiling. Kwasin chopped three more lengths, after which the pieces were dropped down the shaft to discourage the soldiers from looking up it. Hadon said, referring to Paga and the others, "They must all be near the bottom of the lower ladder. Let's go."

On returning to the big shaft, they saw by the torchlight that Hinokly and Kebiwabes were still climbing down. The rest were at the foot of the ladder, looking anxiously upward. Hadon and Kwasin climbed down, the latter holding the end of the torch between his teeth. When they got to the bottom, Kwasin took the lead, and they followed him down a shaft running at an oblique angle. They came out into an immense tunnel fifty feet wide which ran straight into the darkness. They stood on an apron of stone holding, as Hinokly

189

had described, a number of long slim boats and barrels of supplies. They broke open the barrels and put food and some extra weapons in the two boats. Seven boarded one; Kwasin took the other. The torches were inserted in sockets near the prow, and they shoved off into the dark stream and began paddling.

The stone walls were smooth for a while; then openings appeared, out of which sewage poured. They had just skirted one of the noxious cataracts when Paga said, "We are being followed."

Hadon looked back and saw four lights in the distance. He said, "Paddle faster. And be prepared for trouble ahead, too."

The shaft abruptly began to narrow, and its roof angled downward. Hadon had expected this, since there would be no other reason for the overhead runners. In a minute the wooden strips were scraping against the stone overhead, and the boat was pressed downward. They dug their paddles into the water and shoved, forcing the boats ahead, the wood grating against the stone. The water rose almost to the wales, making Hadon wonder if the boat was not overloaded.

Suddenly the tunnel enlarged, and they saw the opening about sixty feet ahead. It was lit by torches and by a light beyond them the nature of which they did not comprehend at once. As they paddled closer, they saw a fiery mass splash into the bay, and they smelled brimstone.

"Khowot explodes!" Kebiwabes said.

Hadon had anticipated guards here. There was a platform of stone about ten feet above the water level, and torches flared there. But the guards had deserted their post.

It was no wonder. As they emerged onto the choppy waters of the bay, they cried out. Another flaming object was falling from fire-lit skies, falling toward them.

21

There was no time to change course. Their fate was in the hands of Kho. The mass struck between the two boats with a roar and disappeared with a great wave and a cloud of steam. Hadon's boat reared up, up, so high and at such a steep angle that he thought surely it would fall back and turn over. But it suddenly leveled and plunged downward. A moment later they were paddling ahead again.

The volcano was spouting flame. A many-miles-broad sheet of bright red flowed down its side toward the city and the area to the northwest. Flames of sulfur filled the air, causing them to cough violently. Flames and smoke arose also from the buildings on the shore and up the hills. What Minruth had not burned, Khowot was now destroying.

Hadon gave the order to drive straight ahead. He had planned to go along the shore northwestward until they came to the entrance of the canal which ran down from the lower lake near the coliseum of the Great Games. But that was too close to the volcano. By the time they got there, the lava might be filling the upper part of the canal. It would be better to go much farther north, past that canal which ran straight to the bay from the larger upper lake. And perhaps, when they got there, they would find that they must continue their flight on the water. The buildings beyond the upper canal were burning here and there, though the whole area was not yet afire.

"At least, we can get lost in the confusion!" Hinokly called to Hadon.

Hadon hoped so. The bay was swarming with boats and ships, all heading toward Mohasi and Sigady islands. A naval galley passed them on their left, its gong master beating a tempo that indicated the depth of desperation and panic of those aboard.

Hadon glanced behind him again and saw three boats

full of men paddling after them. Their bronze armor and helmets gleamed dully in the red light. An officer standing up in the prow of the lead boat was pointing at them and shouting. At least, his mouth was open and working. The rumblings and the explosions overrode everything, even the yelling and screamings of the panicky mob ashore.

"They're not going to quit their chase!" Hadon shouted back. "Faster! Faster!"

The waters were becoming increasingly choppy, no doubt agitated by the quakes. They were shipping water, and though Hadon hated to lose any paddlers, he ordered Kebiwabes to help Abeth bail with helmets.

Presently, with the chasers drawing nearer, they passed the mouth of the lower canal. People swam toward them, shouting for help. Behind them was a horde, heads bobbing in the waves, arms waving. On the shore was a mob rushing into the water. Behind them a wall of flame ravened.

Hadon directed the boat outward then, because he did not want to be slowed down while beating off the swimmers. If several managed to cling to the boat, they would pull it under. His heart ached for them, especially for the children he saw among them. But trying to save even one would cause all aboard to perish.

Ashes were filtering through the smoke now, ashes that burned and stank. Those on the boats became gray, as if they were ghosts, and the surface of the water was thick with gray. For several minutes the visibility was so limited that they could not see their pursuers. Hadon hoped that now they could elude them. But after five minutes, the ashes suddenly became less, and the first of their chasers, phantom-gray, solidified from the cloud. A moment later the second boat emerged. The third, however, seemed to be lost. Perhaps some of the swimmers had grabbed it and overturned it. In any event, the odds were now cut down.

It was a long pull under such conditions. By the time they reached the mouth of the upper canal, only Hadon and Paga had any strength left. Their boat slowed down while the pursuers continued at an unremitting, though slow pace.

The shore here was the closest point to the eastern end of Mohasi island, which accounted for the greater number of swimmers here. To try to put ashore would only bring the boats among them. Yet they could not paddle much longer.

Kwasin, who had been looking back frequently, suddenly turned his boat around and came at them. Hadon ordered his paddlers to steer away. Kwasin bellowed, "Lalila! I will stop the soldiers! When I come back alive, I claim you as my reward! I am doing this for you! You will be mine!"

Lalila tried to yell at him, but she was too tired. She said weakly, "I will never be yours."

Hadon shouted, "Kwasin! You may do what you wish, but Lalila is no cow to be bought and sold! She loathes you!"

Apparently Kwasin did not hear him. Smiling, he shouted back, "I am yours, Lalila! You will have the greatest man of the empire as your lover!"

"He is indeed mad!" Lalila said, and she groaned.

Hadon said, "He can't hold you to that, though I doubt that even he can overcome all those soldiers. He won't be back."

"Let him sacrifice himself," Paga said. "We must go on!"

They bent to their paddles, with Hadon looking behind him at every sixth stroke. When he saw Kwasin leap aboard the lead boat, he did not stop to see what would happen. Instead he dug in, and the boat continued northwest, toward the peninsula of Terisiwuketh. It terminated in two extensions which suggested the gaping jaws of a snake, hence its name of Python's Head. Hadon wanted to land near the base of the lower jaw and continue across it to the northern shore. From there they could go along the shore until they came to a part of the city that was comparatively free of fires. They would go inland and into the mountains north of Khowot.

Hadon's last sight of Kwasin was his smoke-and-ash-blurred figure swinging lustily with his ax while the boat sank under his weight and soldiers fell into the water.

Hadon's group stopped paddling while they laid about them with paddles and swords, beating back the screaming people trying to get onto their boat. Then they were free. Hadon changed his mind and ordered them to go straight north. Though the city ahead was flaming, he had decided to chance crossing the peninsula much farther to the east. His crew was too exhausted to make the base of the lower extension.

At last they inched onto the shore, Paga and Hadon the

only ones able to lift their paddles. They scrambled ashore and got out of the way of a number of women, children, and men fighting for their boat. Hadon led them down a street of mean tenements, the white plaster overcoats of which were black with smoke. Once he looked behind him and saw dim figures. Were they the soldiers on the second boat?

As fast as they could go, which was only a swift walk, they proceeded down the street. When they came to intersections, they ran across to get by the heat striking at them. The fires had advanced within six blocks of their route and were coming swiftly.

They made it to the other shore of the peninsula, though they were now black, not gray, and their lungs seemed seared. They walked along the street that paralleled the shore until Hadon saw that an advance guard of the flame-storm was going to cut them off. He led them into water waist-deep, and they continued along the shore. They had to submerge now and then to coat themselves with water as insulation. The wind, built up by the roaring inferno, pushed them inward into the shore. They resisted successfully, but their pace was considerably slowed. Hadon took the child from Hinokly and told her to cling tightly to his back.

They had gone perhaps a mile when he thought it safe to venture ashore again. They staggered coughing along the street in a steady northeastward direction. Finally, when Awineth and Kebiwabes could not go another step, they halted. All except Hadon lay on the ground. He eased the child down and walked back a few blocks. Seeing no sign of the soldiers, he returned.

After a fit of coughing, he said, "We must go on. If we don't, we'll choke to death on the gases."

They struggled groaning to their feet and followed him. From time to time they waded into the water and soaked their kilts to hold over their noses. After another mile the gases became only a faint odor. The fires were advancing toward them, but at a slower rate. And then came blessed rain, though the wind howled around them and lightning flashed in the distance.

Soon they were past the walls of the Outer City and on a dirt road running by farmlands. Many of these had been burned to the ground by the soldiers of Minruth. Those citizens who would not renounce Kho or those suspected of falsely swearing renunciation had been slain, their houses and barns burned down, and their animals seized.

The houses that remained were dark and silent. Either their occupants had fled, fearing the volcano, or they were hiding trembling inside their walls, hoping that doom would pass by them. Kebiwabes suggested that they take refuge in a house and rest there. They could continue in the morning. Hadon said they would not stop until they had at least come to the bases of the mountains. When they came to a road running inland, he led them down that. At dawn they were trudging along, Hadon holding the sleeping child in his arms. After passing several farmhouses Hadon turned into a dirt road leading to a house set far back from the main road. It was a bad choice; two huge dogs rushed growling at him. He barely had enough time to place Abeth on the ground and draw his sword. One dog stopped; the other leaped at him. Hadon took off its head in midair and ran at the second dog. It ran away, but stopped when Hadon quit chasing it. A wooden shutter of the lower story of the log cabin swung out, and a dark face appeared.

Hadon said, "Call off your dog, or I'll kill it too. We don't mean you any harm. We are just refugees from the wrath of Kho who need food and rest. That is all we ask."

"Go away!" the farmer said. "Or my sons and I will kill you!"

Awineth stepped forward and said, "Would you turn your queen away!"

Hadon cursed under his breath and said softly, "You should not have done that, Awineth! Now the word will be out!"

The farmer scowled and said, "You look like a bunch of tramps to me. Do not try to fool me, woman. I may be a rube, but I am not stupid."

Hadon looked at the tall totem pole near the road. He said, "Kebiwabes, you are a member of the Green Parrot people. Appeal to this man to help one of his own totem."

The bard, filthy, naked, and shaking with fatigue and hunger, called out in a weak voice, "I ask for your hospitality in the name of our tutelary bird, farmer! And in the name

195

of the law that requires that you give a wandering bard food and drink and a place under your roof!"

"When the deities quarrel among themselves, there is no law for mortals!" the farmer shouted. "Anyway, how do I know you are not lying?"

"I, your queen and high priestess, demand that you welcome us as guests!" Awineth said. "Do you want to call down the wrath of Kho on your heads?"

"Big talk!" the farmer said. "You are lying! Besides, even if you were queen, what are you doing here? Resu rules the land now, and you are the slave of Minruth! Perhaps, if I held you for him, he would reward me!"

"I was afraid of that," Hadon said. "Let's go on before they get the idea of holding you for money and glory."

"They would not dare touch me!" Awineth said. "I am the chief priestess! My person is sacred!"

"You're also worth a vast sum," Hadon said. "And the fact that you're a refugee shows that you have no power. To him, he'll be safe under the aegis of Resu and Minruth. Let's take one of his goats for food and go on."

"I will not be insulted!" Awineth cried.

"You can punish him when you're in a position to do so," Hadon said. "Face reality."

The door to the house swung open on its bronze hinges. The farmer and six men followed him out onto the bare earth. He was a short but powerful man of about fifty. Four youth who looked like they must be his sons ranged themselves beside him. The other two were tall thin men who were, Hadon supposed, his hired help. All were holding small round wooden shields covered with bullhide, and short heavy leaf-shaped swords.

The farmer said, "We call on you to surrender in the name of Resu and the king of kings!"

"You are seven men to four men and two women and a child," Hadon said. "But I am a *numatenu*, and I do not need these others to help me fight against only seven bumpkins."

That was a lie. Hadon had not been officially initiated into the *numatenu* class, but the name of *numatenu* must surely terrify these peasants.

There was only one way to find out. Hadon summoned

a loud cry from a parched throat and strength from his weary muscles. He charged, holding the sword before him with both hands. The peasants stopped, their eyes wide, and the two servants fled toward the rear of the house. Why should they face what seemed to them a certain death for a family which had overworked and underfed them?

Whatever their original spirit, that of the father and sons was shaken by the desertion of their servants and by a man who looked as if he intended to rage among them as a leopard among sheep. They turned and fled into the house, or at least they tried to. The doorway was not wide enough for two to get through at once. They coagulated there in a shouting, clawing frenzy that would have been comical under other circumstances. Hadon could have cut off the heads of most of them if he had wished, but he was weary of bloodshed. He laughed and walked away, saying, "To the barn!"

There they took some freshly laid duck eggs and a kid on a leash and proceeded up the road. Awineth, raging, demanded that the house be burned down and the peasants slaughtered as they ran out.

"We shouldn't leave any witnesses!"

Hadon agreed with her on the latter point but did not say so. Though the farmer could tell the king's men which direction they had gone, they would be in the mountain forests by then, perhaps over the mountain.

With the frequent halts, they walked until noon. By a clear running mountain stream they slaughtered and cooked the kid and sucked out the contents of the eggs. They also stuffed themselves with berries Abeth had found on a bush nearby. All but Hadon then fell asleep.

An hour passed. Hadon fought heavy eyelids. The sun was hot, but the breeze was cool in the shade of the grove in which they were hiding. He was thinking of rousing Hinokly to replace him as the guard when he saw Lalila sit up. She yawned, looked gravely at him, and rose. She said, "Is it all right if I get a drink of water?"

"There's no one in sight," he said. "Go ahead."

She walked down the steep grass-covered hill to the brook flowing at its foot. He watched her while she drank and then washed off the dust and mud. He long yellow hair and her shape were indeed beautiful, and she had a gentle yet strong soul to match their beauty, he thought. The bruises on her face angered him. Should he ask her about them, or did she prefer not to speak of them?

After a while she returned, her skin glowing, her large violet eyes wondrous. She sat down by him, saying, "I need much more sleep. But I don't think I can sleep. I am too troubled."

"What is it that troubles you?"

"Minruth disturbs me in my dreams."

"He will pay for that someday."

"That will not undo the horror or heal these bruises, though the marks will go away in time. But not the bruises inside."

"You cannot expect such a man to be gentle," he said. "He takes a woman as a bull takes a cow."

"He did not get much satisfaction. I did not fight, which I think he expected and perhaps hoped for. I lay as if I were dead. After he had spent his lust twice on me, he cursed me and said I was no better than a statue carved from soap. He would give me to one of his Klemqaba slaves. I said nothing, and that made him even angrier. It was then that he struck me three times on the face. I still did not cry out; I just looked at him as if he were the most vile creature on earth. Finally, swearing, he left me. I wanted to kill myself, not because of what he did but because of what he might yet do. But I could not leave Abeth motherless, and I would not kill her. Perhaps, no matter what, I might escape. Or perhaps Sahhindar might come to this land and rescue me."

"He is not here," Hadon said. "But I am."

She smiled and touched his hand. "I know. I also know that you are in love with me."

"And what about you?"

"Time will have to tell me."

"Then there is . . ."

He stopped and held his hand up in the air as if he would catch something. He rose, listening, scrambled up a tree, and then came quickly down.

"Soldiers! They have dogs with them! And the farmer's sons!"

They woke the others, explained the situation, and went on up the hill. This led to another even higher; beyond that were more hills, with the mountain waiting behind them. Their progress was slow and arduous. They were tired and had to push through heavy brush and thorny berry bushes. Nor could they see how close their pursuers were.

Finally, panting, bleeding from thorns, they came to the mountain itself. Before them was a very steep slope on which grass grew in patches and lone trees clung. They toiled on up, with frequent looks behind them. After a while Hadon heard the dogs. Looking back he saw them burst out of a heavy patch of forest. After them came five men hanging onto their leashes, and thirty soldiers, the sun shining on bronze helmets and cuirasses and spear points. Behind them were the farmer's sons.

He turned back in time to see Lalila, crying out, fall back down a rocky slope, sliding in a cloud of dust as she grabbed for a hold she could not find.

He ran as swiftly as he could to her. Her face was twisted, and her hands were grasping her right ankle.

"I've sprained it!"

Hadon told the others to go on. He sheathed his sword, stooped, and hoisted her up. Carrying her in his arms, he climbed up, though his legs turned to water. When he reached a narrow rocky pass with high walls, he let her down. The others were waiting for him, their faces pale where their sweat had washed off the grime.

After he had caught his breath, he said, "You all go on ahead. I will help her walk."

He lifted her up but had not gone more than six steps when he knew that it was useless. She could travel only if carried, which meant that they could never keep ahead of their pursuers.

He let her down again and said, "There is only one thing to do."

"And what is that, Hadon?" Awineth said.

"This pass has room for no more than one person at a time. I will stand here, in the narrowest part, and hold them off as long as I can. The rest of you must get away as swiftly as you can. Hinokly, you carry the child."

Lalila cried out, which caused Abeth to run crying to her mother's arms.

Awineth said, "You will die here for Lalila?"

"For all of you," Hadon said. "I can hold them here long enough to give you a head start. Don't argue! They are getting closer every second. This must be done, and I am the only one who can do it."

"If you stay here with her," Awineth said, "you are deserting me. Your duty is to protect your queen and high priestess."

"That is exactly what I am doing," Hadon said. "They must be held up long enough for you to get far ahead of them."

"You can hold them off for a long while, perhaps," Paga said. "But some will eventually climb up the slopes outside the pass and come at you from behind."

"I know that," Hadon said.

"I order you to leave the woman, who will die in any event, and accompany me!" Awineth said.

"No," Hadon said. "She will not be left to die alone."

"You *do* love her!" Awineth cried.

"Yes."

Awineth screamed and jerked her dagger out of its sheath. She ran at Lalila, but Hadon caught her wrists and twisted, and Awineth, with a sharp cry, dropped the dagger.

"If she dies now, there is no reason for you to stay!" she shouted.

"Awineth," he said hoarsely, "if you had the sprained ankle, I would do the same for you."

"But I love you! You can't leave me for her!"

Hadon said, "Kebiwabes, take her away."

The bard picked up the dagger, put it back in its sheath, and drew her, weeping, away. Hadon took the child from Lalila's arms and gave her to Hinokly. Abeth, crying and struggling, was dragged away.

Hadon watched them until they had disappeared. Then he said, "I'll help you up to the narrow way. And we will both rest there until we can rest no more."

When he had eased her down behind a rock, he looked down the pass. Far below, the dogs bayed, and the men toiled upward.

"It will be a good fight," he said. "I can feel my strength flowing back. It is too bad, however, that Kebiwabes is not here to see this. He could fashion from it a fitting climax to his song. If he lives to sing it, that it. If he does, he will have to depend on his imagination. Which means that the fight will be even more glorious than it will be in reality."

"I hope that my child will be all right," Lalila said.

"Is she the only one you think of?"

"The main one. I am not eager to die, and I do not wish you to stay here with me, though I am grateful to you. But if you would kill me, so that those men will not be able to harm me, I would be even more grateful. Awineth is right. You should go with them. Then my child will have a protector."

"Paga will protect her, and Hinokly and Kebiwabes will help take care of her. They are all good men with good hearts."

"But you are sacrificing yourself in vain!" she said. "And you are giving up all chances of becoming the ruler of Khokarsa."

"Let's save our breath," he said. "I, at least, will need it."

He sat down by her side and picked up her hand. Presently she kissed him long and warmly, though the tears still ran.

"I think I could forget Wi," she said. "Oh, I don't mean that I'll ever *forget* him. But love is for the living."

Hadon broke into tears then. When he had wiped them away, he said, "I wish I could have heard those words while we were still in the Wild Lands. We would have had much time to love each other then. Perhaps, when we go down into the realm of Sisisken, we can love there. The priestesses say that some men and women are selected to go to a bright garden where they live happily, even if they are phantoms. Surely we will be chosen to go there. If there is such a place. Sometimes I have been guilty of doubts about what the priestesses say. Do we really have a life after death? Or do we just become dust, and that is our end except in the memories of those who won't forget us because they love us?"

"I do not know," she said.

He kissed her again and then arose.

Huge clouds of smoke still rose from Khowot. At its foot

lay a blotch that was ruined Khokarsa. Nearby, a bird sang sweetly. A mouse ran out onto a shelf of rock from its hole and twittered at him.

They would be alive after he was gone. They would sing and twitter in the bright sun below the blue sky while he lay a bloody, unseeing, unhearing, unfeeling corpse.

But then, what would they know, if they lived to be a hundred, of love? Of his love for Lalila?

He leaned on his sword and waited.

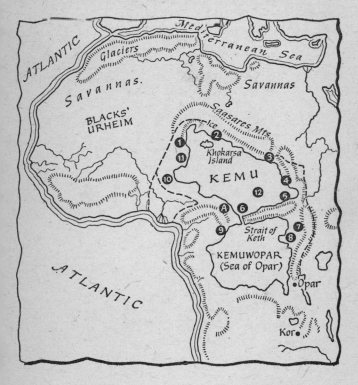

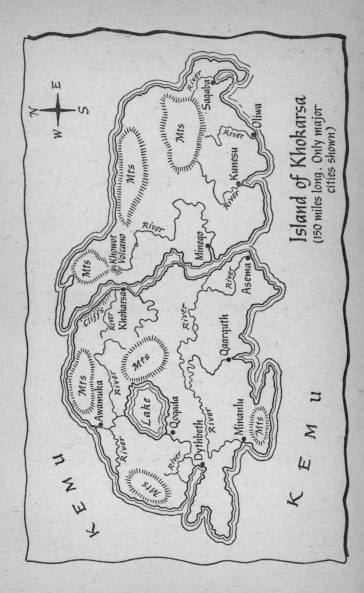

Island of Khokarsa
(150 miles long. Only major cities shown)

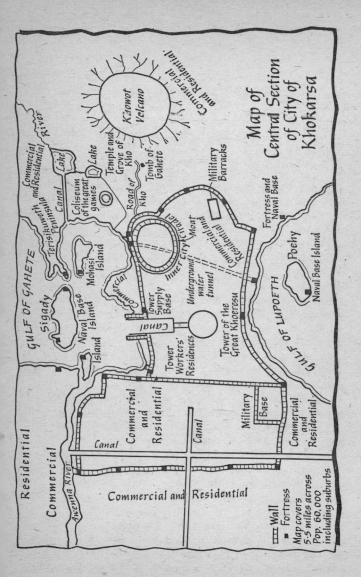

Description of Maps

Map 1 shows the major part of Africa circa 10,000 B.C. This is a modification of the map presented by Frank Brueckel and John Harwood in their article: *Heritage of the Flaming God, an Essay on the History of Opar and Its Relationship to Other Ancient Cultures,* The Burroughs Bulletin, Summer, 1974. Their map, in turn, was based on that in Willy Ley's *Engineers' Dreams,* Viking Press, 1954, though also much modified.

The world in 10,000 B.C. was in the dying grip of the last Ice Age. The present Sahara was mountains, plateaus, vast grasslands, parks of trees, rivers, and freshwater lakes. Elephants, rhinoceroses, hippopotami, crocodiles, lions, antelopes, and ostriches numbered in the millions. The two inland freshwater seas actually existed, though their boundaries as shown here are highly speculative.

The outlines of the mountains won't satisfy a professional cartographer; they're provided to give the reader a rough idea of their extent. The Mediterranean coastline was from 100–200 feet lower than its present level.

While the rest of the world was in the late Old Stone Age, a maritime civilization had risen around the northern inland sea, the Kemu (the Great Water). Some colonial cities, including Opar, had been founded in the Kemuwopar (Sea of Opar). Excluding the cities of Khokarsa Island (see Map 2), the major cities were: 1, Mukha; 2, Miklemres; 3, Qethruth; 4, Siwudawa; 5, Wethna; 6, Kethna; 7, Wentisuh; 8, Sakawuru; 9, Mikawuru (the pirate stronghold); 10, Bawaku; 11, Towina; 12, Rebha (the pile-city). A - Klemqaba country.

Opar and Kôr are called out on the map, but Kôr was built after Hadon was born.

Note: The Khokarsans had their own system of measurements and weights, but in this novel only the English equivalents are given.

Chronology of Khokarsa

Introduction

About 13,500 B.C. the coasts of the two seas of Central Africa were inhabited by a hundred small groups of paranthropoids, neanderthaloids, and human-neanderthal hybrids. The latter dewlt on the northern coast of the north sea; the neanderthaloids, on its west and east coasts; the paranthropoids, farther south. The total population along a coastline (including both seas) almost equal to that of the present Mediterranean was perhaps ten thousand.

The inland seas were the last refuge of the neanderthaloids. Elsewhere they had been exterminated or assimilated by Homo sapiens. The paranthropoids were hairy subhumans related to the *yeti* and the *sasquatch* of today. These were more numerous than now. Paranthropus lived in the forest and jungle areas, retreating before the advance of Homo neanderthalensis and Homo sapiens.

Some time before 13,000 B.C., a number of Caucasian tribes wandered down from the lush savannas of what is today the Sahara. These people called themselves the Khoklem. They gradually pushed out the hybrids and the neanderthaloids to the south, or else assimilated them.

About the same time, another group of Caucasians, the Klemsuh, began drifting into the middle-eastern coast of the north sea. These had physical characteristics which, if history had not decreed otherwise, might have seen the Klemsuh develop into a separate race. Their skins were a yellow-brown; their hair was straight, coarse, and dark; and they had slight epicanthic folds. These are Mongolian characteristics today, but the Klemsuh (the Yellow People) were definitely a stock of the Caucasian race.

The hybrids, who were to be called the Klemqaba (People of the Goat) by the Khoklem, eventually settled along the coast and in the hilly and mountainous interior northwest of the strait between the two seas. Though very peaceful in the beginning, many hundreds of years of belligerency by the Khoklem taught them the art of war. Until the end of the Khokarsan civilization, they were to be a thorn in its side.

The Khoklem, like the others, subsisted mainly on fishing, hunting, and food-gathering. Most of their protein came from the Kemu (the Great Water). Due to the absence of cereal plants in this area, it is doubtful that they would ever have amounted to anything if it had not been for the appearance of the man they called Sahhindar.

This mysterious man was regarded as a god by the Khoklem, and with good reason. He brought with him a variety of plants (apparently during a number of visits in a period of fifty years) and taught them how to domesticate these as well as the animals and birds of the area. Sahhindar also showed them how to mine copper and tin, how to make bronze tools and weapons, and how to make bricks and mortar. He also instilled in them a respect for sanitation and taught them the concept of zero. It is no wonder that he held a position in the Khokarsan pantheon analogous to that of Thoth in the Egyptian pantheon.

These gifts explain why the Khokarsans anticipated the Agricultural Revolution of Mesopotamia by about four thousand years. It also explains how these old Stone Age tribes leaped over the Middle and New Stone Ages into the Bronze Age.

Eventually, groups in dugouts and on rafts landed on the island of Khokarsa, which was about the size of Crete. These were Khoklem belonging to a tribe known as the Klemreskom (People of the Fish-Eagle). Their chief goddess, Kho, was a fertility deity titled the Bird-Headed Mother. She was represented in rock paintings and on bone and hippopotamus-ivory carvings as a steatopygic, huge-breasted woman with the head of the fish-eagle. Other tribes came in a little later, and some of these represented her as having the head of a parrot. No doubt this was because the island was swarming with parrots.

Sahhindar was also the god of Time, though the religion

had it that he stole Time from his mother Kho and that was why She exiled him from the land. Sahhindar was said to have been able to travel in time before Kho had taken away this power. Undoubtedly, he was a time traveler from the twenty-first century who had been stranded about 12,000 B.C. (See my *Time's Last Gift*, Ballantine, 1972.) Apparently he was not in the least responsible for the development of civilization elsewhere (in the Near East and on the Indus), but regarded Khokarsa as a private project. He will be referred to throughout this series but will play only a minor role in a few of the novels.

That Sahhindar appeared a number of times in Khokarsa over a period of two thousand years can only be attributed to an age-delaying elixir of some sort.

Major Events

12,000 B.C.   Khoklem spreading out on northern shore of the Kemu. Appearance of Sahhindar.

11,800 B.C.   The hero Gahete is the first man to land on uninhabited island of Khokarsa. On succeeding trips, brings his tribe, the Fish-Eagle Totem. Their chief priestess dedicates a sacred oak grove high on a volcano, Khowot (Voice of Kho). Khokarsa (the Tree of the Hill of Kho) gives its name to the island. Painted fire- or sun-hardened pottery used.

11,700 B.C.   Other tribes have also landed elsewhere on the island. First beer from millet and sorghum made. Priestesses develop an early pictographic writing. Village of Khokarsa becomes the first walled area in the world. Potter's wheel invented. Trephining of skull to relieve chronic headaches introduced.

11,600 B.C. (1 A.T.)   Large stone-block temple to Kho built on plateau by the sacred oak grove. King Nanla seizes the town of Miklemres, the gateway to the tin, copper, and salt mines in the Saasares mountains (the present Ahaggar and Tibesti). Mead-making becomes a major industry, controlled by the chief priestess, Nanwot. Alkaline-glazed pottery. Ox-drawn wagons.

11,550 B.C. (50 A.T.)   Chief priestess, Awineth, establishes a chronology, starting from completion of temple to Kho fifty years before. (A.T. stands here for After Temple.) Wine from grapes first made.

11,530 B.C. (70 A.T.) The priestess-bard Hala composes the first epic poem, *The Song of Gahete*, based on folk songs. Painting and sculpture are more lifelike but still stiff.

11,520 B.C. (80 A.T.) The sundial and the processing of olives invented. First temple-tomb (for Awineth) built. (The kings at this time were still being sacrificed at the end of a nine-year reign. They were buried under large mounds of earth on top of which was set a bird-headed monolith. Heroes and heroines—that is, extraordinary men and women—were buried under mounds with a pointed monolith on top.)

11,450 B.C. (150 A.T.) King Ruwodeth of Khokarsa crushes the revolt in Miklemres. First appearance of the Klemsaasa, a tall people speaking an unknown language, in the mountains north of Miklemres. Lead-glazed pottery.

11,400 B.C. (200 A.T.) Expeditionary fleet led by King Khonan founds the port of Siwudawa in the country of the Klemsuh. This marks the beginning of a long series of campaigns against the Klemsuh of the rural areas. Lost-wax process for casting bronze invented.

11,350 B.C. (250 A.T.) Port villages of Towina and Bawaku flourishing. The "oikos" system of settling the coast frontier is founded. (Bands of adventurous men and women build little wooden forts along the coast and dig in. These were led by men of the hero category whose residences later became small palaces and who ruled large estates. They founded the leading families of these areas, and many of the "oikos" became thriving towns in time.) By this time all six cities of the island have become powerful trade centers. Population of the city of Khokarsa: 15,000. Dythbeth, Saqaba, Kaarquth, Asema, and Kunesu have populations of from eight to ten thousand. Glass invented. Salt-glazed pottery and porcelain.

11,250 B.C. (350 A.T.) Barter is still the basis of economy.

212

Gold and silver first extensively mined in the northern mountains. From their villages in the Saasares, the Klemsaasa raid outlying districts of Miklemres. They incorporate their patriarchal sun god with Kho's son, Resu. Hourglasses using sand invented.

11,153 B.C. (447 A.T.)   The genius Awines born in Dythbeth.

11,118 B.C. (482 A.T.)   By the age of thirty-five, Awines has invented a syllabary, founded the science of linguistics, created a theory of atomism (much like Lucretius'), discovered the circulation of blood, formulated an elementary algebra, and invented wooden printing blocks, catapults, Greek fire, the water clock, the magnifying glass and a solar calendar.

11,113, B.C. (487 A.T.)   Awines is exiled to Bawaku because his syllabary and calendar are considered sacrilegious. Bawaku revolts and defeats the Khokarsan fleet with Awines' catapults and Greek fire.

11,111 B.C. (489 A.T.)   Awines is killed while trying to fly with artificial wings from a mountain.

11,110 B.C. (490 A.T.)   Keth of Kenesu reports discovery of the strait of the southern sea. Apparently, however, others had preceded him. The port village of Mukha becomes a city due to salt mines discovered near it.

11,000 B.C. (600 A.T.)   The Klemsaasa, having adopted agriculture, have become more numerous. They seize and control for a decade some tin and copper mines and require tribute from some outlying provinces of Miklemres. First mint established with coining of electrum.

10,985 B.C. (615 A.T.)   Under King Madymin of Khokarsa, Bawaku is retaken, its citizens are massacred, and it is resettled with colonists from Khokarsa. A group of Bawakans, led by the hero Anesem, escape and found the first City of Pirates, Mikawuru. (In Khokarsan, *mi* means *city*, and *kawuru* means both *crocodile* and *pirate*.)

This was on the fjord coast northwest of the strait into the southern sea (still little-known at this time). First silver and gold coins. First recording of use of brass.

10,968 B.C. (632 A.T.) A great earthquake and tidal wave. The Klemsaasa seize the city of Miklemres. Towina, Bawaku, Dythbeth, and Kaarquth revolt successfully. Aboriginal population of Siwudawa revolts, massacres Khokarsan troops and merchants, and establishes independent state.

10,954 B.C. (646 A.T.) The Mikawuru are driven from their stronghold by the Klemqaba. Led by Wethna, they cross the Kemu and found Wethna on its eastern shore. Use of perspective in art begins to spread.

10,915 B.C. (685 A.T.) A Bawaku expedition under the hero Nankar travels the length of the Bohikly (the Niger River) and brings back from West Africa the red protein berry *mowometh** and the ebony, African mahogany, and okra trees. These begin to spread rapidly around the Kemu. First biremes built. First contact with the Negroes of the west by the hero Agadon of Towina. King K'opwam of Khokarsa retakes Dythbeth and Kaarquth.

10,878 B.C. (722 A.T.) The first great plague. (Smallpox, previously unknown, was probably brought in by black captives.) A quarter of the population of the island and of the cities of Towina and Bawaku die. A few years later, smallpox ravages all the population of the other areas.

10,875 B.C. (725 A.T.) A chief of the Klemsaasa leads them and an army of Miklemres allies to Khokarsa and seizes the city. He marries its sole surviving priestess and ascends the throne. He adopts the Khokarsan name of Minruth; assimilation of the Klemsaasa begins. Those

* *Dioscoreophyllum cumminsi.* A recently discovered red berry, native to West Africa. It's three thousand times sweeter than sugar on a weight-for-weight basis. It is a protein, not a carbohydrate. See *Signature* magazine, March, 1973.

left in the mountains become known as the Klemklakor (Bear people).

10,866 B.C. (734 A.T.)   Minruth I completes the conquest of all the cities of the island and Towina and Bawaku. He refuses to honor the age-old custom of sacrifice of the king after nine years of rule and institutes custom of sacrificing a substitute. The Klemsaasa pantheon is entirely incorporated into the Khokarsan. Resu, the sun god, is proclaimed to be the equal of Kho. Nevertheless, in practice, most of the people for a long time regard Resu as secondary to Kho. This year marks the beginning of the long struggle between the priestesses and the priests. Old lunar calendar is abandoned and Awines' solar calendar is adopted. New one has twelve months of three ten-day weeks each, with five festival days at end of year. Year starts on the vernal equinox.

10,846 B.C. (754 A.T.)   Syllabary of Awines adopted. Governmental postal system, based on that of the temples, is adopted. First copper coins stamped.

10,832 B.C. (768 A.T.)   First trireme built. Coastal highway of stone blocks begun from Miklemres east and west. The hero Kethna circumnavigates the southern sea. This was originally called the Kemuketh but later became known as the Kemuwopar (the Sea of Opar).

10,824 B.C. (776 A.T.)   The city of Kethna founded. This will eventually control the strait and be a source of trouble to Khokarsa.

10,810 B.C. (790 A.T.)   The priestess-heroine Lupoeth discovers gold-, silver-, and diamond-bearing clay at site of Opar and founds a mining village. Depiction of deities as human-headed in art and sculpture spreads from Khokarsa.

10,800 B.C. (800 A.T.)   First Negro slaves brought into Opar.

10,757 B.C. (843 A.T.)   A second Mikawuru (City of Pirates) founded on northwest shores of the Kemuketh. These settlers were not from Wethna, which had become respectable, but were criminals and political refugees from all over the northern sea.

10,700 B.C. (900 A.T.) Colonists from Mikawuru establish a stronghold on east coast of the Kemuwopar. It grows in later years into a city called Sakawuru.

10,695 B.C. (905 A.T.) The city of Opar completed in all its grandeur. The port of Wentisuh founded by colonists from Siwudawa.

10,600 B.C. (1000 A.T.) The climate is warmer and drier. The ice sheets in the Saasares are dwindling. A great plague and a series of earthquakes usher in another Time of Troubles. Revolts of tributary states and falling apart of the empire. K'opwam II murders his wife in attempt to impose patriarchy and flees to Miklemres during the uprising that follows. He is captured and sacrificed at the great temple. For a hundred years the chief priestesses of Khokarsa have husbands who are denied the kingship. Many temples of Resu torn down or converted to temples of Kho. Human sacrifice, except in times of great tribulation, is abandoned. This custom spreads throughout the two seas, except at Sakawuru.

10,560 B.C. (1040 A.T.) Beginning of the *numatenu* (heroes of the broadsword), a warlike class similar to the samurai. By custom, only the members of the *numatenu* are allowed to use the slightly curved, blunt-ended broadsword lately introduced, but this is not strictly observed.

10,499 B.C. (1101 A.T.) The Klemqaba take Bawaku and massacre its citizens.

10,490 B.C. (1110 A.T.) A combined Klemqaba and Towina fleet attacks Dythbeth. A *numatenu*, Toenuseth, consort of Dythbeth's chief priestess, destroys the fleet. His wife makes him the king, and he sets out on the conquest of the island of Khokarsa.

10,485 B.C. (1115 A.T.) to 10,480 B.C. (1120 A.T.) Toenuseth conquers Saqaba and Kaarquth. The city of Towina, now an enemy of the Klemqaba, drives the Klemqaba from Bawaku with the aid of revolting Bawakans.

10,478 B.C. (1122 A.T.) Toenuseth killed by a spear thrown by the chief priestess of Khokarsa during the siege of that city. This is considered a judgment of Kho, and it discourages the idea of the kingship for some years.

10,460 B.C. (1140 A.T.) The chief priestess of the city of Khokarsa institutes the Great Games (later known as the Great Games of Klakor, after the winner of the first games). These mark the return of the kingship. By the Law of Pwymnes, the victor of the Great Games becomes the husband of the chief priestess (if she accepts him) and is crowned king of Khokarsa. Any man is eligible to compete unless he is a slave, a neanderthaloid, or a Klemqaba. The Games occur when the old king has died or the chief priestess dies. However, the reigning king may keep his kingship if he can induce the dead wife's daughter to marry him, or if she lacks daughters, the nearest relative to assume the priestess's throne. Pwymnes, too old to bear children, retires after the hero Klakor wins the Games, and he marries her daughter, Hiindar (meaning Gray Eyes). It must be kept in mind that the king governed only military, naval, and engineering areas. The queen controlled the judicial courts, the law-making, currency, religion, taxation, and commerce. It had, however, long been recognized that men were responsible for the impregnation of women, that Kho or her sons and daughters (gods and goddesses) were not the agents of fertility of women (except that they might cause a man or woman to be sterile). That men caused pregnancy was the main argument of the priests of Resu for the superiority of Resu and for the dominance of males in society. Officially, the fact was ignored, and it took a long time for the idea to be accepted in the rural areas. Work on the Great Tower of Kho and Resu begun by Klakor.

10,452 B.C. (1148 A.T.) Klakor completes the reconquest of the island of Khokarsa. Kwamim, the greatest of the epic poets, born in Miklemres. At the age of twenty-eight, she will create the *Pwamwotkethna*, or *Song of Kethna*. This is based on the wanderings of Kethna and the founding of his city but is historically inaccurate. The songs of much earlier heroes and heroines are incorporated in it, making them contemporaneous with Kethna, and much mythological matter is embodied. The language is based on that of the city of Khokarsa, but Kwamim borrows words from other dialects and even coins new words.

10,449 B.C. (1151 A.T.) Fleet of Miklemres destroyed by Klakor, and Miklemres capitulates. This event marks the beginning of the conquest of the queendom of the coastal Kemu.

10,448 B.C. (1152 A.T.) Opar conquered by Sakawuru pirates under Gokasis. They control the precious metal and jewel trade. Plumbing invented and installed in the palace in Khokarsa.

10,443 B.C. (1157 A.T.) Klakor's herald, the bard Roteka, arrives in Opar to demand surrender. His head is sent back to Klakor, arriving there in 1159 A.T. But Klakor has died.

10,440 B.C. (1160 A.T.) Kethna seized by allied Oparians and pirates of Mikawuru and Sakawuru.

10,427 B.C. (1173 A.T.) Gokasis proclaimed himself king of kings of the Kemuwopar after taking Wentisuh. The first Khokarsan expedition against the alliance destroyed outside the strait of Keth. Awodon, the Praxiteles of Khokarsa, born. Owalu, Qethruth, and Mukha become major cities. The poetess Kwamim, a guest at the court of Wentisuh, is taken prisoner and carried to Opar.

10,423 B.C. (1177 A.T.) to 10,420 B.C. (1180 A.T.) The hero Rimasweth, leading a Khokarsan expedition, strikes Kethna from overland and, leaving a holding force, bypasses Wentisuh, and Sakawuru and raids Opar. He slays Gokasis (son of the first Gokasis) in hand-to-hand combat, massacres the citizens, and takes Kwamim. His fleet is caught at the Strait of Keth and destroyed, but he and Kwamim, with three *numatenu*, escape.

10,417 B.C. (1183 A.T.)   Kwamim first sings the *Pwamwotrimasweth*, the *Song of Rimasweth*. This is the second-greatest epic of Khokarsa (some critics consider it the greatest). It is the first to sing of living heroes. The barbarian Klemklakor are numerous enough to require large punitive expeditions.

10,397 B.C. (1203 A.T.)   Awodon begins work on his masterpiece, *Kho and Her Children*, a frieze of sixty-four figures along the marble base of the Great Tower of Kho and Resu. A fourth expedition levels Kethna and Wentisuh but is destroyed in the Battle of the Bay of Opar.

10,390 B.C. (1210 A.T.)   Siege of Opar begins. Mikawuru and Sakawuru blockaded but resists storming. Expeditions sent out to West Africa, the Mediterranean, and Nile Valley. (But none return.)

10,389 B.C. (1211 A.T.)   Opar taken. Spectacles invented.

10,387 B.C. (1213 A.T.)   Sawakuru taken, its citizens executed, and a ship sent out to arrange for colonists from Khokarsa to repeople it. Mikawuru resists successfully.

10,386 B.C. (1214 A.T.) to 10,266 B.C. (1334 A.T.)   A hundred and twenty years of comparative peace, prosperity, and expansion of population, Awodon completes his great work at the age of seventy, dies two years later, and is buried in a hero's tomb. Work on the Great Tower proceeds apace. Networks of stone roads built out from coastal cities along the shore and inland, and a network completed on the island of Khokarsa. Census in 1334 A.T. shows that population of the two seas is an estimated two million (This was the peak.) The town of Rebha, built on piles in a shallow spot in the southeastern Kemu, becomes important in sea commerce. Border forts built to strengthen defense against Negroes of the Western Lands. Another successful expedition against the troublesome pirates of Mikawuru. The explorer Dythphida discovers that an arm of the Kemuwopar is about to cut through the middle-west mountains on the western shore. This portends the eventual drainage of the two seas, but this should not start until another estimated two or three hundred years have passed. The chief priestess of Khokarsa, Aquth, proclaims that this drainage can be averted only by a downgrading of Resu and a return to more conservative forms of religion. Minruth III considers building a gigantic dam, but since this will halt work on the Great Tower, he takes no action.

10,256 B.C. (1335 A.T.)   Opar half-destroyed by an earthquake, but rebuilding begins at once. The Whooping Plague first appears in Towina.

10,261 B.C. (1339 A.T.)   The plague has spread all over the empire. Crop failures and a deadly disease among the fish cause great famine. The Klemqaba devastate Bawaku but are themselves struck down by the plague. The city of Khokarsa is half-destroyed by an eruption of Khowot, and the citizens flee.

10,257 B.C. (1343 A.T.)   The population has been reduced to three-quarters of a million. The empire has fallen apart. The majority of the royalty has died. A *numatenu* from Opar, Riqako, marries the only surviving priestess able to bear children in the city of Khokarsa. He becomes the Reskomureeskom, the king of kings, literally, the Great Fish-Eagle of the Fish-Eagles.

10,061 B.C. (1539 A.T.)   Heliqo discovers connection between malaria and mosquitoes.

10,050 B.C. (1550 A.T.)   The climate is getting warmer and drier. There is, however, still ice and snow in abundance on the peaks of the Saasares. The level of the Mediterranean has risen. Khokarsa is once again in the ascendancy. All the states of the Kemu acknowledge its suzerainty, but the fact are semi-independent. Kethna sends tribute but acts as if it were independent. Though the population has increased, there are still some areas that have not recovered. The pirates of Mikawuru are giving more trouble, and there are pirate bases in the Kemu. There has been little progress in technology. Iron weapons and tools were introduced circa 1340 A.T., but since the main iron-ore deposits are deep inside the Saasares, it is expensive. Bronze weapons and tools are still much used.

10,049 B.C. (15551 A.T.)   Minruth IV wins the Great Games of Klakor, marries Demakwa, the chief priestess.

10,042 B.C. (1558 A.T.)   Bissin, inventor of a crude steam engine, is born.

10,036 B.C. (1564 A.T.)   The herculean and ill-fated Kwasin, Hadon's cousin, is born in Dythbeth.

10,034 B.C. (1566 A.T.)   Demakwa dies, Minruth marries her cousin, Wimimwi, and so no Great Games are held.

10,031 B.C. (1569 A.T.)   Hadon of Opar born. His father, Kumin, is a crippled *numatenu* who has been reduced to sweeping the floors of a temple. His mother, Pheneth, is the daughter of an overseer of slaves, so Hadon has a poverty-stricken childhood, and his parents are of a low social class. Both parents are members of the Ant Totem. Awineth, daughter of Minruth and Wimimwi, born in the temple of Kho on the slopes of Khowot. Electroplating of metal by means of a primitive battery is invented.

10,018 B.C. (1582 A.T.)   Kwasin, drunk, ravishes a priestess of Kho and kills some temple guards. He is exiled instead of being executed when the oracular priestess of the temple of Kho at Dythbeth (where the sacrilege took place) says he should be sent out of the land but permitted to return when Kho so decrees. He wanders off into the Western Lands carrying his great brassbound oak club.

10,013 B.C. (1587 A.T.) Wimimwi dies. Awineth becomes the chief priestess. The Great Games are scheduled to be held within three years. (Enough time has to be given for all states to be notified, the preliminary Lesser Games held to choose three main contestants and their three substitutes from each state, and for the contestants to journey to the city of Khokarsa.) Minruth asks his daughter to marry him, but she refuses. Minruth (called the Mad behind his back) plans to keep the throne by hook or crook. Ruseth, a fisherman, invents the fore-and-aft sail.

10,012 B.C. (1588 A.T.) Hadon becomes one of the winners of the Lesser Games in Opar.

10,011 B.C. (1589 A.T.) The events of *Hadon of Ancient Opar* begin.

More top science fiction available from Magnum

T. J. Bass
4133467 The Godwhale   65p

Alfred Bester
4133457 Extro   60p

John Brunner
4133458 The Wrong End of Time   55p

Philip K. Dick
4133654 Dr. Futurity   60p
4133655 The Unteleported Man   50p
4133653 The Crack in Space   70p

Clifford D. Simak
4133690 Way Station   65p
4133768 Time and Again   75p
4133760 Cemetery World   70p
4133695 Time is the Simplest Thing   70p

These and other Magnum Books are available at your bookshop or newsagent. In case of difficulty orders may be sent to:

> Magnum Books
> Cash Sales Department
> PO Box 11
> Falmouth
> Cornwall TR10 109EN

Please send cheque or postal order, no currency, for purchase price quoted and allow the following for postage and packing:

UK   19p for the first book plus 9p per copy for each additional book ordered, to a maximum of 73p.
BFPO   19p for the first book plus 9p per copy for the next 6 books, thereafter
& Eire   3p per book.
Overseas   20p for the first book and 10p per copy for each additional book.
Customers

While every effort is made to keep prices low, it is sometimes necessary to increase prices at short notice. Magnum Books reserve the right to show new retail prices on covers which may differ from those previously advertised in the text or elsewhere.